THE PRETTY ONES

A KATE REID NOVEL
BOOK 6

ROBIN MAHLE

HARP HOUSE PUBLISHING, LLC.

Published by HARP House Publishing
January, 2017 (1st edition)

1

A t an hour that drifted somewhere between absolute
darkness and morning light's salvation, he lingered.
The slow grind of the rising zipper fastening his
hooded jacket eclipsed the ambient noise of the city streets. The
one for whom he waited had announced her arrival by way of
high heels striking a fractured sidewalk as she approached the
neighborhood roads ahead.

An admirable command of strength complemented her mien.
She would not fall prey easily. It was clear she had an understanding of these streets and this was not her first time traveling
them alone. She exuded purpose, and so he had to rise to the
challenge.

A flicker in her eyes was his signal. A brief flash of uncertainty
as to her safety meant this was the time. From the shadows of the
alleyway, he emerged. A looming figure, obscured in heavy clothing, eyes concealed by the brim of a baseball hat and hair that
hung in tight rings against his shoulders.

This part of the city had been all but abandoned by law enforcement, who were otherwise engaged in efforts to eradicate gangs, drugs, and all that had befallen these forgotten streets of South Los Angeles. That was why he had chosen this place, a few blocks from the more populated avenues and just in front of the residential homes in much need of improvement. This was where he could easily pick off the least affluent; those who used public transportation, worked double shifts, and were usually too tired to fend off predators.

The woman stopped in her tracks and clutched her purse. "I don't have any money."

"I don't want your money." He watched her cast her gaze in search of a place to run or a person who would help. "There's no one here who can help you. You're alone."

"Please don't hurt me. I'll give you everything I have." She lowered her bag from her shoulders and held it out for him.

"I can make you beautiful. I can make you legendary." He gripped her arm and pulled her into the alley. "You'll be famous when I'm through with you. I promise."

She struggled to free herself and opened her mouth, ready to scream, but he slammed his hand over her lips.

"Don't."

As anticipated, she had been difficult, but he'd accomplished the task and was ready to place her on display for all to see. The working conditions had been a bitch, but the end result was stunning. He stepped out of the shadow of the alley and noted the hint of grey light appear on the horizon. The streets would again awaken and his time was running out.

The spot had already been chosen because he left nothing to chance. With visual assurance of their solitude, he carried her to the bus stop. Physical strength was a prerequisite to the successful execution of his plan and he accomplished the task with ease. Timing was always the unknown component and that was what he fought against now. It would only take a car or a pedestrian to pass by for all to be spoiled.

In rapid succession, he secured her to the bench and wrapped her coat over her shoulders to cover the blood that soaked through her shirt. But it was on her face that he took care to ensure no blemishes appeared. Made up to perfection, he tilted her head and raised her shoulder for support. With his hands, he pushed her hair from her face and tucked it behind her ears. She was ready and it was time for him to leave but not before one last thing.

He retrieved his cell phone and pressed record. The lens captured her essence and beauty as he scanned her unmoving figure, posed in a provocative manner. It was all the time he had, but it had been enough.

As he prepared to leave, the sound of a cough reached his ears. He turned his head in the direction of the noise but saw no one. He listened further, but it had stopped. Had someone seen him or what he'd done?

Only a moment later, he heard a thud. "Son of a bitch." Leaving behind his work of art, he followed the noise with a steadfast march that turned into a charge. By the time he'd reached the adjacent corner, he spotted a man running away. Whoever it was had been watching him. The idea of such an intrusion filled him with anger. It was as though someone had observed an unfinished piece. A draft that wasn't ready to be received.

This invasion could not go unpunished. He would find the

person and the avenue with which to make that happen would be where he broadcast his performances. Surely whoever did this knew of his work. Who else would watch such an atrocity and not intervene unless it was one of his followers?

Far enough away from the scene of his societal tribute, he began to upload the video from the shelter of his car. And in the vein of other great artists, he would, from this point forward, leave clues for his spectator. Draw him out once again and make right what he had sought to spoil; the intimate creation of magnificence and immortality.

IN THE SHADOWS OF THE STUDIO WHERE CAMERAS, TELEPROMPTERS, and those who operated them moved about in skillful choreography, the producer twirled her finger, signaling to the anchor the need to wrap up.

"Thank you for tuning in and goodnight." Marc Aguilar flashed his sparkling white smile in the moment before the camera's red light extinguished. The blistering studio lights diminished as quickly as his friendly valediction and Marc stood from behind the anchor desk. "Great show tonight, everyone. Thank you." He began to walk backstage to his dressing room before being halted by his producer.

"Marc, you got a second?"

"I really want to go home, Lisa. Can it wait till tomorrow?"

She held a piece of paper in her hand. "You got an email from a reporter at KTLA. He copied me on it. Looks like he's got something for you. Thought you might be interested."

Marc was always interested in a story, under the right conditions, but was surprised to hear from his former colleague. While his career had started in San Diego, he'd spent some time in the LA market before taking the lucrative gig at CBN in New York. That was owed, in part, to his old friend, Kate Reid, and the unfortunate circumstances surrounding her former life that he'd exposed.

"Just check it out. Let me know what you think tomorrow. It has promise on the national scene, but I'll let you make the call."

"Yeah, okay." Marc held the paper in his hands and briefly glanced at the email subject header. *"Second body found in a week on the streets of South L.A."* At first glance, it didn't strike him as particularly unusual. Lots of bodies turned up in LA. "I'll take a look at it tonight. You should go home and get some rest too." He pushed open his dressing room door. "I'll see you tomorrow." Marc turned on the lights of his vanity mirror and began to remove his makeup, which revealed an older man, perhaps appearing older than his forty years. Gone were the days of his spray tans. This wasn't southern California anymore and CBN didn't much care for the orange look. So he wiped away the more natural-looking tone his makeup artist had chosen.

Marc had changed over the past few years and mostly for the good. People should always try to improve themselves and he figured that was what he'd done since his days at Channel 9 News in San Diego. And glancing at the potential news story that now rested on top of his vanity, he recalled those days. He'd have jumped all over a story like that, but this was CBN and things were different here. Marc had to learn to think nationally; globally. But still, he would consider the story as a favor to his former colleague, who he was certain would want something in return for such a gift.

Marc rose from his chair and loosened his tie. A glance at his phone showed a time of 9:45. "Might make it home at a decent hour tonight." He walked out of the dressing room and into the hall where the next batch of anchors, producers, and assistants were filing in. It was a twenty-four-hour news service. No matter if the same story was churned multiple times in a day, reported in every angle imaginable, they had to stay on the air.

"Night, Marc." His counterpart on the ten p.m. show passed by, her blond hair unmoving as she vacated the hairstylist's chair.

"Night, Jill." He reached the rear exit door, walked into the chilled air of an unheated parking garage, and soon regretted leaving his overcoat in the car. Unlocking his Mercedes, he slumped into the driver's seat and headed out toward the Upper West Side. That was where he called home now. A ridiculously small two-bed, two-bath condo that set him back a cool 1.5 million. Marc considered calling his old friend at KTLA, then remembered there was a three-hour time difference and he might still be on the air. "Maybe in the morning."

THE DOORMAN SMILED AS MARC APPROACHED. "GOOD EVENING, MR. Aguilar. Great show again tonight." With a swipe of his electronic key card, he pulled open the door. "You have a good night."

"You too, Gene." Marc entered the lobby of his apartment building and headed up to the third floor. Upon stepping into the corridor, he continued toward the end of the hall where his unit was located. The light sconces that hung on the walls were dimmed and cast a soft yellow glow onto the grey carpet, making it appear almost green.

Marc keyed the door and made his way inside. After hanging his coat, the sound of his footsteps on the wood floors squashed any hope of a surprise entrance.

A brunette woman with dark round eyes and olive skin glanced over her shoulder as she sat on the sofa, watching the news. "You're home." Wrapping her robe around her slender waist, she began to rise.

Marc moved closer and leaned toward her for a kiss. "No need to get up. Thanks for waiting for me."

"You looked good tonight, babe." Lucinda tucked her hair behind her ears. "Come sit down. You hungry? I can get you something to eat."

"No, no. I'm okay." Marc lowered onto the couch and pushed off his shoes. "I'll go fix myself a drink in a minute after I get changed. I just wanted to see you first. How was your day?"

"Great. We're almost finished with the property in Lincoln Square."

Lucinda was a partner in an interior design firm and was also Marc's live-in girlfriend. The two met when he'd hired her firm to decorate his apartment about a year ago. That was when he renewed his contract with CBN and figured he could officially call New York his home.

"Good. I know that one was a hassle for you." Marc eyed the television as the news ended. "You wouldn't mind if I head off to bed? It's been a long day."

"No. I don't mind at all." She regarded him with mild concern. "You feeling all right?"

"Oh yeah." He kissed her again and walked down the hall to their bedroom. The lamp on the nightstand flicked on as Marc pressed the switch and walked inside. A writing desk fronted a shallow bay window and was where Marc often preferred to work. His laptop rested on its center and Marc pulled out the chair and raised the lid.

A moment later, he began to draft an email to his friend at the

LA station. His request was simple: send him as much information as possible on the story and he would do what he could to pitch it to his bosses.

THE SHOPS ON MANHATTAN'S FIFTH AVENUE ALREADY HAD THEIR Christmas window displays in full view, ready to snare pre-Thanksgiving shoppers. The trees were still shedding their red and gold leaves.

He was on his way to meet Lucinda for a late lunch before heading into the studio to prepare for his first broadcast at seven p.m. *The Daily Beat* ran from 7:00 to 7:30, then he co-anchored another show from 9:00 to 9:30, which involved stories that actually had some meat in them. That was where his preference lay, but his contract was what it was and so he had to do the puff pieces in order to get the better stories. This usually meant his days started around three or four in the afternoon. Stories had to be edited, showrunners needed to stage the set. All of these things took hours, so it wasn't like he didn't have to work a full day like everyone else. It was just that he got paid a hell of a lot more for doing it.

Lucinda raised her hand as she stood outside the restaurant, wrapped in a black pea coat, hat, and scarf. Her smile still had the capacity to melt away his stress and he loved her for that. They'd lived together six months and he already knew he wanted to marry her, but hadn't had the courage yet to ask. She was a fiercely strong and opinionated woman, and just a little bit intimidating.

"Hi, babe." Marc kissed her cheek. "Let's get inside. It's freezing out here." He pushed open the door and the warm, softly lit restaurant was instantly soothing. "Table for two, please."

"Of course; follow me." A young woman in a black t-shirt and dress pants guided them to a small table. "Will this be all right?"

"Yes, thank you."

"The waiter will be with you two shortly." She politely smiled and walked away.

"I'm glad you were able to get away for a while." Marc pulled out Lucinda's chair.

"I always clear my schedule for you." She sat down and began to view the menu. "The salmon salad looks nice."

"You always order the salmon salad. Have a burger."

"I'm a woman in my late thirties and well beyond the capacity to consume a burger without damaging side effects."

"Sure, okay." Marc rolled his eyes and cast his gaze to the menu. "Well, I'm having a burger." He remembered a time in the not-too-distant past when he would've ordered the salad. But California was a different market with different priorities. It was a difference he appreciated more and more every day.

Marc was already digging into his food when his cell phone buzzed on the table. He quickly glanced at Lucinda, knowing what she was about to say.

"Don't. Just don't."

"You know I have to." His eyes pleaded with hers. "Technically, it's my job."

"Your job starts when you arrive at the studio and ends when you walk through our front door. You know I don't like interruptions during a meal. It's just rude."

"Fine." He took another bite. "But if it's a lead and someone else runs with it..."

"Oh, good Lord. Just answer it, then." She poked at her salad and exhaled a resigning breath.

Marc reveled in his minor victory and retrieved his phone. An email had arrived from his friend in LA. "Oh, now see. I was waiting for this."

Upon opening the email, his former colleague revealed that another body had been found less than a mile from the previous two. Attached were the police reports from the first two victims, but he hadn't yet received one on this third and newest victim.

Marc suddenly began to eat faster.

"What are you doing?" Lucinda asked. "What was that about?"

"A possible story. It's too difficult to view the attachments on my phone, so I'll have to wait until I get to the studio."

"Which, by the looks of it, you're trying to do as quickly as possible."

"I won't lie. That's exactly what I'm doing. This could be a big one—maybe—and I'd like to get my hands on it before anyone else."

Lucinda waved her hand. "Just go. I'll get the bill. I can see I've already lost your attention anyway."

"I'll make it up to you tonight." He wiped his lips and placed the napkin on his plate.

"Sure. When you get home at 10:30 and I've already eaten dinner."

"Okay, then. This weekend. I'll make it up to you this weekend." He pushed away from the table. "I'll see you tonight. Love you."

MARC ARRIVED AT THE STUDIO AND HURRIED TO THE SMALL OFFICE he shared with his producer that was adjacent to the dressing room. He turned on his computer and began to examine the email attachments. The first one was a police report on victim number one. Selena Ruiz, twenty-two years old, found in a section of what used to be called South Central, but was now called South Los Angeles in an effort to remove the negative association that had been established over the previous three decades.

As Marc began to read the report, an eerie sense of recognition began to crawl into his mind. This was not a drug crime, not even a robbery. This was a crime of passion. And what could well be a desperate need for attention.

He opened the second police report. Another woman. Older, thirty-five, Renee Jones. Nothing about these two women struck Marc as having anything in common, except that they were women. Different body shapes, different color hair, and different ethnicities. But there was a sense of familiarity that took him back to a time he preferred not to recall. A time when he thought he was doing a friend a favor by letting her in on the deal. But what happened in the end was that it cost her the love of her life and altered her path forever.

Marc picked up the phone. "Vince, it's me, Marc. I got your email." He continued to scroll through the reports. "You have anything yet on the third victim?"

"No. Police haven't released the name."

"Do you think it's related?"

"Oh yeah. No doubt about it," Vince continued. "They've already identified the body as that of a woman and she was found in the same vicinity as the others."

"The cops must be starting to get nervous. What were these women doing in that part of town?"

"The younger girl was walking home from a house party. I guess her car broke down or something and she was waiting for her ride to show up and decided just to start walking."

"Jesus," Marc replied.

"The other, I don't know why she was on West Adams. Maybe she was USC faculty, I haven't confirmed with the police, but she was also walking alone at night."

"That could still be a pretty far walk and by herself?"

"Agreed. We'll have to wait on the rest. Does this mean you want this one?"

Marc had to broach the topic because he knew it was coming. "You looking to make a move out of LA?"

"Maybe. I think I'm ready to see what else is out there."

Marc considered his remark. "Let me ask you something. You know I helped break the Highway Hunter case, right?"

"Of course."

"Then you might remember what they did to the bodies."

"I remember."

"Is that why you called me? I looked at the crime scene photos you sent. You were on the scene before they took the body away?"

"I was. They taped off the area, but I got there before they loaded her onto the truck."

"Has anyone else seen these pictures?"

"No. Cops asked me not to include them in the story. Said they didn't want any copy cats and they needed to leave out specific details to help them find the real killer."

"Right. So the public doesn't know that this—person—is slicing and dicing the bodies, but seems to be making up the faces? I mean, it doesn't appear as though these women would've been wearing that much makeup. It looks intentional."

"So far, that's been left out. I believe he is applying makeup to them as if he was getting them ready for a photo shoot. It looks highly staged; professional. You know it won't be long before that gets out. He's leaving them out in the open. Propped up on a park bench, or like this last one, they found her at a bus stop."

"Get back with me when you know more about this third victim. We'll work something out. Thanks for the heads-up, Vince." Marc ended the call.

This was far removed from the stories he'd covered over the past year or so. While there weren't any specific markings like the Highway Hunter cases, this guy was sending a message nonetheless. But he wondered; would his old friend, who'd suffered enough losses, want to hear from him again? Would she want to bring this to her BAU boss, Agent Nick Scarborough? This was still a case for the LA police and it wasn't likely to be handed over to the feds unless they asked for help.

Marc detested the thoughts that were forming in his mind, but he was a man who could still go places. Places that would pay him more money, where he'd have more prestige. But he would have to break something bigger than the Highway Hunter and Vince wanted something in return too.

His contacts with the feds were few and far between. Kate Reid was about the only person who might be interested in this. And if she was, he knew she would be his go-to. But then, he was the one who brought Edward Shalot to her doorstep. Had she forgiven him for that? *Could* she forgive him was probably the better question. He supposed the only way to know for sure was to call up his old friend.

2

A young professional in a bespoke suit raised his index finger to the bartender, signaling he was ready for another drink. However, given the mass of thirsty patrons, it would be several more minutes before he was handed his second vodka tonic.

It had been standing room only for the latecomers, but fortunately, Kate Reid and Alicia Vasquez had arrived early at the popular bar. It was a rare day when they could leave work at a decent time and the two, who had grown closer in recent months, elected to have a quick drink before heading home.

It was Alicia who'd spotted the well-dressed businessman at the end of the bar, eyeing the two of them when he thought neither was looking. "What about that guy over there?" She cocked her head just slightly in his direction.

"Who are you talking about?" Kate asked. "That guy?" Her eyes shifted to the man in the dark grey suit, who was sporting a heavy five o'clock shadow.

"Yeah. He keeps looking over here."

Kate smiled. "Probably because we're the only two women here without a man."

"We are not. And I know he isn't looking at me."

"He could be."

"I don't think so. And even if he was, he's not exactly my type. He has a penis."

Kate tossed her head back in a full-bellied laugh. "That is true. But he's not my type either."

"You're so full of shit, Kate. He's brooding, mysterious, piercing eyes. I've known you long enough to know he's exactly your type."

"Well, you might be right, but it doesn't matter. I'm taking a break for a while." Kate sipped on her white wine. "I've got some big decisions to make and I don't need a man clouding my head."

"So you decided to move?"

"I think so. I'd like to be closer to work. I mean, what the hell do I need a house for? A little one-bedroom apartment in the heart of D.C. would suit me just fine."

Alicia raised an eyebrow. "Uh-huh. I guess you could get rid of that piece of shit car of yours if you did that."

Kate shook her head and smiled. "Yes, yes, I could." Movement out of the corner of her eye caught her attention. "Damn it. Don't look, but that guy is coming over here."

Alicia immediately spun her head around.

"I said don't look."

"Evening, ladies."

"Evening." Kate fashioned a polite smile.

"You two seem to be having a good time. I've been hearing quite a bit of laughter over here." He placed his half-empty vodka tonic on the table and extended his hand. "I'm Noah Quinn. Nice to meet you."

"Pleasure." Kate took his hand. "I have to tell you, Noah, that my girlfriend and I are having a very nice time blowing off some steam, so if you don't mind, I think we'd prefer to spend time alone. You understand."

"Of course. My apologies for interrupting. You two have a nice evening." He began to walk away.

"Girlfriend? Are we dating now?" Alicia displayed another raised brow.

"I'm not in the mood to deal with the likes of Noah Quinn. Come on; that cannot be his real name. That's the name of a character in a mommy-porn novel."

"That's a little harsh and judgmental, isn't it? He seemed nice enough."

"So did Ted Bundy."

"Yeah, you've been working here too long." Alicia studied Kate for a moment. "How's things with you and Scarborough?"

"Fine. Why do you ask?"

"Kate, I'm not stupid. Things have been weird between you two for a while. And then you broke up with Mike a couple of months ago and it's like there's this thing, this wall, between you. Scarborough changed after the death of his friend's son, and I know he blames himself, but it's more than that. He's closed off, all business. That's not the guy I know."

Kate hadn't revealed to anyone the conversation she and Nick had that morning at his place. But if Alicia had picked up on the tension, then she was sure not only Dwight would have, but probably most of their colleagues had as well. It was what she had tried so hard to avoid. Things were weird and she hated it because she missed how close they used to be. In the few months that had passed, she thought it would get better, but it hadn't and it was becoming a problem for both of them.

"No, it isn't. But I've decided that I can't help him through this. He has to do it himself. We've all been through the wringer and you know that. I'm done feeling sorry and I'm done feeling like I have to take care of him. I know how that sounds, but Alicia, I don't have the strength to shoulder his problems along with my own."

"What are you saying?"

Kate's phone began to ring and she glanced at the caller ID. "Oh my God. Hang on a second. I need to take this." She slid out of her seat and headed out the front door and into the cold night air. "Marc? Is that you?"

"Kate! How are you?"

"Good. I haven't heard from you in a long time. But I've seen your show. I can't believe you're on CBN. It's fantastic!" She eyed a woman who seemed annoyed that Kate was standing near the bar's entrance and talking on her phone. She stepped aside and nodded as the woman, draped in a heavy wool coat, entered. "So to what do I owe the pleasure?"

"I'd like to send you something I got from an old colleague when I worked in LA. I guess there've been some things going on that I thought might interest you."

"Things?"

"There's no way to put this delicately. Three women have been found in South LA, their bodies left in pretty bad shape, but their faces untouched. And they've been left posed, I guess is the only way to describe it. Like on a park bench. Sat upright."

"Oh my God. So, what does this have to do with me?" Kate adored Marc and the two had been through their share together, but she knew he wouldn't be calling her if he didn't want something.

"Well, you work on these kinds of cases, don't you? Serial killers and bizarre murders and things like that."

"I do, but it sounds like LAPD is running this one. It's not something I can just jump right into. And besides, why would you want me to?"

"Look, I'm not going to pretend not to remember the last time I called you up and asked for a favor. I know what that favor cost you."

Kate raised her head to the starless sky. "That's not on you, Marc."

"I suppose what it boils down to is that my former colleague wants me to pitch this story to CBN. He's angling to get out of the local market. But I don't think they'll be interested unless the feds are. And that's where you come in."

"You have to understand that things don't work that way. I can't barge into LAPD and demand they hand over the case files. On something like this—local—they have to ask for our help. Allow us to offer up a profile of the unsub; assist them with the investigation. And so far, this is the first I'm hearing of it. So I don't think they've reached out to us yet." She considered again what it was that he wanted out of this. "What happens if you pitch this to CBN?"

"You mean, what do I get out of it?"

She didn't reply.

"I deserve that," Marc said. "And I imagine the AP has already covered this, but no one else seems to want to pick it up."

"Except you. And you haven't answered my question."

"Come on, Kate. You've seen the type of BS fluff stories I get. Don't get me wrong, I'm grateful to be where I am and, honestly, I have you to thank for that. I guess I'm the only one who benefited from the Highway Hunter case. But the fact of the matter is, I need a strong national headliner. This can't be all there is for me."

"Marc, you're a good friend and I don't hold you responsible for anything Edward Shalot did. You need to understand that. Even if I could reach out to LAPD, which is above my pay grade, I can guarantee you, I wouldn't be the one running the show. I couldn't give you any scoops or anything like that. I don't think I'd be much help to you at all."

"Before you dismiss it completely, will you just take a look at what I've got? If anything, you're damn good at your job and you might see something they don't. You know you got that crazy sixth sense thing."

Kate had to laugh. "Sure." She rubbed her arm for warmth, as the temperature seemed to have dropped ten degrees just since she began this conversation. "I need to get back inside. I'm freezing my ass off out here." She paused and cast her gaze among cars passing by, their red taillights hazed by the visible exhaust floating in the air. "Send me what you've got. I'll take it upstairs and see what we can do."

"Thank you, Kate. That's all I'm asking."

"Uh-huh. It was good to hear from you, Marc. Hey, you miss the warm weather back home?"

"Sometimes."

"Me too. I'll catch up with you later. Goodnight." Kate returned inside and found Noah Quinn sitting with Alicia. Her eyes widened and her palms turned up, a silent questioning of her friend's intentions.

"Kate," Noah said. "Your friend here was explaining to me that you might have been mistaken as to your current relationship status."

"Oh, did she?" Daggers shot from Kate's eyes toward her soon-to-be former friend.

Alicia offered a phony smile and shrugged her shoulders.

～

"COME ON, BABY. IT'S TIME TO GO TO SCHOOL." DINA KNIGHT placed her hands against her son's shoulders and began to usher him toward the door. "Andre?" she shouted up the staircase. "Andre, we're leaving."

A moment later, Andre Knight appeared at the top of the stairs and began leaping down to meet them at the bottom. "Have a good day at school, little man." He kissed his son on the top of his head.

"Look at your tie. Come here." Dina began to straighten her husband's tie and smoothed it down his chest. "Much better. I'll see you tonight." She kissed his lips.

"I might have to work late."

"Again? Andre, come on. That's the third time this week. You're going to miss dinner again?"

"I said I might. I'll let you know as soon as I do. You know I got to put in the hours if I want a promotion."

Dina pursed her lips. "Right. And I'm sure they'll remember that you were working twelve-hour days when the time comes."

"Mom, we're going to be late."

"You'd better go," Andre replied.

"All right." She pulled open the door. "You let me know if you're going to be home for dinner, you hear me?"

"Yes, ma'am." Andre closed the door behind them and pressed his back against it with a heavy sigh. He quickly recovered from the morning chaos and made his way into the kitchen, grabbing his insulated coffee cup for the commute to his office. A quick check of the time and he knew if he didn't leave now, chances were better than fair he'd be late for work.

He stepped outside and walked along the concrete path toward his car, which sat on the driveway. With his eyes briefly cast toward the sun, he realized it would be a warm day. It was November and he still hadn't gotten used to the weather in Los Angeles. Andre was a transplant. His native Detroit no longer provided him and his family the stability of a good job, so he moved them here last year.

Andre took to the road and headed into Downtown LA where he worked as an accountant for a telecommunications company. The pay wasn't great, but at least it was a job. Dina worked in a clinic that offered medical services for those with little or no health insurance.

Their home was a rental in a not-so-nice neighborhood in LA, but it was all they could afford for now. He carried a gun with him at all times and insisted Dina carry one too. She sometimes worked the second shift and he didn't like her walking into the parking lot alone at night.

Andre arrived at work just in the nick of time and quickly made his way inside the six-story building. "Morning, Stella."

"Good morning, Andre. Right on time, as usual. You have a good day, now."

"I will, ma'am. And you too." Andre continued past the receptionist and toward his cubicle, which was near the back of the building. With the obligatory pleasantries exchanged, he sat down and got to work.

Andre only had a couple of friends at the office, but they weren't close. Lunches and the occasional beer after work and that was about all. He'd been invited, along with his family, to attend barbeques and birthday parties and the like, but Andre always had an excuse for not being able to attend. He never even made mention of the invites to Dina. He was a man who preferred to keep to himself and that was the way he'd always been.

"Hey, man. What's up?" Miguel Perez worked in customer service and the only time he made his way to accounting was when one of his customers argued against a charge on their bill. "You got a second to look something up for me?"

Andre regarded the man with the pomaded hair and loud tie. "Sure. What is it?"

"This *puta* says she has a charge on her bill and says it's higher than it's supposed to be."

"What's the account number?" Andre despised Miguel but luckily didn't cross paths with him that often. Still, just looking at the punk made his pulse rate rise.

Miguel handed him the information and Andre began to search for this erroneous charge. "It's right. She's wrong." He turned the screen so Miguel could see it.

"Okay. Thanks, man." He turned on his heel.

Andre began to imagine himself catching up with Miguel, grabbing him by the shoulder, and whipping him around. And before he would know what hit him, Andre would stab him in the eye with a fork. A smile crossed his face as he continued to type on his keyboard.

The day passed by with little notice and numbed by the banality of his job, Andre hadn't realized it was already time to leave. He never stayed a single minute beyond five p.m., no matter what he still had to process. For thirteen dollars an hour, they didn't deserve his extra time. He logged off his computer and reached for his briefcase, which he never really needed but liked to carry anyway. It made him feel important and made him look important in his wife's eyes.

He began walking out of the building and, again, nodded his way through, never saying much to anyone. Andre reached his car and pressed the remote to open it. He keyed the ignition of his 2004 Honda CRV. The engine sputtered, then caught and began to purr. The parking lot was emptying quicker than an elevator after someone had a back-end blowout. He waited several minutes for his chance to escape.

At last, he was on the 405 and now was when he could finally let go. Let go of all the bullshit stress of a bullshit job. He yanked off his tie and turned up the music.

It took him almost forty minutes, but he'd arrived. Andre pulled alongside the curb fronting the park and plunked money into the meter. There weren't many cars parked on this stretch of the road and it was mainly a residential area. The people from this part of town didn't really give a shit about anyone else's business, which was a good thing for Andre.

He scanned the area. A few men stood outside a liquor store across the street, smoking their cigarettes and holding cartons of them in their hands, selling them for less than what they could buy inside the store. The small park on the other side was deserted. No one hung out there for too long once the sun started going down. It seemed Andre was in the clear.

He moved around to the back of the CRV and opened the swing gate. Lifting the floorboard, he reached inside the compartment that contained the tire jack. He pulled the bag from below and closed up the car. After another glance in both directions, Andre walked toward the park where a small building stood. It was a public restroom, but it had already been locked up for the night. Or perhaps it was always locked up. Sometimes they never bothered to open them up in the first place.

Tucked behind the corner of the building and with no one in his periphery, Andre reached inside the bag and retrieved a wig. He carefully placed it on his head, the fake locks resting just below his ears. Another search inside the bag and he pulled out a hat—a baseball hat, to be precise. He placed that over the wig and pressed it snugly against his scalp. His own hair was kept in a buzz cut, so it was easy to ensure a secure fit. The final piece was to do a quick change and slip on his t-shirt and shorts that hung low on his hips, exposing the band of his boxer shorts.

Without a mirror to confirm nothing was out of place, he had to take his chances and began to walk back around the building and faced the park. The sun was lowering below the horizon and the few streetlights that worked flickered on. Andre approached a bench and took a seat. All he had to do now was wait.

3

When the BAU-4 Section Chief called, Nick wasted no time clearing his schedule to accommodate him. It was a call he rarely received and one that could hold a variety of meanings.

He looked upon the many certifications and degrees mounted on the wall of the chief's office. Some time had passed since he'd been asked to instruct at Quantico and perhaps that was the reason for the call. But Nick could speculate among a thousand different reasons because he now waited for the man in his office and had nothing but time to think about such things.

"Sorry to have kept you waiting, Agent Scarborough." The chief, SSA Colin Halpern, offered a greeting.

"No problem at all, sir." Nick stood awkwardly to accept the chief's greeting and quickly returned to his seat. It seemed his nerves had gotten the better of him the longer he sat in wait.

"I'm sure you're wondering why I called you." Halpern placed a file on his desk and pulled out his chair to sit. He continued without waiting for a response. "I wanted to get a feel for how things were going with your team at WFO."

"Fine, sir. Couldn't be better."

"I know how difficult these past few months have been for you after your friend got into some trouble."

That was putting it mildly, but Nick wasn't about to correct him. "Yes, sir. But things have returned to normal for the team. We're busier than ever."

"Good. Glad to hear it. I guess I should get to the point then." He opened the file on his desk. "I've been going over your records and wanted to relay to you that I think you've done a fine job at WFO."

"Thank you, sir."

"Apart from the letter of censure." He raised his eyes to Nick. "Which, frankly, I think was a raw deal for you." He returned his attention to the file once again. "You've had an exemplary record. And that brings me to why I asked you here today. Your work at WFO and your experience inside BAU has made you a top candidate to be considered for the Senior Unit Agent here at headquarters."

"Candidate?" Nick began with some trepidation. "What about Agent Cole?"

"He's being promoted to Unit Chief and we need someone to fill his position."

Nick shifted in his seat. "You want me to come to Quantico?"

Halpern smiled. "Yes. You're at the top of our list for consideration. Nick, you and I both know you've gone as far as you're going to go at WFO. There's no place there for you to move. Now, I know you and your team are tight, but it's time you consider your options here. I don't need to tell you the financial benefits, so I'll tell you that it would mean leading a much larger team, more complex and varied cases, and much more room for growth."

The unexpected news was exactly what Nick had wanted to hear for a very long time. It was all he'd worked for and the prospect of it actually coming to fruition caught him off his guard. "You said I'm a top candidate. So there are others in consideration?'

"Yes, there are. However, you're the only one who has instructed here at Quantico, who has been an SSA for the past five years, and whose time has come to be rewarded for his hard work."

Nick's thoughts immediately turned to Kate. While their relationship had, for the most part, returned to a state of normal, this would mean no longer working with her. It would also likely mean that Dwight would be promoted, which he rightly deserved to be. Maybe it was for the best? Quantico wasn't far away. He wasn't leaving the city. He owed Dwight and perhaps this was the best way to repay him. And it was a position he'd coveted.

For a moment, Nick couldn't figure out if he was trying to convince himself to stay or to go, but Halpern continued to look at him, waiting for an answer. "Thank you, sir. This is something I would be very interested in pursuing. It's an incredible opportunity and I'm honored you're considering me for the job."

"That's what I was hoping you'd say. You had me nervous for a minute. Now, there will be testing for the position, but I have no doubt that will prove all too easy for you. It's really just a formality."

"When would this go into effect, assuming I'm green-lighted."

"We're still in the process of shifting things around here. It will likely be the first of January." Halpern rose to his feet and extended his hand. "It'll be a pleasure having you here, Agent Scarborough."

As promised, Marc sent Kate the police reports he'd received from his colleague and she was now studying them at her desk. She wasn't sure how his colleague had obtained the information in an ongoing investigation, and for a moment, wondered if she should have this to begin with. But in her short time with the Bureau, she'd learned that not everything was black and white and that sometimes she had to operate in the grey, and perhaps this was one of those times.

"What's that?"

Startled, Kate looked over her shoulder to find Dwight peering down. "Nothing." She clicked off the screen. "Just a friend wanting me to take a look at something."

"Someone asked you to consult on a case?"

"No. Nothing like that. I don't think it'll amount to anything significant for us." She turned her chair. "What are you working on?"

Dwight regarded her with narrowed eyes. "Waiting on Scarborough to get back. I wanted to go over the caseload. I received a few requests for consults and we need to prioritize them."

"Where's he at?"

"Was called out to Quantico."

"They want him to train?"

"Don't know. He didn't say. Just said he'd be back later this afternoon." Dwight glanced at his phone. "Should be any time now."

Beyond Kate's cubicle were the elevator doors and as she

peered over Dwight's square shoulders, she spotted Nick step out in the distance. "Speak of the devil."

Dwight turned. "Great. I'll see when he can meet. How does the rest of your day look? You got some time to get together and go over these requests?"

"Yeah. Of course." Kate kept her eyes on Nick as he veered toward his office.

"Good. I'll get back to you with a time."

She'd seen the look on Dwight's face and regretted that he had been caught in the middle of this. He was a smart man and there was no denying the strain between her and Nick. It was a tension she'd created, or at the very least, did nothing to resolve. And so it would continue until more time passed and eventually all would be forgotten, or rather, ignored.

Kate returned to her screen and pulled up the files to continue reviewing the case. The police had no leads. No one in the area was willing to talk. That, however, was no surprise. It was a community fearful of the police, the gangs, and everything in between. No one could blame them for their silence. Except that they were now in the crosshairs of a murderer with a penchant for pretty faces. Still, she could see no reason that would warrant reaching out to the LAPD. They hadn't asked for help and the toes that would be stepped on if she approached them would be many and large.

As she continued to read the most recent report, an email arrived in her inbox. The alert at the bottom of her screen indicated that it was from Marc. "Well, that didn't take long." She clicked it open and, after reading it, began to type her reply.

"I'm looking at it now. Give me today and I'll let you know what I think. But as of right now, I can't see a way to offer help to the LAPD."

She pressed "send," dropped her hands into her lap, and

considered perhaps she could bring it up in the meeting later today. If nothing else, just to let Marc know that she tried to help.

DETECTIVE RAY SHARPE RACED UP BEHIND A POLICE CRUISER, ONE OF nearly half a dozen, by the looks of it, and shifted his car into park. He stepped out of the unmarked Chevy Tahoe and pulled on his black leather jacket. Los Angeles was in the throes of a cold spell and, combined with the pre-dawn hour, meant it was chilly by Southern California standards.

He walked toward the several officers who fronted the police-taped crime scene in order to hold off bystanders. "Morning."

"Detective Sharpe." The officer nodded and raised the tape for him to pass through.

Sharpe continued into the park and headed toward the beams of light shining on the ground. The park was otherwise bathed in darkness as it had closed several hours earlier and there was no mistaking the body was the subject on which the lights shined.

An officer broke from the crowd and approached. "Detective Sharpe, thanks for coming out."

"Did I have a choice?" He raised a corner of his mouth, deepening the fold of his laugh lines, although there weren't many of those, and his forehead told a better story of his life. Deep lines etched across it along with those in between his brow. It appeared he'd spent most of his life in a state of worry or anger; perhaps both. "Same as the others?" He began to move near the body.

"Appears so. She was on the bench, but um—someone came across her and nudged her. When she fell off, he called the police."

"Is he here now?"

"They took him to the station."

"Okay. Make sure he doesn't leave before I have a chance to talk to him."

"Will do." The officer turned his attention to the others surrounding the woman. "Excuse us."

Sharpe moved in and squatted next to the crime scene investigator. "Anything of interest?"

"It's looking like it's the same perp. Heavy makeup. No trauma to her face, but as you can see, the rest of her didn't fare so well." With a pen, he raised the blouse of the woman enough to make visible the multiple stab wounds.

"No." Sharpe eyed the wounds, assessing a pattern, noting their depth and length, and assumed that whoever committed the act did so in a hurry, except when it came to the face. It appeared as though extra time and care were taken to ensure it was perfect. Still, the killer would have taken an extraordinary amount of time and someone had to have seen him. "When's the ME supposed to arrive?"

"Any time."

"Good. We need to get her the hell out of here." He returned upright and surveyed the growing crowd. With unyielding eyes, he looked upon each individual. Most seemed to have enjoyed a boisterous Friday night. Their glassy stares and slight sways suggested they'd consumed an excessive amount of alcohol and perhaps other substances.

But what Sharpe was looking for, he did not see in the gathering. However, if they didn't break up this little party, things would turn ugly. They always did. He returned his attention to an officer. "Make sure we keep things orderly. When the ME gets here, get her bagged before dragging her out in front of everyone."

"Ten-four."

The detective made another pass in the area and jotted down a few notes. The killer would have had to perform the act itself in a place of seclusion and so he searched for just such an area inside the park, noting there didn't appear to be a place that offered complete isolation. The night skies would have helped. There were no blood trails, meaning he would've carried her from one place to another. That would mean he was strong, probably larger than average.

Sharpe again surveyed the area. Someone had to have seen something once he brought the victim to the bench that was only thirty-odd feet from the street, but he wouldn't get any help from around here. It was understandable but frustrating nonetheless. Young women were being murdered and he'd begun to feel that without the community's help, they would continue to die.

4

A short train ride and Kate had arrived, stepping onto the platform and ready to head into Manhattan. The autumn skies were brisk and the winds blustery. She buttoned her wool coat and wrapped the scarf around her neck as she prepared to meet with Marc Aguilar for the first time in a long time.

It had also been a long time since she'd visited New York. Not since her parents had taken the trip to see her graduate from the Academy.

She continued toward the studio, passing the storefronts that already had Christmas for sale in their windows. The tree at Rockefeller hadn't yet been lit, but it was in the process of being decorated and, as she passed by, the tree looked much larger than what she had seen on TV all of those years.

Kate entered through the glass doors of CBN's building and approached the front desk attendant. "Good morning. I'm Kate Reid and I'm here to see Marc Aguilar. He's expecting me."

"One moment and I'll buzz him for you."

Kate waited for the man to get the approval and surveyed the beautiful lobby. She smiled at the thought that Marc had come so far and of the origins of their relationship.

"Here's your badge. He'll be down in a moment."

"Thank you." She stepped away from the desk and meandered inside the great lobby until moments later when she spotted him. "Oh my God! Look at you!" Kate opened her arms wide.

"It's so good to see you, Kate. I can't believe you're here." He pulled back from the embrace to arm's length and let his eyes consume her. "You look gorgeous as ever."

"And you haven't changed at all." He had but in a good way. She noticed his skin wasn't as orange and his teeth weren't as paper white. It was a look that suited him well. "So, are we grabbing something to eat or are you going to show me around here first?"

"I'm starving. Let's get some food and then I can give you the nickel tour. Most everyone's gone right now anyway for lunch. When we get back, I'll introduce you to some people you'll probably recognize."

"You're assuming I watch your network."

"You don't?"

She smiled. "Of course I do—sometimes, and only to see you." Kate patted him on the back as the two made their way outside.

THE DRIED LEAVES FELL FROM THE TREES AS KATE PEERED THROUGH the window. She sipped on her glass of water and waited for Marc to finish up a call. The restaurant was busy and a bit too loud for Kate's taste, but it was nice and she thought Marc picked it because it was trendy. Maybe he was trying to show off a little that he was an official New Yorker now. Though to her, he'd always be Marc Aguilar from Nine Action News.

She supposed that he might have thought the same about her. Working as an evidence technician for San Diego PD, she had been a small fish in a big pond. Now she was a small fish in an even bigger pond.

"Sorry about that." Marc dropped his phone into the pocket of his coat, which hung over his chair. "My producer. She doesn't like to be far from me."

"It's fine. I was enjoying the scenery. Does it just feel unreal that we're both sitting here right now? I mean, given where we started."

"It's a little mind-blowing, yeah." He swirled the straw in his ice water. "So, you looked at what I sent you?"

"I did."

"What do you think?"

"I think it's not my case. I think LAPD has their hands full with this one, but as I mentioned before, Marc, I just don't think I can do anything to help you."

"Is it because of what happened the last time I got involved in one of your investigations?"

"No. Of course not. And if you're carrying some kind of guilt around with you, then you need to stop. Please. There's nothing any of us could have done to prevent what happened." That wasn't entirely true for her. She always shouldered the blame. Shalot had been after her and her alone. "Besides, that was a long time ago and I'm different now. We're all different now, aren't we?"

"I guess so."

"Why did you want me to come here today? We could've discussed this on the phone."

"You don't like the city?"

"You know what I mean. Don't get me wrong, it is really good to see you, but you know you'll always be my friend and we can see each other any time you'd like."

"I know."

"Then what's behind this? Why do you want BAU to take this on?"

"Not just BAU. You. I think it's you who should help them out with this one. Forgive me, but you probably have more experience than LAPD does in this type of case."

"Don't underestimate their abilities and their expertise. They know what they're doing, Marc. I can assure you of that." She paused for a moment. "Is it just for ratings? A better gig? I mean, if we're going to be honest, then let's be honest here. You owe me that much."

"Partly, yes. As I said before, I'd like to run better stories. But I don't want it to sound as though I'm using our friendship."

"Aren't you, though?" She felt bad for laying it on the line and wished she hadn't said it at all.

"I don't mean to be. I really don't. I need your help. That's what it boils down to."

"But you don't." She leaned over the table. "You can run on this yourself. You don't need me involved. It's a story. A sad one, but it's a story."

"No way would they run it unless either the feds were involved or a whole lot more people were being killed. Look, it's a shitty business—journalism. I've known that for years, but it is what it is and I want to be better than that. I want to do real stories that have real meaning to people."

"I understand that, I do." Kate stopped to consider his request.

"And I know you're not trying to take advantage of my position because, honestly, I have zero clout."

"But it isn't just that. You do have a knack for certain things. I've seen you in action. Whether or not you want to admit it, you do have some innate ability to solve puzzles. Find clues that would otherwise be overlooked."

"Okay. You've buttered me up enough. I'll talk to my SSA."

"Agent Scarborough?"

"Yes. I'll talk to him. See what he thinks. But I have to follow the rules here. You understand?"

"Of course. I'd never ask you to bend the rules for me, Kate."

"Sure you would." She smiled again as their food arrived. "Now, can we talk about something else? Who's this woman you're living with and will I get to meet her?" Kate dipped a spoon in her soup.

"She's great. And yeah, I'd love for you to meet her."

COLLEGE FOOTBALL GAMES WERE BROADCAST ON EVERY SCREEN IN the bar, but Nick had his eye on only one. Nebraska. His Cornhuskers were winning against Illinois and they were doing well in their division this season. Saturdays brought with them a certain elation for Nick and today appeared to be going much the same.

"Hey, buddy." Dwight approached from behind and placed a hand on Nick's shoulder.

"Hey. There you are. Take a seat."

"How's the Huskers doing this year?" Dwight pulled out a stool and sat down. "Penn State isn't doing shit right now, but I'm holding out hope."

"Not bad. What are you drinking?" Nick asked.

"Just a beer for me, thanks." Dwight noticed his colleague's half-empty bottle. "How long you been here? Sorry I'm late. Had to take the kids back early. Their grandmother is celebrating a birthday and Megan wanted them to be there, so I gave up my time."

"You two have to be the easiest-going divorced couple I've ever known."

"We have our moments. Trust me on that." The bartender handed Dwight a bottle of Sam Adams. "Thanks." He took a swig and turned his attention to Nick again. "So what's going on? I'm glad to see you're getting out and about these days. That's an improvement. How's um—you know." Dwight tossed a glance at Nick's beer.

"Okay. I'm managing."

"No disrespect. I just..."

"None taken, man. I appreciate your concern. You have every right to be and I know that. I guess I'm doing all right." He began to tear at the label on his bottle. "You know Friday at our team meeting?"

"Yeah?"

"I wanted to tell you something then, but I just didn't know how."

"Okay, what is it?"

"You know I had that meeting with the section chief?"

"Yeah, sure."

"They want me to come back. Be their senior unit agent."

"What? Are you serious? That's great—isn't it? I mean, it sucks for us, but man, that's fantastic for you. That's what we all want, right?"

"I guess." He held Dwight's gaze. "It'd mean leaving the team. Leaving you and Kate."

"Well, I guess that's true, but shit. It's a hell of an opportunity. We'll be fine."

"Nothing's set in stone yet. I'm up for consideration only and it won't take effect until the beginning of January. It would mean leaving a position open for you at WFO. You know I'd recommend you for that in a heartbeat, right?"

"Of course. And I'd be grateful if it came to pass, but this isn't about me. It's about you. Yet for some reason, you seem hesitant. And I can only hazard a guess as to why."

Nick turned away, sheepishly drinking his beer until the bottle was empty. He raised a finger to the bartender.

"I've known for a long time," Dwight said.

Nick regarded him as though he'd just cast an aspersion.

"Don't give me that look. The hotel? Hell, even before that, I suspected, but I kept my mouth shut because no one was getting hurt. But that all changed a few months ago, didn't it?" Dwight took another drink. "You guys have a lot of history. There's no denying that. You helped her through her grief. She helped you through your breakup. It's no surprise—to anyone. And now, you're thinking, well, if I take the job, I won't see her; won't work with her, and she'll move on. And you know what? You're probably right."

Nick remained silent while his partner and friend, whom he hadn't realized had been fully aware of the situation, offered a gentle reprimand.

"Kate has shared things with me. Things that still haunt her, goals she's striving for. We talk. But there's one topic we don't discuss and that's you. I thought you might've played a part in her breakup with Burgess, but I never asked her about it. Not my place. And if she wanted to share it with me, she would have. Point being, this has to stop. It's not good for either of you. You need to either shit or get off the pot." Dwight downed the rest of his beer.

"You think I haven't told her how I feel? I did. And she still walked away."

"I'm sorry. I didn't know that. She never said anything."

Nick peered again at the football game and noticed the score. "Ah hell. I missed a touchdown." He turned to Dwight. "So I guess that was what I wanted to tell you. That, depending on how things go, I might be moving on. But I think if it happens, it'll be a good thing for you. You deserve to be running the show over there. You're one of the best agents I've had the pleasure to work with."

"Hey now. You don't need to grease me up if you're looking for a letter of recommendation. You know damn well I wouldn't hesitate."

DETECTIVE SHARPE GLANCED AWAY FROM HIS COMPUTER SCREEN AT the officer standing in his doorway. "What is it?"

"They brought the body in. Thought you might want to take a trip down to the morgue."

He rose from his chair and pulled his jacket off the back of it. "Let's go."

Within minutes, they'd arrived at the ME's office and were escorted to view the body of the woman Sharpe had been standing over only hours earlier in the park.

"Jesus, man. Have you even gone home yet?" the officer asked.

Sharpe only shook his head.

"No one can fault you for lack of dedication." A door was just ahead. "This is it."

"I know." Sharpe followed behind the officer and approached the medical examiner. "Dr. Hahn."

"Detective. You're looking well."

"No need for fabrications, Dr. Hahn. How far have you gotten?"

"I've just finished with the photographs and removing the bags from her hands and feet. I've scraped under her nails too. So far, everything points to this young woman as being the victim of the same person as the previous victims, I'm afraid."

"I figured." Sharpe didn't intend to be curt, but he hated wasting his time, especially here in the morgue. "What about the face?"

"We'll send samples to the lab for confirmation, but I suspect we'll find the same makeup used."

"What is it about this perp and makeup? Why is he playing dress up?" the officer asked.

The detective rubbed his chin, which had grown stubbly from the long shift he was pulling. "I don't know. Maybe he feels guilty about how he destroyed their bodies. Maybe it's a fetish. Right now, I don't know shit because we have no goddam leads. No one knows what this person looks like. We assume it's a male based on your findings, Dr. Hahn. But other than that, we have no idea who this guy is or why he's doing this."

"He might have left us a clue on this victim and that's what I'm here to find out." The doctor began pressing down on the woman's chest with his razor-sharp scalpel as he slid it along her torso.

5

After considering how best to approach her current predicament, Kate decided to rip off the Band-Aid and just ask. Uphold the promise she'd given Marc and ask Nick if he would allow her to make contact with the LAPD, whether they wanted her to or not.

And with two coffees in hand, Kate now stood in the doorway of Nick's office. "Morning. You have a minute?"

"Sure, come in. Have a seat."

"I thought you might need one of these." She handed him the coffee.

"Wow. Thank you. You have a good weekend?"

"Yes, thanks. That's kind of the reason I'm here."

"Oh? Everything okay?" He sipped on his drink.

"I went to New York to visit Marc Aguilar."

"Really? Haven't heard that name in a while. How's he doing?"

"Very well. He's an anchor for CBN. Mostly nights. But he wanted to talk to me about a case out of California—LA."

"Why? What's happening in LA?"

"There've been some murders in South LA. Not the usual drug or gang-related ones. Three women have been found. No leads, from what I gather."

"Okay. What's that got to do with us, or Aguilar, for that matter?"

"He thinks we should reach out to LAPD and offer assistance." She failed to mention Marc specified her involvement. "There are some characteristics to this case that point to serial killings of a particularly unusual nature."

"As if any of them are normal."

"Good point. But by that, I mean whoever's doing this is making up these women's faces, maiming their bodies, and leaving them on display in very public settings."

Nick closed his eyes for a moment and inhaled a breath. "Okay. I'm failing to see how this would involve us, though. Has LAPD been looking for federal help?"

"No. And that's the problem. I think Marc wants to take the story national and he wants our—my help doing it."

"I see. He hasn't changed much, has he?"

"He's got good intentions. What I'm asking here is, do you think it's appropriate to reach out to the detective in charge and offer our help?"

"Depends on the detective. And, we haven't ventured out west in a while. I'm thinking it'd be better suited to the LA field office."

"What if I could help? And of course, I could also consult with the LA office. I've been thinking about specializing in profiling. I'll be finished with my probation in a matter of weeks and it's an area I've always been interested in learning. Frankly, I have unique experience in the matter."

"That you do." Nick leaned back in his chair. "How much do you know about the case? What did Marc tell you?"

"He sent me the police reports he got from a former colleague in LA. I reviewed them on Friday and then again yesterday after I got back from New York. The first thing that came to mind was that because the unsub carefully applies makeup to his victims, to me, that says he's attached to them in some way. He cares for them; wants them to look pretty."

"Out of guilt?" Nick asked.

"Possibly. I don't know yet."

Nick studied her for a moment before continuing. "If this is an area you'd like to consider, then maybe it would be a good idea to reach out to the detective. I don't know if you'll get a bite, but it can't hurt to ask. I wouldn't count on ASAC Campbell letting you fly out there just yet. I would suggest a few phone calls, Skype, whatever to make contact and get a feel for the case, again, assuming they want our help. It wouldn't be any different than the cases we discussed last week from offices that were asking for consults."

"Thank you. I appreciate you letting me pursue this. I don't know how much I can help Marc. Maybe not at all, but this one's different. Not like anyone I've come across—yet." Kate rose from her seat and turned to leave.

"Kate?"

She stopped and spun back around. "Yes?"

Nick was silent for several moments, holding her gaze, and appearing ready to speak. "Let me know how it goes."

"I will."

THE FRONT DOOR OPENED WITH A QUICK SWOOSH AND THE KIDS RAN inside, dropping their backpacks to the floor.

"You two better get back here and hang those up before your mom gets home." Andre dropped his keys in a bowl kept at the end of the breakfast bar. He pulled off his tie and began to walk upstairs to change. It was his night to get the kids and start dinner while Dina worked the second shift at the clinic. But she would be home within the hour and expected the kids to have their school uniforms hung up and their homework finished. She ran a tight ship.

Andre pulled on his sweatpants and t-shirt before checking to see that the kids had changed. "You have any homework tonight?"

"No, Dad," Amber said.

"Okay." He watched as his daughter switched on her small television and began watching cartoons before closing her door and making his way back down the stairs.

Ty sat in the living room, TV on and cartoons blaring while playing with his tablet.

"You have homework?"

Ty looked at him with guilty eyes. "Yeah." He slumped down from the sofa and walked into the hall to get his backpack.

After a few moments of returning emails from his cell phone, Andre decided he'd better get dinner going. Dina would be home soon. Tonight was taco night. He wasn't much of a cook but could manage the simpler meals while his wife often ventured into more upscale cooking. And that usually resulted in the kids not eating at all.

He stood over the stove, skillet sizzling with browning meat when he heard the front door open. Her rubber-soled shoes squeaked on the tile floor until she appeared in the kitchen, wearing her green scrubs, the dry cleaning slung over her shoulder.

"Hey, baby." She draped the clothes over a barstool. "How was your day?" Dina moved toward him, wrapping her arms around his waist and kissing his cheek while he still stirred the meat.

"Fine. How was yours?"

"The usual. Did about a dozen ultrasounds and gave a lot of flu shots. It's that time of year." She walked back toward the pile of clothes. "Oh, hey, the dry cleaner said he couldn't remove some sort of grease stain from one of your dress shirts."

Andre stopped stirring. His mind's eye flashed images of him placing his work clothes in a bag and tossing them into the back of his Honda. He must not have pulled the drawstring closed enough.

"Andre?" Dina placed her hands on her hips. "Did you hear what I said?"

He broke free from the memory and turned to face her with a smile. "That's okay. I've got plenty more. Why don't you go get changed? Dinner will be ready soon."

The table was set and dinner was being served. "If you eat both tacos, you can have dessert," Andre said to Ty as he placed the plate in front of him. "Same goes for you, Amber."

He sat down and crunched down on his own taco. The television was on in the living room, where they had a clear view from the dining area.

Dina turned as the news story appeared. "I can't believe that." She returned her attention to Andre. "You hear about that? I should change the channel." She looked at the kids before standing and reaching for the remote that sat on a side table in the living room. On her return, she continued. "Those poor women."

"What women?" Ty asked.

Andre cast a stern glance. "Never mind. Just eat your dinner."

"Detective Sharpe, thank you for taking my call." Kate sat alone in the conference room and made the call with Nick's blessing.

"What can I do for you, Agent Reid?"

"I know how busy you must be right now, so I'll keep this brief. You're handling the investigation into the murders of women in South LA?"

"That's correct."

"I wanted to reach out to you and offer any assistance you might need on the case. I work under the resident agent of BAU Unit 4 in Washington."

"That's a very long ways from here."

"It is, sir, but with your blessing, I'd like to possibly take a look at your case files?"

"Agent Reid, we have this situation under control and currently do not need the FBI's help. I appreciate your concern, but we're handling things just fine over here."

"Of course, and I certainly don't mean to imply otherwise. However, I have a unique perspective in these matters and am beginning to focus my efforts on profiling the likes of the person you're dealing with now."

"So you're in training?"

"I can assure you that I have the necessary skills to handle such a case. I've been directly involved in others, too many others, of a similar nature." She didn't want to pull the "victim" card. But it did give her a uniqueness that probably no other profiler or other type of agent had.

"Okay, Agent Reid. Without formally requesting the FBI's help, I'll send you what I have so far. I'm awaiting the autopsy results from the latest victim, but I'll send those as soon as I have them. If you can tell me the type of person I'm looking for, I suppose it can't hurt."

"Thank you, detective. I'll get started as soon as I receive your files. I'll be in touch after that. Have a good day, sir." Kate flinched at the sound of the line going dead. He'd hung up without saying another word.

She walked back into the hall and happened across Dwight on her way to her desk. "Hey. Looks like I might be consulting with the LAPD on a case."

"Really? Why don't you tell me about it at dinner tonight? I'm inviting you and Nick out. Can you make it?"

"What's the occasion?"

"I'd like you both to meet someone. Is that all right with you?"

"Yeah. I'll be there. What about Nick?"

"He's coming whether he wants to or not." Dwight smiled and started past her again. "See you at eight. I'll send you the address."

SHARPE MARCHED INTO THE HALL AND TOWARD HIS CAPTAIN'S office. Without waiting for an invitation, he pushed his way in.

"Sharpe," the captain said as he sat at his desk. "Come in, why don't you?"

"Did you put a call into the feds about the Pretty Face investigation?"

"What are you talking about? Why would I do that?"

"I just got a call from someone at BAU. She wants the files to run a profile on our suspect."

"We don't have a suspect yet. But no, I made no such call. Who is this person?"

"Agent Kate Reid out of the Washington Field Office."

"Washington? Well, shit, if I was going to ask for help, I'd contact the LA field office."

"Agreed, but they don't get involved unless asked, so you didn't ask?"

"No, Sharpe. I didn't ask. But it's a profiler. I'm thinking it's not a bad idea. Especially on this one. You still have no leads."

"I'm waiting on the latest autopsy results."

"Regardless, unless this time the suspect left behind DNA, we could use help from the people who deal with these kinds of killers all the time." He studied Sharpe for a moment. "Who is this agent? Any good?"

"Kate Reid. Don't know her from Adam—Eve. Says she's worked on a bunch of similar cases."

The captain placed his glasses on his face and began typing on his computer. "Let's just see what we can find out about this person. If we're going to get help, I don't want it to be some hack."

"You can just look her up?"

"No. But I've got a friend in the LA field office. I'll shoot him an email and find out who she is. And make sure they don't get butt-hurt if they're circumvented." He turned back to Sharpe. "In the meantime, just do what you're doing. Get those results back as soon as possible. I don't care if you have to camp out in front of the ME's office. Just get them."

"Will do." Sharpe walked out of the office less staunch than when he arrived, feeling better that his captain hadn't under-mined his authority. Ray Sharpe had been on the force for fifteen years, working these very same streets since the beginning. Put his time in the Gang and Narcotics unit for five years. Took the detective exam and moved over to Special Ops support. And now he worked in Homicide, which, in this part of LA, meant he had to stay on his toes. This was "Death Valley," the part of LA County that had the highest homicide rate. He didn't need a gung-ho FBI agent tailing his every move.

Still, as the captain said, he'd give her the information. If she was good enough, then she might come up with something of use. No skin off his teeth.

Sharpe walked back into his office and reached for his phone. "Damn it." He'd missed a call from the ME. He ripped his jacket off the back of the chair and walked back out into the hall.

"Where you going?" an officer asked.

"ME's got the report. I'm heading over there now." He continued through the halls of the station until exiting through a staff door. He never went out the front if he could help it. Too many people he'd seen in his earlier days. Most were repeat offenders and he didn't want to make a scene.

Within minutes, he was on the road, heading south to the medical examiner's office. He could've just called him back and got the report emailed, but he preferred to do things in person. Less room for misinterpretation. Sharpe was a little old school like that. Not that he was old. A cop in his forties. Hell, he could still retire in five years. Full pension. But that wasn't who he was. He'd probably never stop working unless he took a bullet.

Sharpe entered the parking garage of the building and again slipped on his jacket and walked inside. He was a Southern California boy born and bred, and it was always cold as hell inside that place.

"I'm here to see Dr. Hahn," he said to the receptionist.

She nodded and made the call. "Go on back, detective. He's ready for you."

Sharpe pulled open the ME's door and the whiff of ammonia almost made his eyes water. "Dr. Hahn. You have something for me?"

"Have a seat, detective. Thank you for coming down, though it was completely unnecessary."

"You know how I like to work."

"Unfortunately, I do." The doctor began to retrieve the file in question on the latest victim. "I have a thumb drive ready for you to take, but this is what I've come up with." He opened the file folder and pushed it toward the detective.

Sharpe began to review the report, flipping the pages and not saying a word. A moment later, he looked up. "Same MO, then. Sexual assault postmortem. Multiple stab wounds. Never touching the face except to take care to apply makeup."

"Yes." Dr. Hahn nodded. "There is one thing I did find that was not on the others." He reached for the report and flipped the page. "Here. I found a synthetic fiber, like from a wig."

"The victim's?"

"I don't think so. I found no evidence of any other matching fibers on her scalp or clothing."

"He's disguising himself." Sharpe reviewed the report again. "No DNA anywhere?"

"I'm afraid not."

"Then all I've got is a fiber."

"Yes."

With a nod and downturned mouth, he began, "I can work with that."

6

The rain was coming down in icy sheets by the time Kate arrived at the restaurant. Standing under the awning, she closed the umbrella and brushed off the drops of rain that had accumulated on her coat.

"Good evening, miss." A man stood at the restaurant's entrance and pulled open the door for her. "You'll warm up once you're inside. Have a nice evening."

"Thank you." Kate walked through the door, offering a gentle smile to the man.

A hostess stood at the podium, awaiting Kate's approach.

"Hi. I'm here with the Jameson party."

"Yes, of course. Right this way." The hostess led Kate farther inside the restaurant.

She smiled at the sight of Dwight and a woman whom she was excited to meet. "Thank you. I see them." She continued her approach. "Evening."

Dwight immediately stood. "Kate. You look very nice. Thank

you for coming. I'd like you to meet someone." He turned to his date. "This is Abby. Abby Whitman."

"It's a pleasure to meet you." Kate offered her hand to the woman, who appeared somewhat daunted.

"Kate. I've heard so much about you. Very nice to meet you as well. Please, sit down."

Kate surveyed the restaurant. "Where's Nick?"

"Something came up, I guess," Dwight began. "He won't be able to make it tonight."

"Oh. That's too bad." Kate could see in Dwight's eyes how disappointed he was. She knew nothing could've been so important that Nick couldn't have taken a couple of hours out to meet Dwight's new girlfriend and she was disappointed in him too. "Well, his loss, then." Kate opened the menu. "What's good here?"

NICK SAT IN HIS CAR IN THE PARKING GARAGE OF HIS BUILDING. HE'D already excused himself from attending the dinner, but guilt pervaded over the past couple of hours. Dwight had been there for him so many times, he'd lost count. And now the one time Dwight needed him, he'd bailed.

But Dwight wasn't the problem. He'd wanted to go and meet this new girl he'd seemed so excited about. It was the first time in years, Nick had seen him so happy. Perhaps he was a little jealous. The real problem was seeing Kate. Especially since he'd confided in Dwight about his feelings and Kate's rejection. Nick felt that being there with all of them would be too uncomfortable now.

And then there was the issue about his possible departure from the WFO. Dwight knew about it, but Kate didn't. Nick was afraid that might come up as well and he wasn't prepared to deal with it.

In the end, here he was now, sitting in his car, ready to fire up the engine and drive to the restaurant anyway. He'd be late, of course, but maybe it was better than not showing up at all.

A calming breath and he was off. He'd considered texting Dwight to let him know he was on his way, but in the end, if they were already gone, he'd at least have tried. He was almost ashamed of his behavior but was at a loss as to how to handle this entire situation. A situation he'd worsened by distancing himself from Kate.

Within minutes, he'd arrived and pulled alongside the valet parking attendant. The attendant opened the door of Nick's SUV.

"Good evening, sir. Here for dinner?"

A bit of an obvious question, but Nick let it pass. "Yes." He handed the man his keys, jogged toward the restaurant's entrance beneath its cover to avoid the rain, and waited for the valet ticket.

"Here you are, sir. Enjoy your evening." The man smiled.

Nick stood outside the entrance for a moment and peered through the window. It was busy inside and he didn't see his friends. He reconsidered his actions.

"Let me get that for you, sir." The doorman opened it up and waited for Nick to walk inside.

It seemed he had no choice now and entered the restaurant. "The Jameson party," he said to the hostess.

She kindly walked him back and gestured toward their table. "Right over there, sir. Enjoy your evening."

Dwight noticed him. "Nick? Hey, buddy. I didn't think you could make it tonight." He stood up to greet him. "We've already started eating."

"That's fine. My fault I'm late. Turns out I was able to wrap things up and make it down here." He glanced at Dwight's date. "Hello. And you are?"

"This is Abby Whitman. Abby, this is Nick Scarborough."

"Of course." Abby greeted him warmly. "Dwight has said some wonderful things about you."

"I'm sure he has." Nick sat down between Dwight and Kate. "Evening, Kate."

"Hi. I'm glad you could make it after all." She eyed him carefully.

"Me too. I'm sorry I'm so late."

The two held one another's gaze for several moments before Nick finally broke away to look at the menu. "Maybe I'll just get an appetizer."

"We're in no rush," Dwight replied.

Nick placed a quick order and turned his attention to Dwight after the waiter departed. "So, Abby, how did you and Dwight meet? I have to say, he's been pretty quiet about you until now."

"Well," her entire face lit up as she began to speak, "our kids have been on the same soccer team for the past two seasons, and one day, just before a game, he came up and started talking to me. We sort of hit it off after that."

"It's not often I can attend the games, as you know," Dwight looked at Nick. "So I thought I might not get the chance to see her for a while and figured, why not?"

"Why not?" Kate smiled. "Well, you both seem very suited to one another. Dwight is a great friend and a wonderful man. I'm thrilled for you both."

"Thank you." Dwight squeezed Abby's hand as it rested on the edge of the table. "She's pretty great too."

~

Detective Sharpe arrived early, which wasn't unusual for a man who'd been rising with the sun practically since birth. He might rise a bit slower now but never arrived at the station beyond seven in the morning and today was no exception.

As he sat down at his desk and placed his steaming coffee next to his keyboard, Sharpe waited for his computer to wake up. And when it did, several emails awaited him, but only one that caught his eye immediately.

The subject line was in all caps and the sender was his captain. *"This is **the** Kate Reid,"* it read. Sharpe clicked it open and began to read.

"You wanted to know who this was and, according to my people, this is the same Kate Reid from a few years back who tracked down her abductor."

Sharpe was well aware of the Hendrickson case and the Highway Hunter investigation, which also involved Ms. Reid. Within striking distance of San Diego, he'd even known a few cops who were originally involved. This was unexpected news indeed. And Sharpe now was most interested in knowing more about Ms. Reid's skills as a profiler. He hadn't known she'd gone on to work for the FBI. She'd kept a very low profile since the funeral of that detective he couldn't quite recall the name of. But he'd been at the funeral. Most of the precincts in southern California had attended. It was just what you did when a cop was killed in the line of duty.

Perhaps she could be of some use after all. Now that there was confirmation the killer was disguising himself, he could present this new information to her as well. There could be similar cases he was as of yet unaware. He'd begun to like Kate already. How could he not appreciate someone who'd been through hell and made it out the other side?

"Agent Reid?" Sharpe asked when she answered the call. "This is Detective Ray Sharpe with LAPD. We spoke the other day?"

"Yes, of course. Hello, detective. I haven't received any files from you yet, so I'm actually glad you called."

"I apologize for that, but I'll be sending them over shortly. We did receive some new information based on the autopsy performed on the latest victim. It seems our suspect likes to disguise himself. A synthetic fiber, such as those found on inexpensive wigs, was discovered on the body. And it doesn't appear to have come from the victim."

"That is interesting. I'll keep an eye out for the information. I'd like to start digging into it right away."

"Certainly. Give me a call after you've had a chance to review the information."

"Will do. Thank you, Detective Sharpe. I appreciate your confidence."

"Goodbye, Agent Reid."

"Who was that?" Agent Vasquez approached her cubicle.

"You remember me mentioning a friend of mine, Marc Aguilar, and how he wanted me to look into a case in LA?"

"Yeah. Something come of that?"

"It did. That was the lead detective. He's sending me the file so I can develop a profile of the unsub."

"That's great. I think it's high time you started getting involved in that type of work. I know you've been interested in it for a while. And without Agent Myers..." Vasquez trailed off.

"Right. She left a pretty big hole," Kate replied.

It was only minutes later that Kate received the information from Sharpe. She opened the files and began to study the reports, some of which she already had, thanks to Marc, though she hadn't mentioned that to Sharpe. However, it did bring to mind that she needed to let Marc know what was going on. This was important to him, even if she didn't fully agree with his reasons. He'd been there for her in the past and she would return the favor.

Kate picked up her phone again and began to write a text to Marc. *"I'm working on what we talked about now. I'll call you later about it."*

She began to run a search into similar investigations, looking to find a link to other unsolved cases with similar signatures. While there was plenty of information out there, none seemed to quite match this one. Here was an unknown subject who was killing women, leaving them posed in public, and making up their faces as though they were modeling. And then it occurred to her. Could this person have been taking photos and perhaps uploading them?

Kate rose immediately and began walking toward Nick's office. He would know how best to approach this and could offer guidance. "Hey, can I talk to you a minute?" She stood in his doorway.

"Come in. What's going on?" He turned away from his computer.

Kate moved in. "That detective in LA? Sharpe? He sent me the case file on the killer. They're calling it the Pretty Face murders, I guess. Anyway, I got to thinking, he's making up these women and essentially putting them on display. Do you think he could also be taking pictures and posting them online on some website?"

Nick folded his arms and creased his brow. "That's entirely possible but would be extremely difficult to track down."

"I understand that. I guess where I'm going with this is in terms of the unsub's personality. His fetishes."

Nick began to nod. "I'd say it's definitely something worth considering. Have you approached the detective about it yet?"

"No. I've only just begun to scratch the surface on this and I didn't want to run to him without more information."

"There could be a way we can find out."

"Run a facial recognition search on the web." This solution seemed to just dawn on Kate.

Nick nodded and smiled.

"I'm on it."

"Hey, Kate?"

"Yeah?" She stopped short of leaving.

"If you need to go out there, I'll authorize it."

"Thank you. I'll let you know."

Upon return to her desk, Kate began searching the FBI's FACE system. The Facial Analysis, Comparison, and Evaluations services program accessed not only Next Gen but also databases from several state and local law enforcement agencies, including motor vehicle divisions. At her fingertips, she had access to more than thirty million photos. However, that wasn't the only place for her to look. Search engines also provided facial recognition searches, which in this instance, might be of more use. They would utilize a photo that had been uploaded and find similar images. This was where the real money was for Kate. The FBI's systems would be useful in their own right, but she needed to know if any of these victims were online and on what sites.

"You working on that case in LA?" Dwight approached with a half-eaten sandwich in his hand. "Scarborough was mentioning that to me earlier."

"Yes. I'm searching for online images of the victims to find out if the unsub is posting pictures of them."

"Not a bad idea. Although, if he was, I doubt it would be easily accessible. I'm thinking if the guy's smart, he's using the dark web if anything."

Kate stopped for a moment and closed her eyes. "Damn it. You're right. A site with that type of imagery would surely be flagged and taken down by the ISP provider."

"And then reported, most likely," Dwight continued.

"And then reported." She nodded.

"Still, don't give up. It's a good lead and you have to start somewhere. Just remember, what you're doing here is trying to develop a profile."

She turned around in her chair. "And that has everything to do with posting pictures online."

"It does, but you need to be looking into other areas of his personality. What do you know about him right now?"

"The lead detective says he's using a disguise. He found a fiber from a wig on the victim."

"Okay. That's good. What else?"

"He's making up their faces and posing them in certain ways."

"Good. Start there. I'm not saying toss out everything you're thinking as it relates to websites. There could still be something there. But work with what you know for a fact right now and build out from there."

"Of course." Kate studied Dwight as he took a bite of his sandwich. "Thank you."

With a half-full mouth, he replied, "There are still a few things I can teach you, Agent Reid."

"I'm well aware of that, Agent Jameson." Kate smiled and returned to her computer.

7

The keys rattled in Kate's purse as she attempted to pull them out and open the garage door to her house—a house she still rented from an old woman and her son. And the lease was up soon and she still hadn't given them notice. Putting it off much longer would be unfair to them, even though she still hadn't come to a firm decision one way or the other.

With the keys firmly in hand now, she opened the door and walked into the kitchen. The carrier bag on her shoulder was heavy with files and her laptop, and she managed to set it down on the breakfast bar. Bringing her work home was nothing new and, in fact, she often preferred it to the distractions that accompanied working in an office. She hadn't gotten as far as she wanted and there was a killer on the loose. Only moments from walking inside, her cell phone, which of course was stuck at the bottom of her purse, rang.

"Damn it." Kate scrambled again and finally retrieved the phone. "Marc, hi. I just got home."

"Do you want me to call you back?" he asked.

"No, no. It's fine." Kate kicked off her shoes and grabbed her computer, setting it on the kitchen table before pulling out a chair for herself. "So I got approval to help LAPD and the captain there pointed me to the lead detective. His name is Ray Sharpe."

"Don't know him."

"Anyway, he sent me everything this morning and I'm really just starting to get into the meat of it. I'll be developing a profile for him."

"So you're not going to be handling the investigation yourself?"

"No. Not this time. At least, not from what I gather. I'll be working *with* LAPD."

"Well, that's a start. What do you think about me pitching this story yet? You have anything worth noting?"

She did but hesitated to say anything. It was much too soon and telling Marc that the suspect wore a disguise would certainly jeopardize the budding relationship she was developing with Sharpe. "No, nothing yet. And, Marc, you still need to understand that I can't feed you details that aren't being released by LAPD. I can't jeopardize their investigation. You do understand that, right?"

"Of course, yeah, I understand. And I wouldn't ask you to. It's just..."

"I know. It's just you're anxious to move in on this. I get it. But not yet. Give me some time. Couple of days to get my head around this. I'll keep you in the loop, okay?"

"Okay. I appreciate that, Kate. I really do. But I have a feeling if another victim is found, it'll be out of my hands. I'm sure it'll get picked up nationally. And if it does, will you help me?"

"I'll do what I can. Right now, I'd like to help find this person before another victim turns up." Kate turned her attention to the sound of a knock on her door. "Hang on a second. Someone's at my door." She made her way to peek through the security lens. "I'm gonna have to call you later, okay?"

"Sure. Thanks, Kate. Bye."

Kate lowered her phone and opened the door. "Hey. Everything all right? Come in."

"Everything's fine." Nick walked inside. "Sorry to drop by unannounced. I was just on my way home and, well, you're only a few minutes away. You don't mind, do you?"

"No. Not at all. Come have a seat." Kate closed the door. "You want something to drink? I don't have much. Soda, maybe wine. I think I'm out of beer."

"I'll just take some water." Nick followed her as she made her way into the kitchen. "I heard you talking to someone." He began looking around. "Do you have company?"

"No. I was on the phone with Marc Aguilar." She noted his suspicion with curiosity before grabbing a bottle of water from the refrigerator. "Here you go. You haven't said why you're here." Kate walked toward the sofa and curled her leg up on one end of the couch while Nick sat on the adjacent chair and propped his elbows on his knees. He looked painfully serious and she began to worry. "What's going on?"

"I—um, I've been meaning to talk to you about something and I guess, well, I guess I haven't found the right time. And so, I thought maybe it'd be better to discuss it outside the office."

"Okay. You have my attention."

He held her gaze and finally began, "Last week, late last week, I was asked to meet with the section chief at BAU headquarters."

"I remember you mentioned that briefly in our meeting."

"What I failed to mention was the real reason why I was asked there." He began rubbing his hands together and stared at them with great intent. "Kate, I was put up for senior unit agent."

"Well, that's great. Why would you hesitate to share such good news with me?"

"It would mean me leaving the WFO. I'd be transferred back to Quantico for the position."

"Oh." She cast her gaze everywhere except on him. "Still, that's fantastic news, right? I mean, you'd be in line for unit chief after that, right?"

He nodded. "Eventually. If I get the position, it'd likely take effect after the first of the year."

Kate swallowed hard. "Wow. That's like what, less than eight weeks?" She nodded to the point that verged on obsessed. "So, what would happen to our team?"

"Dwight, of course, would be the next in line. He's ready for the spot."

"You already told him about this?"

"I did."

"Oh. Okay. And how does he feel about it?"

"He's excited for me. He's excited for the opportunity for him. And, you know, you're not on probation now, or won't be by that time, so you'd eventually be in line to follow in his shoes. And I'm sure they'd bring in another agent."

"Why didn't you tell me when you told Dwight?"

"I don't know. I guess I was nervous. I wasn't sure how you'd react."

"Did you think I wouldn't be happy for you?"

"No, not at all. I—I don't know what I thought."

"Well, of course I'm thrilled for you. And for Dwight. You both deserve recognition for your work. You've put in the time. I know you have. And you've had to make some very difficult calls."

"Yeah." He looked down at his hands, which he rubbed together with increasing agility. "You're not pissed at me?"

"What for?"

"Because I told Dwight before I told you?"

"I understand. I do. Things have been—difficult—between us these past couple of months. I know you've felt it too and, well, maybe this is the best thing for everyone. Don't get me wrong, Nick. I'll miss the hell out of you, but you need to do what's best for you."

He pushed off the chair. "I'll let you alone. I just wanted to come by and talk to you. I know I shouldn't have waited so long, but..."

Kate followed him to the door. She tried to hold a smile, but couldn't. "Thank you for telling me. Goodnight, Nick. I'll see you in the morning."

He took hold of the door handle where her hand remained fixed and peered into her eyes. The two seemed to bore into one another with their stare. Nick leaned forward and reached his free hand around her back, pulling her close.

She knew he was going to kiss her and a million thoughts raced through her mind all at once. It would be a mistake. She didn't love him. She was sure she didn't love him. But he was leaving and the possibility that he would no longer be there for her day in and day out, well, Kate wasn't as strong as she thought she was.

His lips finally touched hers and she didn't pull away. In fact, quite the opposite. Kate pushed into him firmly and held him as close as she could. She wasn't ready for things to change so dramatically, no matter how much she thought she was. The simple task of deciding whether or not to move from this house almost paralyzed her. Why couldn't she act? What was stopping her when she'd been so damned determined to move on with her life and had, up until now.

She was encouraging him and, with that, he held her more tightly and with greater passion than she'd expected. A moment's regret flashed before her, but Kate couldn't stop. Nick had been by her side for so long. Helped her through so much and she him. Why was she so afraid of this? She knew why, but those thoughts faded with an expediency like never before.

Nick stopped and pulled back, staring at her, consuming her with eyes that held an infinite desire.

He was asking for her permission without saying a word. And he would do as she wanted without saying a word, whatever that might be and however difficult. But she could see his longing and it mirrored her own.

A tilt upward from the corner of her mouth. That was all it was, but it was all he needed to know that they wanted the same thing. Kate reached for his hand and turned away from the door, leading him to her bedroom.

Inside, she freed her hair from the elastic band and let it fall against her shoulders.

Nick caressed her silky locks and again held her close. "I didn't think it would happen like this. I didn't think it would happen at all."

"Do you want to stop?" she whispered, unbuttoning her blouse.

"God no."

NICK SAT UP ON THE EDGE OF THE BED AND BENT DOWN TO REACH his clothes.

"What are you doing?" Kate pulled the blanket over her now chilled body.

"I'm sure you'd like to get some rest. I was going to head home." He glanced over his shoulder at her and smiled.

"You don't have to leave."

"I know." He stood to pull up his dress pants and turned toward her.

What a strange feeling to see him this way, Kate thought. He was a handsome man, that she already knew and so did everyone else. But to see him standing in front of her, bare-chested and about to slip on his shirt; it was surreal. This was Nick. The man who convinced her to change her life and it seemed he was about to do it again, even if he hadn't realized it.

"I just think it'd be better to go on home so you can get some decent sleep." He began to walk around the bed with his shoes in his hand and leaned in to kiss her. "Goodnight, Kate." He held his palm against her cheek and smiled.

Kate thought she spotted regret behind that smile but didn't ask. Maybe he'd seen regret in her eyes too, although that didn't seem to be exactly what she was feeling. She didn't really know what to feel right now.

"Don't get up. I'll show myself out."

Moments later, she heard the door close and had to get up anyway to re-lock it. She slipped on a t-shirt and walked into the living room where the headlights from his car moved across her front window.

She locked the deadbolt, turned to the darkened room, and walked into the kitchen for some water. "Well, I sure as hell opened one giant can of worms." She returned to the couch and turned on the television. It was then that she realized it was only 9:00 and turned on the TV to CBN just in time to watch Marc's show. His on-screen persona had changed dramatically from his earlier days and she was glad for that. He seemed humble, sincere, even truthful, which was a feat for any journalist, she supposed.

As she watched him deliver stories of no real significance, Kate's phone buzzed on the side table. Upon reaching for it, she noted it was an incoming text from Nick.

"You okay?"

She typed her reply. "Yes. You?"

"Yes," he responded.

"Get some sleep." She sent another, but he didn't reply.

ANDRE KNIGHT STARED AT THE CEILING OF HIS BEDROOM IN THE darkness. A glance at the red glowing numbers on his clock showed it was one a.m. He'd come to bed more than an hour ago and had yet to find sleep. Dina had, though, and she was snoozing right now as he struggled to control the thoughts in his head. He turned to look at his wife. She was facing away from him and curled up on her side. That was how she always slept. He likened it to a child. She was a petite woman too, which made her appearance all the more child-like. He turned back to the ceiling and flashes of the ones whose lifeless bodies he'd seen appeared as though on a slide show.

He'd begun to lose control and he would have to do something to rein it in. It was on the news almost nightly. Although, in this city, murders were always making headlines. So much so that he'd begun to think people probably stopped paying attention. Except for Dina. She'd commented the other night and Andre nearly shit his pants.

But he paid attention to the stories. He knew the cops had no leads. That was one benefit of living here. No one talked. The oil on his shirt, though. That could've been disastrous and he would need to take greater precautions.

At least his job was a good cover. He could use the old excuse of having to work late and Dina would never question it. She had absolute, unwavering trust in him. And he used that to his advantage.

For now, Andre would need to cool his heels. Let some time pass before getting back out there. He had to be smart—smarter than the cops. Wait for the story to die down, but that was out of his control.

So Andre would go to work tomorrow and the next day and the next. He would wait. But there was only so much patience in him.

He began to turn on his side when he heard Dina's voice.

"You still awake, baby?"

"I'm okay. You go back to sleep." He felt her hand caress his shoulder and gently slip away as she returned to dreamland.

8

Raquel's skin glistened from the heat inside the nightclub, but as she and Vanessa grew tired of waiting for a cab and decided to walk home, the cool night air brought her relief. High heels dangled between their fingers, and the young women laughed and stumbled their way along the two-mile walk.

"It's cold as shit out here, right?" Vanessa rubbed her free hand along the opposite arm. "We should've just called Uber."

"Stop your bitchin'. We'll be home in fifteen minutes. Besides, it'll help you sober up."

"Me? What about you? You're fucking drunk as shit." Vanessa continued alongside her friend in the early hours of the morning. The street lamps shone down on them, illuminating their breath as they exhaled.

"Fuck!" Raquel grabbed her right foot. "I fucking stepped on a piece of glass!" She reached out to Vanessa for balance. "I gotta sit down and pull this shit out."

Vanessa made a clicking sound with her tongue and rolled her eyes. "Come on. Don't be such a fucking baby."

"I'm sorry, do you see this blood?" Raquel raised the bottom of her foot.

"All right. Shit. Over here. We can sit down over here." Vanessa helped her to a low wall that bordered the sidewalk and a vacant piece of land where a building once stood.

The girls perched atop the masonry wall and began to examine Raquel's foot.

"We should've waited." Raquel cringed as she gripped the shard of glass with her index finger and thumb.

"We should've kept our shoes on is what we should've done." Vanessa scanned the sidewalk. "All the fucking broken beer bottles and shit." She looked at Raquel again. "Just take it out so we get home. I'm getting really cold now." Her tiny form-fitting dress offered little in the way of warmth but always got her free drinks in the bars. And for a twenty-two-year-old with only a part-time job and taking a few online college classes, that meant something.

"Can you just call your moms?" Raquel asked. "She'll pick us up."

"No way. It's two in the morning and she has to be at work by six. She'll be pissed if I get her up, not to mention if she sees how fucked up I am."

"Whatever." Raquel shook her head and proceeded to pull the glass from her foot. "Fuck me!" With the piece of glass in her hand, she showed Vanessa. "Look at the size of that. You think I need stitches or some shit?"

Vanessa noticed the blood that now began to drip from her foot. "Maybe. It does look pretty bad."

"Now will you call your mom?"

Vanessa reached for her cell phone when a man approached,

stopping square in front of the girls. She looked up to see him concealed in dark clothing and shadowed by the street light that shined behind him. "What the fuck do you want?"

"You ladies need some help?"

"Nah, man. We're okay. Just waiting on our ride." She cast a suspicious glance at Raquel.

The man with the shoulder-length curly hair and baseball cap hovered over them. "You sure? That looks bad. I can take you to urgent care."

"I said we was all right. We got someone coming." Vanessa's heart pumped hard in her chest.

He raised his hands in surrender. "Okay. Shit. I was just offering to help you out, but whatever." He began to walk away. "Fucking bitches."

Vanessa immediately called her mother. "Mom? Me and Raquel need a ride home. Can you please come get us—now?" She continued to eye the man as he walked away. "We're on Crenshaw and 10th. Thanks, Mom."

Raquel waited until Vanessa ended the call. "What the fuck was that guy's problem?"

"I don't know. My moms is coming now."

THE MAN WITH THE DARK CURLY HAIR CONTINUED DOWN THE QUIET stretch of shuttered liquor stores, pharmacies, and check-cashing joints. The girls he'd passed along the way were long out of his periphery now and he'd begun to focus on the road ahead. Soon he'd approach Death Valley, where he was sure to come across a few junkies, but he wasn't interested in junkies or street thugs or anyone else like that who frequented the streets at this hour.

There was one place he'd had his eye on and that was where he would go. The only place that would be open.

He approached the still-dark building only blocks from where he'd started his journey and waited. Soon, the early shift would begin and the donut shop would start baking for their morning crowds. He'd eyed the shop for the past few days and knew exactly when she arrived.

He adjusted the cap on his head, lowering it over his brow, and pulled down on the strands of hair that hung below it. The parking lot was in the back and there he waited. And this time, he tested the fortitude of his spectator. Even considered allowing him to watch before surprising him with an unexpected turn of events. The breadcrumbs had been left. Time would tell whether or not the interloper would appear, but this time, he would be ready.

Minutes later, the first car arrived. A white, older model Kia pulled onto the lot, its headlights flashing before him. He tucked himself behind the dumpsters to avoid the spotlight. The car stopped and the engine died. A young woman emerged, wearing her black uniform and comfortable tennis shoes, preparing for the long and busy shift.

From behind the dumpster, he adjusted his baggy jeans and pushed down his hat. He slipped his hand inside a pocket of his fleece, ensuring his gun was in place. Behind his waistband was the knife, which he would retrieve at the appropriate moment.

Only sparse light was cast from a distant lamp in front of the building and it seemed the parking lot lights weren't operational. Another bonus.

She must've heard his footsteps crunching atop the chip-sealed surface as he emerged because her head swung in his direction. Her uniform blended into the darkness that surrounded them and it was difficult for him to see what exactly she was doing.

He moved in closer and that was when the familiar look appeared on her face. The immediate recognition that death was coming.

REMARKS JOCKEYED FOR POSITION ON THE TIP OF KATE'S TONGUE AS she was carried in the elevator to the WFO offices. Last night wasn't supposed to happen—not that way, but it had, and now the time had come to face the repercussions of her actions.

The elevator doors had already begun to close before Kate returned to the moment and stepped off at the last minute. To her right was Nick's office; straight ahead was her cubicle. She peered down the corridor and figured it was best to address the elephant in the room before everyone else arrived. Otherwise, they'd be swimming around one another in a sea of unspoken words.

"Knock, knock." Kate leaned into his doorway.

Nick pulled his attention from his phone and smiled. "Hey. Come in."

"Morning." She walked inside with hesitation behind each step.

"Good morning. You sleep well?"

Kate nodded. "You?"

"Sure." He appeared ready for a sermon espousing the reasons last night shouldn't have happened.

With each passing moment of silence, the air thickened with thoughts each seemed prepared to express, but both were afraid to do so.

"I was going to put in a call to the LAPD detective later today,"

Kate began. "You want in on that conversation?" She'd lost her nerve and now it seemed if the topic was to be discussed, Nick would be the one to have to bring it up. And the look on his face suggested he would.

"No. I'm sure you can handle it. What—um—do you want to talk about last night?"

A moment's pause was needed to reflect on her next words because it could make all the difference in how they intended to move forward. She finally sat down. "In all the years we've known each other, I never thought it would get this arduous. I've always been able to come to you with anything." The corners of her mouth raised slightly. "I guess that's all changed now and I don't really know how to handle it. After we talked—a while back—and I broke it off with Mike; I wasn't quite sure why I had done it. I thought maybe it had just been too soon. I hadn't been ready for a serious relationship and Mike, well, he was more than ready." She cast her eyes down, staring at her hands, which were folded in her lap. "I've always felt something for you, Nick. I just couldn't quantify it. You've been more than a friend, more than a boss or colleague."

Before she could continue, Nick interrupted. "You broke up with Mike after we talked. Was I the reason?"

"Not the entire reason. But ever since then, it's been difficult for us to work as closely as we had before."

"I know. And I'm sorry about that. That's on me."

"No, it's not. Look, I would never want to be anything but honest with you and I think last night happened because I was afraid of losing you."

"Because I told you I might be transferred?"

"Yes."

"Not because of any pent-up feelings; just out of fear?"

The light she'd seen in his eyes when she sat down had all but disappeared from view now. "Nick, you know how screwed up I am. You know everything about me, what I've been through. Hell, what we've been through together."

"Hey, I'm no walk in the park, in case you'd forgotten."

"Well, that's true." She chuckled. "I'd like some time to sort through this, if that's okay. I have a lot of things to figure out. Things I've been putting off for far too long in the name of work. But I can't put them off any longer."

"Am I one of those things?"

"You are now." Another gentle smile formed on her lips. "I'd like to take you up on your offer to meet with the LAPD on this investigation. I think being there – boots on the ground, so to speak – might give me a better opportunity to help them find their guy."

"And get some time away from me."

"Time for myself more than anything. You've let me spread my wings in the past and this is another good opportunity. After all, you'll be gone soon. You can't hold my hand forever." She hadn't meant to bring up the past, but those were similar words he'd said to her during a particularly rough patch when he was dealing with Campbell. And it seemed he'd recalled it too.

"I understand. Go. See what you can do for those guys. I think it's a good idea. Jameson and I have a handle on things right now. It's probably a good time."

Kate pushed up from the chair. "Thank you."

She disappeared from view and Nick continued to stare into the hall as though she might return and rush to his side. But this wasn't some fairy tale. Kate was in a class all her own. This wasn't how he expected the morning to go, but it was really no surprise. Deep down, he felt as though last night had been a mistake and he should've walked away, but he couldn't; not from her.

SUFFERING ONE HELL OF A HANGOVER, VANESSA ROLLED OUT OF BED and walked gingerly toward the hall bathroom to down a couple of aspirins. Her mom had taken pity on her and Raquel when she arrived to pick up the young women and noticed Raquel's injured foot. However, in the light of day, she might well be prepared to offer an admonishment and Vanessa wasn't exactly eager to find out.

Instead, she returned to her bed, noting the light that had already begun to crawl along her walls, and decided another hour of sleep would be necessary if she were to face her mother's wrath. Fortunately, though, her mother wouldn't be finished with her shift until this afternoon and, upon noticing the time, Vanessa had a good few hours before that happened.

But her plan was short-lived when her cell phone blasted an obnoxious ringtone that sounded something akin to helium-induced, high-pitched squeals. Vanessa moaned and answered the call to end the piercing sound that would make anyone's ears bleed. "What? Why are you calling me so early?"

"Early?" Raquel began. "I'm at work, stupid. Where the fuck are you?"

"Asleep."

"Jesus, Vanessa, it's eleven o'clock. Don't you have some school shit or something to do?"

"Well, now that you woke me up." Vanessa opened her eyes a little wider. "What do you want?"

"Did you hear about that body they found?"

"What? No. What body?"

"They found a fucking body next to the donut shop on Vermont Avenue this morning."

"So?"

"That's only a few blocks from where we were last night."

Vanessa sat upright. "Are you serious?"

"Yeah, I'm fucking serious, bitch."

"That's scary shit."

"I know, right? Vanessa, what about that guy we saw? That creepy motherfucker? You think he did it?"

She began to recall the man in question and the fact that he had been creepy as hell. "No way. It was probably some drug deal bullshit gone bad. Don't stress yourself."

"I'm telling you, it's too weird, you know? This guy comes up to us and we blow him off and then he, like, disappears and shit."

"I don't know, Raquel. So what if it was him? What are we supposed to do about it?"

"Tell the fucking cops and shit."

"Hell no. I ain't talking to no cops about some guy we saw. Are you serious right now?"

"What if it was that guy? He's still out there, Vanessa. What, we sit back and do nothing? That could've been us."

Vanessa lowered the phone from her ear and closed her eyes. Her head was still pounding and she was thirsty and could hardly think straight. A moment later, she was ready to answer the question. "Look, we don't know shit about shit, you feel me? I said I ain't talking to no fucking cops. You want everyone to think we're snitches or some shit, 'cause I don't. Besides, it wasn't that guy. No way. He was a creep, but he didn't look like no killer."

"Maybe you're right."

"I am. Now get your ass back to work before you get fired from another job. I'll call you later, okay?" Vanessa waited for a reply. "Okay?"

"Okay. Fine. Bye."

Vanessa dropped her phone onto her bed and leaned back against her headboard. She began to recall the man they'd seen last night. His eyes; the way he looked at her. But he had weird hair. Like, who wore their hair like that anyways? And who the hell wore a Chicago Bulls baseball cap around here?

"No way." She shook her head. "No way he killed somebody." Because if he had, and they said nothing about it, then they'd be allowing the killer to stay on the streets. And who knew if he would kill again? Maybe next time, they won't be so lucky.

9

The LAPD had been remarkably expedient in their authorization for Kate's assistance, an unexpected reaction when she called only yesterday afternoon to make the request to fly out and meet with them. Her early flight this morning brought unexpected news as well. According to Detective Sharpe, another body had been found.

Kate now waited inside the 77th Street precinct for the detective. The enormous police station was almost as big as the WFO and it was surprising that this was one of many of similar size and within just a few miles of one another.

A man in a black leather jacket, jeans, and bearing a slight paunch soon approached. He seemed to recognize Kate because he didn't hesitate to offer a greeting. "Agent Reid. I'm Detective Ray Sharpe. Nice to meet you in person."

"And you, detective. Thank you for agreeing to meet."

"Follow me and we'll get started." He began down the hall and turned to her. "How does it feel to be back home?"

"Sorry?"

"You're from southern California, right?"

At that moment, Kate realized why the sudden agreement. They'd discovered who she was. Didn't seem to matter how many years had passed, she'd always be the girl who escaped. "San Diego, but originally from northern California, around Eureka."

"Right. That's right. This is my office here. Please come in." He held open the door.

"You must've done your homework, detective." Kate walked past him into the office.

"Apologies if I've offended you. But I needed to know who I was dealing with and, to be honest, there's a lot of information out there about you." He closed the door and made his way in. "I respect the hell out of what you've done with your life, Agent Reid, all things considered. And so I'm happy to have you aboard."

She began to take a less defensive stance in light of his apology and the chip finally fell from her shoulder. "Thank you. I appreciate that. So you mentioned the discovery of another body?"

Sharpe took his seat. "That's right. In the early hours of this morning and in the same general vicinity as the others. The victim is already at the ME's office."

"And you're confident it's the same unsub?"

"I am."

Kate retrieved the file from her carrier bag. "This is what I've come up with so far, but we can revise any necessary information to include this latest victim." She slid the folder toward him.

Sharpe opened it and reached for his glasses, which were folded inside his shirt pocket. He glanced toward Kate. "It's hell getting old."

She waited while he reviewed the information she'd spent most of the previous night compiling.

Sharpe looked up from the file. "I'm impressed. This is good work, Agent Reid."

"Thank you."

"Here's what I'd like to do to utilize your skills while we continue to investigate. I think it would be a good idea for you to visit the crime scenes and I'll accompany you, of course. I'd also like you to take a look at the bodies. We've indicated several markers, but a second pair of eyes can't hurt." He pushed up from his chair. "That should keep us busy for today and, in the meantime, I'm running forensics on the synthetic hair fiber that was found on the previous victim's body."

"Hair fiber?"

"Yes, a strand of hair, most likely from a wig, was found on the victim and they've excluded that it belonged to the victim and so now we're working to find out if it was, in fact, from a wig and the type."

"Any chance you can find out where it was purchased?"

"Possibly. Our forensics team is still working on it." He walked around the desk. "We'd better head on out. We have a lot of ground to cover today."

"How's the jet lag?" Sharpe asked as he parked in front of the donut shop where the latest victim was discovered.

"Not bad—yet."

"I'm sure it'll hit you later today." He opened the door and stepped outside, hoisting his jeans and sliding on his leather jacket. "This is where we found her."

They walked around to the back lot of the donut shop that

remained closed and taped off for investigators. A few CSIs were still gathering evidence.

Kate began to approach the scene near the dumpster. "You were saying you believe the victim was killed here, then dragged and staged in front of the store a short time later?"

"She wasn't dragged. No signs of those types of abrasions. Carried is more likely the case." Sharpe pointed to a faint trail on the asphalt leading to the concrete path along the side of the building. "See there? Intermittent blood spatters. Drops from when he carried her to the front of the building."

The two began to walk alongside the bloody trail to the storefront.

Kate surveyed the area. "Any cameras?"

"Already obtained the footage." Sharpe pointed to a bank nearby. "We can review it later, but what we found were some grainy images from the CCTV at the front of the bank that rotates roughly 90 degrees in either direction. In the far corner, you can see something resembling people, but it's very distant." He turned the other direction. "And over there is a liquor store, open 24 hours. They have cameras inside and along their drive-through, but no place that would have made the donut shop visible."

"I assume you've already spoken with the liquor store owner?"

"Oh yeah. Didn't see nothin'. No customers at that time either. Place was quiet, so he says. And I suspect the killer knew there were no front-facing cameras before he made his choice."

Kate peered down one end of the sidewalk and then down the opposite end. "Did he drive here? Did anyone pick up a car on closed circuit?"

"A compact Honda Civic, green, older model stopped alongside the road a couple of blocks away at 3:10 a.m., but drove off only moments later, according to the surveillance footage. We requested all within a mile from here." Sharpe looked in the same direction as Kate. "We couldn't see much, so I have no idea why the car stopped."

"That was only—what—less than an hour from the victim's estimated time of death?"

"That's right."

"Did it capture a plate?"

"No." Sharpe noticed her deflate. "Now you see what we're dealing with."

"Yeah. They don't make it easy." Kate turned back toward the building. "Okay. I think I've seen enough here. I'd like to go to the ME's office now."

ANDRE KNIGHT TURNED ON THE EVENING NEWS WHILE THE KIDS played outside and Dina began making dinner. The first thing he saw was a picture of a young woman who'd been identified as twenty-four-year-old Jessica Brown. The image appeared to have been taken at her place of employment, which the story later on disclosed was a donut shop.

"Ms. Brown had been the first to arrive to work and open the store. It was a fellow employee who noticed she was sitting against the front door when he pulled into the employee parking area. He hadn't realized she was dead. And it appears the Pretty Face Killer was the one responsible, though Police have yet to conclude there is a connection."

He turned off the news and stared at the black screen until Dina approached.

"Dinner's almost ready. Would you mind setting the table?" She waited for a response. "Andre? Can you set the table, please?"

He turned to her with blank eyes. "What?"

"Are you okay? What's wrong?"

"Nothing." He walked past her.

"Andre? Andre?" She followed him to the bottom of the stair-case, but he refused to turn around. She huffed and walked back into the kitchen to set the table herself.

Knight turned on his laptop, which rested on a small desk in their bedroom. He opened the proxy server that would disguise his IP address and began to log on to the website. And there she was. Ms. Jessica Brown, all pretty and dead, resting against the front door of a donut shop.

But Knight hadn't expected to see this. He scrolled through the comments section. The others who were followers of the website hadn't been as angry. But then, none of them followed the man behind the camera the way he had. They didn't have the balls to do it. But Andre, who'd decided that he needed to take a step back, hadn't expected another quite so soon. The decision had been easy when the victims were spread apart by several days. The unexpected turn of events and the fact that he had missed the whole thing made his blood boil. How could he do this? Betrayal accompanied the anger and he slammed the lid shut without reaching the end of the video.

His chest heaved as he tried to calm himself because he knew he would have to go downstairs in a few minutes. Knight closed his eyes and opened the lid again. Leaving behind any trace that he'd visited the site was dangerous. It was how he covered his tracks. But before he erased all the evidence, he couldn't help but comment. *"Half the fun is that you build us up, ready us for the masterpiece that will follow. I'm disappointed that didn't happen this time."*

It was all he could think to say because pushing the point could mean he would be blocked and then it would all be over.

How could he go back to a normal life? He desired nothing so much as to watch them and watch him in action. It was the only thing that satisfied him. A satisfaction that not even his wife could compete with.

He shut down his laptop and retreated to the bathroom to splash water on his face. With a few more palliative breaths, Andre made his way back downstairs. As he stepped down each one, his eyes grew brighter and his smile returned, both of which were by force. He walked into the kitchen. "Do you need help with anything?"

Dina turned from the stove and placed a hand on her hip. "Oh, now you wanna help?"

THE KEY CARD SLID INTO THE LOCK AND THE GREEN LIGHT FLASHED. Kate pushed open the door to her hotel room and flipped the switch. It was approaching ten p.m. and she was exhausted. The long day and grisly scenes had taken their toll. She dropped her purse on the desk and flopped onto the bed. That was when her phone began to ring.

Finally sitting back up, Kate answered the call. "Hey."

"It was getting late and I hadn't heard from you yet," Nick began. "Everything go okay today?"

"I just got back to my room, actually. Sharpe took me through the entire gamut. And I know I'm on the right track with a profile, but there's more to consider. How are you?"

"Fine. Got home about an hour ago. Dwight and I have been sorting through the consults, but no cases yet."

"That's good. Does that mean I can stay as long as Sharpe needs me?"

"Absolutely. Hey, if you can help them, more power to you. Sounds like they've got a growing problem there and they need to nip it in the bud."

"Couldn't agree more. In fact, I was going to put a call into Marc Aguilar, but he'll probably be in bed by now. I'll reach out to him in the morning and let him know where we're at. I don't think he wants to wait much longer to pitch this to his bosses."

"The last thing you need to do right now is worry about Aguilar. I'm surprised no one's picked up the story nationally yet anyway."

"Me too. I guess the country is more concerned about what the Kardashians are doing than they are about killers."

"Ahh, you're beginning to sound like me now. Don't you start getting bitter too, Kate. It won't look good on you."

"You're right." Kate yawned. "Sorry about that. Don't mean to be rude. Just the jetlag."

"It's okay. It's late and you're still on East Coast time. I'll let you get some rest. I'm sure tomorrow will be just as busy. Keep me posted, if you wouldn't mind."

"I'll talk to you tomorrow. Goodnight, Nick."

"Goodnight."

Not a single word was mentioned about what had happened. It was as if it hadn't happened at all. At least they were still talking. That was a good sign.

Kate had no idea what would happen on her return. They could only tiptoe around the conversation so much. But the idea that he would be leaving soon did hurt. And she would have to come to terms with it because she would never ask him to stay— not for her. He deserved to move up. He needed it. Work was the only thing that kept him from sliding down the slippery slope she'd had to pull him from only months ago.

The problem was that Kate still needed to decide what was best for her too. She thought work wasn't a crutch, but maybe it was. Maybe she needed it as much as he did.

NICK WALKED INTO THE KITCHEN AND PLACED HIS GLASS ON THE counter. He looked at the half-empty bottle of Jack Daniels next to the glass. As much as he'd wanted to, he knew his battle had deepened and that meant he would need to fight harder to resist. He wouldn't have Dwight and Kate to prop him up anymore. And pulling any shit at Quantico meant he'd be out on his ass. That alone was enough to make him stop—for tonight anyway.

The idea that he wouldn't have to be so close to the investigations now was appealing. At Quantico, they performed case analysis, profiling, database research, and all for the support of other offices and law enforcement. Those guys didn't go out into the field as often and see all the dead bodies. They didn't face the angry and hurt family members. He'd been at this for too long and that was the bright spot in all this. He might have to leave Kate and Dwight, but he'd also get to leave behind the worst of the brutality of humankind. At least, only have to deal with it in textbook form and from a safe distance for the most part. That was what had really worn on him these past few years. And he'd increasingly taken it out on the bottle. That had to stop. Now he would get that chance. Even if it meant leaving Kate.

10

The bedroom curtains ruffled as a cool breeze blew through the open window. Andre, still awake, felt a chill settle on his skin while he rested above the covers. He rolled out of bed and padded to the window, pulling it closed. Shadowed by the grey light, he turned back and noticed Dina stir. Andre was restless, his mind consumed with thoughts of the earlier betrayal. He eyed his laptop and retrieved it from the desk, making his way through the bedroom and out onto the landing.

The wooden treads scraped against the rusting nails as he descended the staircase and headed toward the living room with his laptop tucked beneath one arm. Settling on the sofa, Andre turned on his computer and waited. The blue and white light from the screen burned his eyes for a moment until they finally adjusted. He began to type, gaining access to the dark web, which he often patrolled. Now proficient in all forms of clandestine movement inside the web, Andre fancied himself somewhat of an expert.

He happened upon the site where he visited only hours earlier and discovered he'd been betrayed by the man behind the camera. The man who had promised to keep his followers informed. Except he hadn't done so yesterday. And now, something else caught his interest even more. A new video.

Andre pressed play, confirming the sound was off and watched. He found himself instantly transformed. His base instincts were awakened by the pretty faces that appeared one after the other in a multitude of poses, each more provocative than the last. It was as though he was watching a stop-motion movie, except these were no animated puppets. These were the dead women who'd been presented so expressively by the man with the camera. The same one who'd documented his every move and whom Andre had decided to follow in the act itself. Perhaps others had too, but he hadn't seen anyone else. They were all undoubtedly filled with cowardice and preferred the comfort and safety of their homes, indulging in their fetishes while their families slept. Andre had done that too, but he'd chosen to take the risk, to experience in person the excitement others had only seen on the screens of their various gadgets. Waiting, watching. He only had minutes after the man left to catch a glimpse of his artwork. He tried not to linger, no matter how much he'd wanted to, although he had slipped up before and made his escape before being discovered. It was a mistake that wouldn't happen again.

Was it luck that Andre lived near enough or was it fate? Of course, he'd found the site through a chat room that he had chosen based on geographic location. So it wasn't much of a stretch to find his way to the site operated by an anonymous entity inside the chat room. But Andre had begun to feel as though he knew the man behind the camera. He'd grown close to him and had felt betrayed because he hadn't said where his next victim would be found. Had he been discovered the night of his narrow escape? No, no mention of anything like that was on the website and Andre was sure it would have been mentioned. And then there was the other woman. Again, he'd followed, but had taken more precautions and almost waited too long before indulging in his moment. Still, it brought to mind the reason as to why there was no advance warning about Jessica Brown and the donut shop.

"When will you be out again?" he typed in the comment section of the video, trying desperately to elicit a response, but several minutes passed and there was no reply. Time must've slipped by quicker than he expected as he noticed light filter through the front window blinds. He could wait no more and closed down his computer, carrying it back upstairs, and slipped into bed where Dina remained unaffected by his disappearance.

KATE'S EYES FLUTTERED OPEN AS SHE REACHED FOR HER PHONE ON the nightstand. The screen lit up with an incoming call. "Marc, good morning. Did you forget I was in LA and there's a three-hour time difference from New York?"

"Well, now that you mention it, yes, I had forgotten." He paused for a moment. "Jeez. I didn't realize it was five a.m. there."

"That's okay. I need to get up." She rubbed her eyes and sat up on the edge of the bed. The hotel room windows were encased in blackout curtains that obscured all sense of time. "What's going on?"

"We're picking up the story."

"When? And why now?"

"My old friend at KTLA called me a few hours ago. Said someone called the station with an anonymous tip."

Kate's back straightened in an instant. "What'd they say?"

"Something about they saw the guy a short time before the most recent victim was killed. Gave a description."

"Oh my God. Why the hell didn't they call the police?"

"I don't know, Kate. But my friend called me and I told him I'd run it by my boss and I just got out of the meeting. I'm running it on the morning show as a special commentator. The reason I'm calling to tell you this is that I was hoping you could give me a comment. I didn't think I'd get far if I called the detective in charge, considering he has no idea who I am."

"Marc, I can't give you a statement. I'm most definitely not running the show here. You'd have to reach out to Detective Sharpe. And I've got to tell you, from what I've learned about him, he won't give you the time of day."

"I figured that. You don't have anything for me?"

"No. I'm sorry. I knew this wouldn't stay local for long, but I was hoping we'd have more by now. I'd just like to know where the hell this tip came from. Sharpe won't be happy about it."

"At least you'll have more to go on."

"How can I get my hands on the tipster's description?"

"Call my friend, Vince Sanchez. I'll text you the number. Tell him you know me. I've already said I'd talk to you about it first."

"I guess you got what you wanted," Kate said.

"Not really. I wanted the story, but I wanted to break it as part of a federal investigation with local ties to the LA market."

"What difference does that make?"

"I don't have anything more than the AP, except a vague description, which I don't even have in my hands yet. Vince wouldn't hand it over until I talked to you. I think he's using it as leverage."

"Leverage for what?"

"To make sure I credit him with the story. I've already pitched it, so he knows I'm running it and needs the description."

"Sounds like a great friend."

"It's just part of the game, Kate. I think it'd be best if you could get the description to Sharpe before I run the story. Call Vince right away. I'll talk to you after it airs."

"Okay. Bye, Marc." Kate ended the call and waited for the text to come through with the contact number for his friend. Moments later, it did.

"Hello, Mr. Sanchez? This is Special Agent Kate Reid. I know it's early, but Marc Aguilar suggested I contact you regarding an anonymous tip your station received concerning the Pretty Face Killer?"

"Yes. Good morning. Thank you for the call. I do have that information and, with your permission, I'd like to cite you as a source."

"A source for what? You have more information than I do at the moment."

"I doubt that, but it would lend more credibility to the story if the FBI is involved."

"Sir, I'm afraid I can't allow that. I'm simply consulting with the LAPD and have no direct involvement in the investigation." She wasn't exactly telling the whole truth, but it would have to do.

"I see. Agent Reid, I'm sure you'll understand when I say that this case directly affects the safety of the people of Los Angeles and they should be made aware that the FBI is here working with the local authorities."

"Sir, I have to insist that I not be named as a source. I'm merely asking that you forward the description of the suspect to the lead detective, Ray Sharpe so that he can pursue this investigative lead." She paused for a moment. "If you do not hand over that information, you will be seen as obstructing an investigation. You understand what I'm telling you, Mr. Sanchez?"

The line was quiet for a moment and then he finally began again. "I understand. I'll get the information over to LAPD right now. Thank you for your time, Agent Reid."

She pulled the phone from her ear when she heard the click of the line as it went dead. "Great guy."

DETECTIVE SHARPE WAS ON THE PHONE AND TAKING NOTES WHEN Kate appeared in his doorway. He waved her in and pointed to the chair across from his desk.

His tone was cool and she didn't think he was one to rise quickly to anger. Nevertheless, his irritation displayed prominently on his hardened exterior. His shoulders raised, his brow narrowed, and when he wasn't speaking, his lips were pursed. She immediately assumed he'd been on the phone with the reporter. She hoped to reach him before the reporter had, but she'd been held up in the unexpected traffic.

"Thank you, and any further details, you'll be sure to inform me first?" he said. "Thank you, Mr. Sanchez. Goodbye." Sharpe eyed Kate. "You knew about this?"

She nodded. "I got down here as soon as I could. I was hoping to catch you before you got the call. I want you to know that I refused to be named as a source. This isn't my investigation – it's yours, and I respect that."

His hard features seemed to soften at her confession. "Thank you. I appreciate that. This was going to happen sooner rather than later. It always does."

"Can I ask you something?" She paused for a moment. "Why

would an anonymous tip be called into a news station and not here? You've got a hotline."

"We do. It just confirms to me that whoever called it in is local to the community. You have to understand something. People don't talk to the cops here. It's dangerous and it could get them killed. That's just the way it is. So I'm not surprised. I'm just grateful someone called. At least we have something." He pushed over the scratch paper. "This was what the person described."

"Caucasian or possibly light-skinned Hispanic. Shoulder-length dark hair, curly. Chicago Bulls baseball cap. About five foot ten." She looked at him. "If you could find out who gave this description, you could put him or her in front of a forensic artist and actually get something out there for the public."

"I couldn't agree more. Apparently, it was a female who called it in, according to the station."

"CBN is running the story this morning. I've got a friend from my old days here in California and he gave me the heads up earlier. He knows the anchor here who got the description—the man you just spoke to."

"Son of a bitch." Sharpe leaned back in his chair. "I'll have to let the communications director know what's coming. There'll be pressure from the governor down to the LA city manager to get this guy in a hurry."

"Listen, I know I'm here as a consultant, but my team can help, if you want it. You've got a description, you've got a fiber, and you've got a car that was seen nearby before the last victim was murdered. I just want you to know we have resources. A lot of them."

Sharpe seemed to consider Kate's offer.

"I'm not saying we'd take over. We'd just be here to offer our assistance. This is what we do, detective."

"How soon could they get here?"

"Tonight."

"Let's do it, then." Sharpe rose from his chair. "Better let the captain know. You should be in on this. Come on."

Moments later, they stepped out of the captain's office and Sharpe turned to Kate. "Go ahead and make the call. I need to get the forensics report on the fiber. They said it's ready."

"Will do. I'll catch up with you shortly." She stepped outside to make the call. "Nick, we've had some developments here and LAPD is asking for our help. Can you and Dwight catch a flight out today?" She went on to explain the anonymous tip and the story that CBN was running.

"So your buddy Aguilar wants a little bit of the limelight?"

"He's just doing his job. I can't stop him from running the story. It's all over the news here and the AP has already picked it up. Marc's just doing the inevitable. It just means Sharpe needs to get a handle on this investigation quickly. That's why he agreed to allow us to support his team."

"Okay. Let me clear it with Campbell. I'll let you know what time we're due to arrive."

She held the phone idle in her hands and looked to the street that fronted the station. Virtually no one was walking and cars packed the four-lane road. The only bonus was the warm weather. Other than that, she found she didn't really miss being back here much. And there wasn't much to miss in any case. They were searching for a killer, just like back home.

She returned inside and tracked down the detective. "We're getting authorization now."

"Good. I just got the report on the synthetic fiber." He held it in his hand. "Looks like our anonymous tipster might have had it wrong."

"What do you mean?"

"She said dark curly hair, right?"

Kate nodded.

"This one was blonde and straight and if a man were to wear it, it would likely just reach beyond the ears."

"Not long hair either, then."

"No."

"What do you want to do?" she asked.

"Could be a copycat."

"Or they're working together."

"Maybe. I think the only way to find out is to discover who our anonymous tip was from."

"The car. Had to be whoever was driving that car," Kate said.

"Yeah. We gotta find the car." Sharpe began walking down the corridor but stopped short and turned back. "You coming?"

She began to trail him. "You don't have a plate, so how are we going to find out who it belongs to?"

"I'm going to have to do a make and model search," Sharpe said as he entered his office.

"What radius?"

"Start wide and narrow down from there. I'm thinking fifteen miles, see where that gets me." Sharpe looked at Kate. "You said you wanted to help. I'll need help with this."

"Just tell me where to start."

"Since we're going with the whole dog and pony show with the feds, I'll have IT set you up in one of the comm rooms. I'll have my guys running the search through MVD, but then it'll be a matter of narrowing down the field of vehicles this will pull up. We can determine the model year, so that will help. But from there, we'll need identifying factors that will match it up with our car on the camera. That's where you come in. I need a good set of eyes for this and you're a hell of a lot younger than I am."

It was the first time she'd seen him smile, even if it was fleeting. "Oh, I'm not as young as you might think."

"You might be wise beyond your years, but I know a little about you, Agent Reid. And I'll leave it at that."

"Well, I'm glad to help. I just hope we can find this guy before it blows up on the national stage."

"Let's get you and your team set up and you can get a jump on this before they get here."

11

The sun's rays pierced the windows of the station as it lowered in the sky. Kate raised her hand to her brow to shade her eyes as she spotted Nick and Dwight approach the entrance. A thin smile appeared for a moment on her lips. Their arrival was welcomed, though a small part of her believed she could've handled this on her own.

Nick pushed through the glass doors and his eyes immediately locked onto hers, creasing as his cheeks raised into a smile. "I see her." He mouthed the words to Dwight as they drew nearer.

"You're here." Kate met them halfway. "Follow me. I'll introduce you to the detective in charge."

"What about the captain?" Nick asked.

"Sharpe will want to make the introductions, I'm sure." She continued along the halls, her brunette hair swinging back and forth in the ponytail she always wore while on the job. "Detective Sharpe?"

Sharpe removed his reading glasses and stood from his chair, offering an extended hand. "Ray Sharpe."

"Supervisory Special Agent Nick Scarborough, BAU. Pleasure."

Sharpe turned to Dwight and offered the same welcoming handshake. "And you are?"

"Special Agent Dwight Jameson. Nice to meet you, Detective Sharpe. Thank you for the invitation."

"Well, now that we've got that out of the way." Sharpe placed his hands on his narrow hips, exacerbating his paunch. "I'll introduce you to the captain and show you where we've got your team set up. Follow me."

"I want you all to know how much the LAPD appreciates your assistance," the captain began after the obligatory introductions. "This is a particularly disturbing case and in this precinct, we always have a full plate, so again, your help is most appreciated." He turned to Sharpe. "Feel free to show them to their setup and let them get started. Keep me posted on any new developments. I'm going to be fielding a lot of calls from the press and I don't want to get caught unawares."

"Understood." Sharpe turned on his heel. "Let's get you all hooked up."

The team followed him back into the corridor where they eventually reached a small room that was used for press conferences, but had now been set up with computers for their use.

"This'll do just fine. Thank you, detective," Nick said.

"Good. I don't know how much you're aware of yet, Agent Scarborough, but Agent Reid and I have been looking for a car that was spotted on CCTV in the vicinity of the latest crime scene. We're working to find the owner of that vehicle."

"Yes, I did fill them in, with the exception of your forensics analysis of the synthetic fiber found on one of the victims." Kate turned to her team. "The verbal description that was given to the local news station doesn't match this fiber. It appears to be from a blonde wig, short and straight. Nothing like what was described by the tipster."

"What are you two thinking, then?" Nick asked.

"Either we have two people working together to commit these murders, or we have a copycat," Sharpe replied. "The best thing for us to do is to find the owner of that car because I can bet a dollar to a dime that whoever it was saw the killer." He paused for a moment. "Your agent here has done a hell of a job helping us to profile this man. However, it appears we could be dealing with more than one and now that this story's gone national, we could use the help of BAU to speed things along and wrap this up before we lose anyone else."

"We're glad to help." Dwight pulled out a chair at one of the computer stations. "I'd like to see what you've got so far while Agent Reid continues to search for the car's owner. Just to get a sense of what we're dealing with and the timing."

"Good idea." Nick approached and sat down next to him.

"I'll keep working on this," Kate said. "Detective Sharpe, please, don't hesitate to toss anything else our way if you need to. I know you've got your hands full."

"Thank you, Agent Reid. One of my guys has traced the manufacturer of the wig and the local distributors. We're going to make a visit to those sellers and see who has purchased that wig in the past several weeks. I'll touch base on my return." Sharpe left them to it.

Kate walked toward another station and pulled up the files she had already compiled. "I think we should put this into ViCAP and see if we get any hits. I'll forward what I have to both of you."

"Sharpe seems impressed with the work you've done so far," Nick said.

"He's a tough nut to crack, but I think I'm starting to build a rapport with him. He's reluctant to get help, but I'm glad I was able to convince him that he needs us right now before this thing blows up on him."

"How are you coming along on finding the owner of the car?" Dwight asked.

"Sharpe retrieved most of the information from the MVD and I'm working on narrowing it down to a smaller radius of owners who would likely have been in the area that night. Without a plate, it isn't easy. What concerns me more, though, is the fact that it seems we have a variation on the description of our guy."

"He could be using multiple disguises," Nick said.

"Then that makes it all the more important to find the person who saw him that night and who can give us a better description of facial features. But, as Sharpe said to me earlier, people around here don't like talking to the cops."

RAQUEL WAITED INSIDE THE STARBUCKS WHILE VANESSA PICKED UP their drink order. She cast her gaze outside and watched as people passed by the window. For the past few days, all she could think of was the man who stopped to talk to them the other night. All she could see was his face looking down on them. And now every man she saw looked like that man. Vanessa had insisted they not go to the cops and she'd kept her word. But Raquel didn't reveal that she'd been the one to call the news station. And even that, she felt, hadn't been enough. No sketches had been released and that was what she really wanted, but she hadn't given them enough information and the idea that this person was still out there had begun to haunt her.

"Here. I got some sugar in case you wanted more." Vanessa placed the paper cup in front of Raquel and sat down at the table with her own large specialty coffee. "What's wrong with you? You've been acting funny lately. You're freaking me out."

Raquel slowly returned her eyes to Vanessa. "Sorry. I'm just tired." She sipped on the steaming hot coffee.

"Hey, so I heard about a party that Carlos is having at his house this weekend. You wanna go with me?"

"I don't know. I have to check my work schedule."

Vanessa rolled her eyes. "Come on. This is about last week, isn't it? You're still all stressed out about some guy who talked to us for what, like, two seconds." She leaned in. "Raquel, it wasn't the same guy that killed that girl, okay? I told you, there's no way. You gotta stop with this shit. Move on. Nothing happened to us."

"You're right. Nothing happened to *us*. Thank God."

Vanessa reached for Raquel's hand and, with her thumb, rubbed the side of it along the tattoo. "This is why you can't go to the cops. You understand? You know what that symbol means. You open your mouth and I don't know what'll happen. It ain't worth it, Rocky. Shit ain't worth it."

"Yeah. I guess you're right. Besides, like you said, it was just some guy." She glanced again through the window and took another drink.

"Good. I gotta get back to work. My boss gets her panties all up in a knot if I'm late coming back from lunch." Vanessa stood up from her chair. "Call me after you get your schedule; see if we can hit that party on Saturday."

Raquel nodded. "See you later." She watched as Vanessa passed by the very window she'd been peering through and gave her friend a final nod when Vanessa waved. Her shift was due to start in an hour and she continued to consider Vanessa's words of warning. How would anyone ever know she went to the cops, though? It was possible to go and talk to them, but not give them a name. People did that all the time. Why couldn't she?

Raquel stared at the tattoo on her right thumb. It was only because of her old boyfriend she even got the stupid thing. Some bullshit about loyalty to people she didn't even know, not really. They were his friends, and now he was gone. And she was left with the mark that meant everyone knew to whom she belonged. And now that everyone knew, there was no way in hell she could get rid of it. That would be like turning her back and people around here didn't like that either. She was stuck. Stuck in this shithole of a neighborhood, with a shithole of a job and no money to leave.

And now there was someone killing girls where she hung out. What if he came back and found them? Raquel closed her eyes and shook her head. This was some fucking shit she found herself in now. Too scared to talk, too scared not to.

She couldn't sit here any longer and think about it. Raquel stood up, raised her cup to her lips, and downed the rest of the now-cooled coffee. She grabbed her sweater and headed toward the exit. Tossing the cup into the trash, Raquel walked outside where the sun shone in her eyes and cool air drilled right into her skin.

Wrapping the sweater around her, she headed down the street toward the bus stop where she would take the bus to work. Opposite the sheltered stop was a police station. The massive building stretched at least a block. She didn't often pass it by, but since Vanessa worked close, they chose to meet at the Starbucks nearest to her work, knowing Raquel could catch the bus from there.

As she waited, she stared at the station, watching cops come and go. Some were taking in handcuffed people; others were on their own or with partners. A few people who she thought looked like lawyers drifted in and out as well.

Out of the corner of her eye, she spotted her bus approaching. Raquel stared at it, then turned her attention to the station. Her heart raced as she considered making a choice that could be her biggest mistake. But someone had died and she feared she knew who had done it. People around here died all the time, but this was different. This was a girl on her way to work, just like she was now. Not some drug deal gone bad or gang retaliation. Raquel might have been raised here, but she wasn't like them. She wasn't like her old boyfriend and remembered what he'd become.

"No. Not this time." Raquel stepped away from the bus stop just as it pulled to the curb. A quick wave of apology and she turned her back and made the call. "Hey, it's Raquel. I can't make my shift today. I'm really sick." She paused while her boss reprimanded her for the late notice. "I know, I'm so sorry, but I don't want to get everyone sick." A few more words of disappointment were hurled at her. "I'll be in tomorrow, I promise. Bye." She ended the call before he could say anything more. She might lose her job, but it wasn't much of a job anyway. If she got twenty hours a week, she counted herself lucky.

Raquel walked to the nearest crosswalk and waited for the light to turn. When the walking man appeared on the sign, she began to cross. Everything in her head told her this was a bad idea, but she listened to her heart, which now beat faster than she could ever recall it beating before. Even when she was in school at a track meet.

She stood in front of the columned entry and glanced at the stone steps ahead. Her eyes raised to read the letters mounted high on the wall. "Jessie A. Brewer 77th Street Regional Headquarters." Never once had she stepped foot inside a police station and a sudden wave of guilt pushed through her. For what? Turning her back on her people? Maybe.

Raquel walked up the steps and entered the building. Inside, she surveyed the lobby in search of someone who could help because if she didn't find someone fast, her nerves would get the better of her.

"Can I help you, miss?" an officer at the security desk asked.

His comment caught her off guard, but she turned to him and was silent.

"Miss? Are you all right?"

Raquel stepped forward. "Um, can I talk to someone about something I saw a few days ago?"

"Something you saw?" Right away, the man seemed to understand she had information.

Raquel nodded.

"Sure. Can you tell me a little about what you saw so I can point you in the right direction?"

Raquel moved closer to the desk. "You know that guy they're looking for? The one who's been—you know—killing those girls?"

The officer's expression turned deadpan. "You have information about that?"

"Well, I'm not sure, but I think so—maybe." She stepped back. "I don't have a lot of time; I was just wondering if I could talk to someone."

He was losing her. "Yes, certainly. I think the detective in charge is still here. I'll call him right now. It'll only take a minute."

She nodded and began looking around nervously. She didn't hear what the man was saying on the phone or to whom he was talking. All she could do was look and make sure no one she recognized was here. Paranoia had instantly consumed her.

"Miss, Detective Sharpe will be with you in just a moment. Just stay here, okay?"

"Okay." Raquel folded her arms and began biting her lip.

Moments later, Sharpe walked toward her. "Miss? Hi, I'm Detective Sharpe. You wanted to talk about something you saw?" He offered his hand.

Raquel stared at it as though no one had ever offered to shake her hand before.

"Can I ask your name?"

"Raquel."

Sharpe noticed the tattoo on her right thumb when she finally returned his gesture.

She glanced past him and watched as a cop held the arm of a man in cuffs. He emerged beyond the corridor and approached them quickly. Raquel locked eyes with the cuffed man and he scanned her up and down with ruthless eyes.

He raised the corners of his lips just enough for her to notice. She knew this man. Not directly, but knew of him. He captured her gaze and held on to it until they walked by.

Sharpe, noticing the exchange, tried to regain her attention. "Raquel, why don't we talk in my office?" He reached for her shoulder to guide her.

"I'm sorry. I made a mistake. I have to go." She twisted beneath his grip and turned toward the door. Her hurried steps resonated on the tile floor.

"Raquel?" Sharpe jogged a few steps to catch up with her. "You're safe here. I promise, no one will hurt you."

Just as she reached the door, Raquel stopped. "Not here,

maybe. I'm sorry. I have to go." She was out the door before he could say another word.

Sharpe dropped his shoulders in resignation and returned to the security desk. "What the hell was that?"

"I don't know. Something spooked her. All I know is that she said she had information about the Pretty Face Killer."

"Great. Well, whoever just walked by blew that for us. Son of a bitch. She could've been the one who called the news station." Sharpe slammed the desk with the side of his fist and walked back toward his office. As he made his way inside, he picked up his phone.

"Hey, I need a favor. Can you get me the phone records from Channel 7? I need to get the number of their anonymous tipster." He paused. "Yeah, I know. I'll call them first and get written permission. Thanks." Hanging up the line, he considered his options and quickly started into the hall, almost running into Kate.

"Where are you off to?"

"I think the woman who left the tip with Channel 7 was just here."

"What? Did you talk to her?"

"She left. Got spooked when she saw someone. I'm going to find out who that someone was and how he knows her."

12

Detective Sharpe's return to the communications room revealed his irritation as he closed the door with more force than was necessary. His agitation then took the form of pacing inside the room.

"Let me guess: no luck?" Kate asked.

"Punk says he didn't know her, just thought she was attractive, although that wasn't the word he actually used."

"You think he's lying?" Kate continued.

"Damn right I do. Shit, I almost had her. She came walking right through my damn front door." He pulled out a chair and sat down. "The only thing I've got to go on is the tattoo on her thumb. It's the sign of one of the gangs in the area. I talked to the gang task force and they're telling me it's the Pirus gang, who's based in Compton, but are working to take over more territory."

"Doesn't that put you right in the vicinity of where the last victim was located?" Nick asked.

"Yes. So now Reid has a perimeter to narrow down her search for the unknown green car."

"That's right," Kate began. "This may not have been the ideal situation, but what if we can find her now because we know approximately where she lives?"

"It does make it a little more straightforward, I suppose. I've requested the phone records from the news station. I want to get the number of our tipster and see if it belongs to this Raquel. Problem is, I don't believe that punk kid, and if he does know her and saw her here?" He appeared reluctant. "She might not be around long enough to track down."

"What about the wig? Any luck there?" This time, Dwight turned away from his computer to speak.

"We've requested they send us the names of the people who purchased the wig, but they're refusing until we get a court order, which we're working on now."

"Jesus. How the hell you get anything done around here when no one talks?" Nick asked.

"We learn to work around it. Agent Reid, you think you could talk to your reporter friend? Ask him to put in a call to his buddy over there at Channel 7 and get those phone records?"

"I'll give it a shot. Depends on if those guys want to dig in their heels, which, frankly, I can't imagine they'd do, considering the consequences."

"Whatever you can do, I'd appreciate. I'll let you all get back to it. I'm going to see where this thug lives and ask the task force to take a drive in the area. They might see her around the neighborhood and if that happens, we stand a better chance of talking to her."

"Keep us posted and we'll do the same." Kate waited for him to leave before turning to Nick and Dwight. "You both have reviewed my profile summary. What do you think? Could this guy we're looking for be a gang member?"

"Based on what we know right now?" Dwight began. "I'd say no. It's entirely possible he lives in a neighborhood with active gangs, but no, I don't think he belongs in one. Doesn't fit. This guy is acting alone."

"But possibly has a copycat or is using multiple disguises," Nick added.

"Possibly. Gang members travel together. Their strength is in their numbers. I mean, I'm no expert on the subject, but you could talk to the task force here to confirm. Rule it out, at least."

Kate nodded. "I still think he considers himself an artist. He's putting on a show with these women. The disguises fit; being a part of a gang doesn't. I'd better call Marc and see if he can pull some strings with the station manager and get us those records."

After Kate left, Dwight turned to Nick. "You think she's on the right track?"

"I do."

"But you'd like to ramp this up and take on a larger role?"

"I think we could be of more use to Sharpe if we did. But I can see what Kate was talking about. He wants to be the guy in charge."

"Maybe more like you than you thought?"

"Maybe." Nick smiled. "In the meantime, I've entered markers into ViCAP. Now I just have to wait."

"Waiting's never been your strong suit."

THE INCANDESCENT LIGHT ABOVE ANDRE'S CUBICLE STARTED TO flicker, threatening to burn out. He glanced up at it with squinted eyes and a hint of disdain. He loathed his job and everyone who worked there. And now that he'd watched the morning news, he grew increasingly distressed, scanning those who walked past him in the halls, around his cubicle; everywhere. But it hadn't been him who had been seen. It had been the man behind the camera. A man whose identity he'd taken on in order to catch a glimpse of his beautiful artwork before it was taken away. He hadn't killed those women. Why should he be afraid?

Because the only thing that kept him happy was following the man behind the camera. Slipping into his shoes as though he'd been the one to create such remarkable art. But he hadn't. He was merely an observer, although now someone had seen the true artist or, at least, had caught of glimpse of him. And his entire happiness hung on the man's capture. Oh, he thought the day would eventually arise, but he needed it to continue for as long as possible.

"Just a while longer." His lament was so apparent in his words.

"Andre?"

Miguel Perez seemed to appear suddenly and without warning, yanking Andre back into the present. "What's up?"

"Dude, you see that shit about that fucking guy? You know, the one who's killing those girls and leaving them all like made up and shit? Fucking crazy motherfucker."

"Yeah, I heard about it. So what?"

"So what? What the fuck is wrong with you, man? Don't you give a shit about what's happening in your own city? Shit. That's cold, bra. I mean, you got a family and shit to protect. If I was you, I wouldn't let them out of the fucking house until that motherfucker is caught."

"You came down here to tell me about some guy on the news?" Andre's tone flattened.

"Nah, man. I came down here 'cause I need the weekly report. You were supposed to email me that shit two hours ago, remember? I got a meeting in like half an hour. You got the report or what?"

"I got it." Andre began typing on his keyboard. "It's on the printer now." He turned to Miguel. "Anything else?"

"That's it. Thanks, man. I'll catch up with you later, all right?" Miguel walked away.

FROM THE COMFORT OF HIS LIVING ROOM SOFA, THE MAN BEHIND THE camera logged on to his site. So many kind remarks about his latest work of art. She had been made beautiful, which wasn't easy because he didn't have much to work with. And even less of a desirable area in which to create. He considered showcasing her inside the glass case where the donuts were displayed. Even now, thinking about that, he laughed. But his entire purpose was to ensure the public witnessed his art. So he carefully placed her in front of the store.

He remembered that he needed to replace the batteries in his flashlight because, without that, he wouldn't see the subjects well enough to apply their cosmetics. "Working under such conditions is a challenge," he said to no one but himself. But as he waded through the praise of his followers, he came upon a comment that upset him. "That's him. The one who followed me. It has to be."

With an avatar of the rapper Dr. Dre, the username of the follower was Dre1995. He noted it was the first time he'd left a comment. "Where did you come from, Mr. Dre1995?"

At first, he was flattered someone would go through the trouble of tracking him down, but it could have cost him everything and that was unacceptable. But he'd wanted to goad the man on. Try to lure him again, after a previous attempt had failed. Perhaps then he could put an end to the trespasser. "You think you're going to try to take credit for my work? Is that why you're following me?"

This could not stand, especially when he'd been so careless as to have been seen already. It hadn't taken him long to figure out it was the girls he offered to help. The only time he'd ever veered off script and now there was a description of him; in disguise, but still a description.

So he would need to take matters into his own hands with regard to his overzealous follower. Make an example of him. He began to type a response to Dre1995.

"You guys want a coffee or something?" Kate asked as she noticed the time. "I need some caffeine."

"They got a breakroom around here? I wouldn't mind stretching my legs for a minute. We had a long flight. Dwight, you want to step out for a few?"

"Definitely."

The three of them made their way toward the breakroom when Kate began, "Sort of reminds me of Florida. When we were all down there together?"

"A little. But this place is damn near as big as WFO. This is no little hick town," Dwight replied.

"Maybe not. Bad guys are the same, though. Still, feels good to be out of the office, doesn't it?" Kate entered the breakroom first. "Wow. We need a place like this. It's like a cafeteria in here."

"They're a big city with a big city budget." Nick opened one of the refrigerators. "At least they stock water. No soda, though." He surveyed the room. "I see a machine over there." He reached into his pocket for some loose change. "Anyone want a soda?"

"No thanks. I'll have a coffee with Kate," Dwight replied.

"It's too damn hot in here for a coffee." Nick plunked in three quarters and pressed the button for a Coke.

"There you are." Sharpe walked inside and hiked up his jeans. "Glad Agent Reid showed you the facilities. Listen, Captain wants to know if you three will join us for dinner. I know you haven't eaten and it's about that time. I told him we could spare an hour or so."

"Sure. I could eat," Kate replied.

"He's a good guy, but he's also got a reputation to protect, and being seen with the feds will help settle the people's worries about our investigation. And it's on the department, so you should jump on that."

THEY ARRIVED AT A RESTAURANT CALLED THE POST AND BEAM. With a modern design, it seemed more suited to the downtown LA entertainment district rather than South LA. Seated almost immediately, and likely due to the captain's pull, the five sat down at a round table near the west side of the restaurant that fronted the windows and overlooked the plaza.

"I wasn't expecting a place like this," Nick began.

"You mean here on Crenshaw Boulevard?" the captain replied.

"No offense."

"None taken. The city and developers have worked very hard to rejuvenate the area. This is considered an up-and-coming location." The captain paused to glance around the nearly full restaurant. "I started out on these streets in the late eighties. Things were very different then." He returned his attention to Nick. "But a lot's changed. Improved."

"Some things haven't changed," Sharpe said.

"It's a process. A long process, but we're getting there and I do what I can to make myself seen in the community. Let people know we live here and dine here too. We're just as much a part of it as they are and we care for it just as much."

"Sounds like it." Kate raised her glass of wine. "Thank you for the invitation."

"You're very welcome, Agent Reid. Sharpe here has told me how valuable you've been since you arrived a few days ago."

"She's a very valuable member of this team," Nick replied. "In the time I've known her, she's become one of the best agents I've worked with. Along with Agent Jameson, of course."

"I was getting worried there for a minute," Dwight replied with mild laughter.

"So, Agent Reid, you reached out to your reporter friend. Was he able to offer assistance?" Sharpe asked.

"I think for the next hour, we should table talk of the case and let our guests enjoy a few moments' reprieve," the captain said.

"Absolutely, Captain, My apologies."

Sharpe was a man who didn't do dinners and Kate sensed right away he was only there because his captain asked him. She'd had to face her own political dealings with the Bureau but now realized it was everywhere and there was no escaping it. "I did and he's working on it. And that's the last I'll say about it for the duration of the meal."

At the end of dinner, they began to leave and made their way to the front of the restaurant.

"Again, thank you for allowing us to spend some time with you. It was a real pleasure." Nick offered his hand to the captain.

"It was indeed. I look forward to continuing to work with your team on this investigation." He turned to Sharpe. "Ray, thanks for coming out. I know this isn't your type of thing, but I appreciate it."

"No problem, Captain. I'm going to head back into the office and wrap up a few things before heading home." He turned to Kate. "You three don't need to come back. Go to your hotel and get some rest. I know it's been a long day. I'll see you first thing in the morning, hopefully with some new information." He proceeded into the parking lot.

"He's a man of few words," the captain began. "A good man and a hell of a detective, but doesn't say much. Thank you all, once again, and goodnight."

"Goodnight, Captain," Kate replied before turning to Nick and Dwight. "You guys already get checked in?"

"Not yet," Dwight replied.

"Let's get you a room, then. I'm tired, so I know you must be." Kate walked toward the parking lot and pressed the remote to open her rental car door. "I'll drive." She slid onto the driver's seat and waited for them to get in. "I'm staying a little farther away, nearer to downtown. Shouldn't take long to get there."

"You seemed to have picked up things here pretty quickly. Already know your way around town?" Nick asked as he closed the front passenger door.

"Sharpe and I drove around quite a bit yesterday. And you forget, I lived in San Diego. Been to LA on more than one occasion. Also, I have navigation." She smiled and pressed the button that brought up directions to the hotel.

Twenty minutes later, they arrived. "This is it. Holiday Inn

Express." She parked in front of the building. "See? I stayed within the Bureau's allowance."

Inside, the desk attendant checked the two of them in.

"You don't mind if I get my own room, do you?" Nick asked. "I'd like to have some time to myself to analyze the case a little further."

"Are you kidding? If it means I don't have to listen to you snore, I'm all for getting our own rooms. Why should Kate get all the benefits?" Dwight nudged her elbow. "Just kidding."

She and Dwight exchanged an uncomfortable look as though they half-expected Nick wanted his own room to drink, but neither said anything. Some time had passed and while they couldn't be sure he was handling his drink better, it seemed as though he was and, at some point, they would have to put their trust in him again.

"Here's your key, Mr. Scarborough. And yours, Mr. Jameson. Enjoy your evening."

The two caught up with Kate, who'd already made her way to the elevators.

"All set?" She pressed the button.

"All set," Dwight replied.

As the doors parted on Kate's floor, she stepped off. "Goodnight, guys." Her room was at the end of the hall and Kate walked inside, feeling as though she should call Nick or meet with him just to talk about things. They'd both set aside what had happened and, even tonight, she doubted Dwight had picked up on anything. But now, alone in her room, she thought about him. He wasn't back in Virginia; he was here. And the elephant in the room had grown especially large.

For now, though, she would slip on her t-shirt and shorts and take off her makeup. It felt as though she'd been wearing these clothes for days and wanted nothing more than to get comfortable. Then she could think about what to do.

And while she'd scarcely had the chance to change, her mobile rang. Kate padded from the bathroom in bare feet to answer the call. "Hey. You get in your room all right?" she asked, noticing it was Nick.

"Oh yeah, no problems. I was thinking... could we talk for a while? Unless you're too tired."

"I'm not. And I think that would be a good idea. I'll see you in a few?"

"Be right down."

Kate perched on the edge of the bed, anticipating the impending exchange. She still hadn't faced the consequences of her actions, and neither had he.

The knock on the door sounded and when she opened it, Kate looked directly into his eyes. "Come in."

Nick entered and stopped inches from her. He held her gaze and placed his hand on her cheek. He slipped the other behind her back and began to kiss her.

No words of warning, no chance for her to reconsider. Kate returned the gesture with more eagerness than she'd expected and within moments, they fell onto the bed. The t-shirt she wore rode up, exposing the smooth skin of her stomach. His lips soon rested just above her navel and the sensation forced her back to arch.

Kate's emotions when it came to Nick were confounding, but she knew one thing for sure. Right here, right now, she wanted him. And he wanted her.

13

It was the light from Nick's cell phone that roused him from his sleep; a beacon that sliced through the pitch-black room. He turned toward it and extinguished its glow with haste, but not before noticing the time. It was still early enough for him to get back to his room without eyebrows being raised by his partner, who would show up to knock on his door in a short while. Best not to have to explain his whereabouts, no matter how familiar Dwight was with the two's tenuous relationship. Which, after last night, brought forth even more confusion and uncertainty.

Upon glancing at her silhouetted figure beneath the covers, Kate still slept and he didn't want to wake her. Nick pushed gently from the bed and felt around for his clothes and shoes, still blinded by darkness after the flash of light that stung his eyes.

He dressed quietly in the bathroom and, within minutes, reemerged clothed in a wrinkled shirt that was untucked and frumpy trousers in desperate need of an iron. He smiled at her curled-up figure a final time and slipped out of the room.

Kate's eyes clicked open and she reached for her phone to check the time. She had been aware of Nick's movements but chose not to acknowledge him. Not out of indifference, but out of ambiguity. And, again, there would be an awkwardness between them and yet she did nothing to prevent it or address it. "What the hell is wrong with me?" A question that would have to be sidelined for the time being because she was here to find a killer and there was still much work to be done. She rolled out of bed and into a hot shower.

As Kate applied the final touches of makeup and pulled her hair into her trademark ponytail, she heard the knock on her door. They were already here.

Pulling the door open, she offered a warm greeting. "Good morning. Everyone's up bright and early."

Nick studied her. "Early—yes; bright—not so much. You ready to go?"

"Yes." Kate grabbed her laptop bag from the desk inside the room and returned. "Let's go."

SERGEANT LOUIS MOORE APPEARED IN SHARPE'S DOORWAY. "I GOT something you might be interested in."

Sharpe peered over his glasses, removing them as the officer piqued his interest. "Oh yeah? What do you have?" He began to wave his arm. "Come in, come in. Sit down."

Moore handed Sharpe the piece of paper. "We got those names we wanted. Court order came through. These are the buyers of that particular wig."

"There's a lot of people on this list. I'm going to need some help sorting through this."

"We're already on it. Lopez and I started dividing it up by location and vicinity to our crime scenes."

"You might be tapering it down too much to start."

"We got a hundred names on here, Sharpe. There's no way we can go and talk to each and every one of these people."

"You're right. But what we're banking on here is that this guy used a card to pay for it. What about a cash buyer? If he's smart, he's using cash."

"Then we might as well throw this list out the window because we have no way to track down a cash buyer."

"Let's consider another approach. This list is good and it's a start, in the event the purchase was in fact made on a debit or credit card. We can rule that out first by running the names and determining if any of them have a record, or match the description our tipster gave to the media. Now we're still out looking for Raquel because as far as I'm concerned, we find her and we'll find our man. She saw him and she has no idea how valuable her description would be. But in the meantime, rule out the card users. Find out how many sales were made by cash and based on when those sales occurred, we can pull video from those dates and times and see if our guy was captured on tape."

"It'll take some time, days probably. And probably not soon enough to prevent another murder."

"We can only do what we can do, Moore. This is just a part of it. I've still got the gang task force looking for Raquel. And we still have the feds searching for the owner of the green car. Something's bound to turn up on one of those fronts. It has to."

Moore nodded. "Understood. I'll keep you updated."

He left Sharpe's office, but only a moment later, the feds arrived at his door.

"Morning, Detective." Nick approached.

"Thank you all for coming in so early. We have a lot of work to do. Please come in and I can brief you on our status." He waited for them to take their seats and began, "We have a list of buyers my team is working on. That's a start. The gang task force hasn't located Raquel, but I'll be focused on that today and I was wondering if Agent Reid could help me on that front. I think if we are able to locate her, she'd be more inclined to speak to another female." He turned to Kate. "I hope you don't take offense."

"Of course not. I'd be happy to work with you on that today."

"Good. Agent Scarborough, I believe the captain will want you to assist with putting together a statement for the press. Apparently, we've got all the major networks and cable news channels arriving for a press conference later today."

"Happy to help," Nick replied. "I think Agent Jameson could possibly assist your team with the list of buyers. I'm sure it's comprehensive."

"It is, and yes, we'd appreciate that very much." Sharpe slapped his desk. "Okay, then. Sounds like we all have our tasks. I'll leave you to it. Agent Reid? Whenever you're ready, we can head out."

"Sounds good. I think my team and I would like to touch base if you wouldn't mind giving us just a few minutes," Kate said.

Returning to their makeshift workstation, Nick was the first to speak. "We all good with what they need?"

"I am," Dwight replied.

"Same here. You're going to be the voice of the Bureau, so whatever you deem is appropriate to disclose, I'm sure the captain will agree."

"Then let's touch base later this afternoon." Nick pulled open the door. "Good luck out there today."

Dwight walked ahead and Nick turned to Kate. "Can I talk to you for a minute?"

She noticed Dwight turn back when they slowed and nodded to him, suggesting he could continue. "Sure."

"You mind if we step back inside for a moment?" Nick returned to the room. "Look, I know this probably isn't the right time. It's never the right time, it seems. But I just want to say something about last night and the other night too."

Kate's pulse rose slightly as she'd hoped this conversation would have taken place later. "Okay."

"You know how I feel about you, Kate. I laid it out there months ago and, at the time, you made it clear you weren't ready to hear it. But then you broke up with Mike, doing the exact opposite of what I thought you were going to do. And I think doing the opposite of what you thought you were going to do." He pulled out a chair to sit.

Kate sat next to him, allowing him to finish.

"I left it alone. Never brought it up once. Because like I said, you made it clear. Then I tell you I might be leaving the team and, well, we know what happened after that. And last night, I should've shown better restraint, but it appears I have little self-control when it comes to you."

"I'm just as much at fault for last night," Kate said.

"You regret what happened?"

"That's not what I mean." She began to stumble on her words. "Nick, I know we need to hash this out. I do. But I can't. Not right now. I think you know that."

"I do. It's just—hard. Hard not to know what's going through your head."

"I know. And I'm sorry for that. I don't want to complicate this more than it already is." She reached for his hand. "I'm confused. Unsure. And yeah, the probability that you're leaving the team? It scares me. But for now, we have to put this on the back burner whether it's good for us or not."

He pulled his hand from beneath hers. "We'll put a pin in it, as they say." A forged smile appeared. "Go. Do your job. You're good at it."

"Consider it pinned. I'll see you later." She returned to the halls and made her way to see Detective Sharpe. "I'm ready when you are."

"Great. Let's go." Sharpe reached for his leather jacket and slipped it on.

"Aren't you warm in that?"

"No. Aren't you cold in that?"

She laughed. "No."

"Okay, then. We're going to stop by the gang task force and have a quick word."

They arrived in the bullpen area where the task force was located, which was near the opposite end of the building.

Sharpe approached one of the officers. "Anything on the girl named Raquel?"

"Nothing yet," the officer replied. "Her affiliation with that gang means she should reside somewhere around that neighborhood, but no luck spotting her yesterday. What do you want us to do?"

"What about the guy you have in custody? The one who eyed her pretty hard when he spotted her in the lobby."

"He's been transferred to County. He can't get to her."

"No. But that doesn't mean he can't get the word out that he saw her talking to us."

"You think she could be in danger?" Kate asked.

"It's highly probable," the officer replied. "It would be better to find her sooner rather than later." He looked at Sharpe. "We can make another pass."

"Hang on." Sharpe turned to Kate. "Any word back from your friend? You said he was working on getting the records last night."

"That's right." She retrieved her phone. "Let me call right now and see where he's at with that."

"Otherwise we have to get a subpoena and that will take too long."

"I understand. Give me just a moment." Kate stepped away and began to dial Marc's number. "Marc? It's Kate. What did your friend say?"

"I'm glad you called me, actually. I wasn't sure when you'd be up, but he said he'd send the information directly to the detective you're working with. Ray Sharpe?"

"Yeah. That's him. Did he say when he could get it to him? Marc, a young woman's life could be in danger. It's very important we find her."

"What do you mean? She just gave an anonymous description. Why is she in any danger?"

"If it's the same person Sharpe believes it is, someone spotted her here yesterday talking to the cops. A gang member. She appeared to have known him because she freaked out and left before talking to Sharpe. Word gets out that she's talking to us, no matter the reason, she'll be the one at risk."

"Damn it. I'll get on the horn with him now and push him along. I'll call you right back. You gonna be around?"

"We're waiting on you, Marc."

"Got it." He ended the call.

Kate returned to Sharpe and the other officer. "He says the

anchor agreed and was working on it. I think we should put a call into the station manager and prod them along a little bit. But we should hopefully have something in the next few minutes. It'll be coming directly to you, detective."

"Then all we can do is wait."

DWIGHT FIGURED SOMETHING HAD GONE DOWN BETWEEN NICK AND Kate last night, but he didn't say anything. This was between them and it wasn't his place. Still, it bothered him that whatever they were going through could or already had spilled over onto this investigation. He didn't want to step in, but if they couldn't get their acts together, he would. He was growing tired of becoming the negotiator and something had to give. Perhaps Nick's impending promotion would solve the problem. Nick's head was clouded and it had been for a while. The problem was, Dwight didn't know if it was booze or Kate that was the cause. Maybe both. But for now, he'd go and help these guys track down whoever owned the wig whose fiber ended up on one of the victims.

"Morning," He offered his hand. "I'm Special Agent Dwight Jameson. Detective Sharpe said you all could use some help."

"Absolutely." Sergeant Moore accepted the greeting. "Thanks for pitching in. Come on over to my desk. "We'll get started. So, what's it like working in BAU? You must see some crazy ass shit."

"You mean like this psycho you're dealing with now? I suppose I do. But it seems like it's everywhere."

Moore laughed. "I guess so. Take a seat." He continued around to his desk. "Here's the list of credit card buyers. This'll be the easiest to decipher and so we'll start here."

"Sounds like a plan. Where should I start?"

"We've made it to the Ds. Can you work from the bottom and we'll meet in the middle?"

"Ten-four."

"I've got a desk for you over there. And a login to our database."

"Perfect. I can have our agent back in D.C. help with this too. She can run the names through the national database as well."

"Can't hurt. You guys have a lot more toys than we do. Might as well use them."

Dwight moved to the desk and set up shop. He scanned in the list and sent an email to Agent Vasquez, asking her to run the names through ViCAP and to check for any serious offenders on the list.

As he started to whittle away at the names, he turned to Moore. "What if he used cash? What's the plan there?"

"Surveillance. Check the dates the purchases were made and ask for the store video to see if we can get a match to the description the tipster left. We're hoping Sharpe can track down the girl who left the tip. I guess they have a name, but that's it."

"From what I gather, the fiber they have didn't match her description anyway."

"It doesn't. Sharpe thinks we could be dealing with a copycat or he's got multiple disguises."

"Right." Dwight returned to his screen and continued while he waited for word back from Vasquez. It was going to take some time and that was always in short supply when it came to tracking down a murderer. This guy had the upper hand right now and they needed to change the odds.

14

It was the message Kate had been waiting for. The moment it appeared on her screen, she hustled to see the detective. "I just got it. Should be in your inbox too."

"I'm looking at it now. That's it? Is it her?" He pointed to the name on the list.

"Seems to be. Raquel Garcia. And that's her address."

"That's got to be her, then. Right in the same area as they were looking before." He looked at Kate. "Thank you. That's good work. Let's get over there now." Sharpe marched through the building, bulldozing anyone who crossed his path.

Kate hurried to keep up with him and on their way toward the front of the building, she spotted Nick. "We found the girl. I'm heading over there with Sharpe now."

"Good. Be careful and keep me posted." Nick continued back toward the captain's office.

"Agent Reid? You coming or not?" Sharpe wasn't a patient man and held the door open for her to catch up.

"Right behind you, detective."

They jumped into his car and once again began driving through the streets of South LA until they reached the neighborhood where they would hopefully find Raquel. Sharpe's unmarked SUV still appeared suspiciously like a cop car, at least around these parts.

"I don't see a car in the driveway." Kate peered through the windshield as they rolled to a stop in front of the small, Craftsman-style home that had been neglected over the years. "You think she's here?"

"I don't know. She might not own a car." Sharpe opened his door and began to step out. "There's only one way to find out."

Kate checked her sidearm and exited the vehicle, moving closer to Sharpe. "You said she was pretty freaked out when she saw that guy. You think she'll talk to us?"

"God, I hope so. She's the only one who can tell us what the killer looks like. We need to make her feel safe and protected." Sharpe reached the front porch and pulled open the screen door to knock. "Raquel Garcia? This is Detective Sharpe, LAPD. Can you open the door?" He glanced at Kate while they waited and listened for movement inside the home.

Several moments had passed and Kate shook her head. Sharpe extended his hand, suggesting she should try.

"Raquel, my name is Agent Reid with the FBI. We just want to talk to you about the other day. It'll just take a minute. Please, Raquel. It's very important."

They almost gave up when Kate spotted one of the front window curtains pull back just a hair. She turned to Sharpe and revealed a thin smile. Within moments, the deadbolt unlocked and the door opened a crack.

"Raquel Garcia? I'm Agent Reid. May we talk to you?" She turned to Sharpe. "You remember Detective Sharpe?"

"How did you find me?"

"Well, miss, you called the news station. They tracked the number back to you."

"You can't be here." Raquel's eyes darted back and forth. "You have to go—now."

"Raquel, we just need to ask you to come back down to the station and meet with a forensic artist so we can get a better idea of the man you saw the other night. The man who might have killed that other young woman?"

Raquel closed her eyes. "If I agree, will you leave?"

"Yes, of course. But we can protect you if that's what you're worried about," Sharpe said.

"Maybe you can protect me, but you can't protect *mi familia*. You think showing up here is helping anything?" She cast her eyes beyond them once again, in search of anyone who might be witnessing the exchange. "Look, I can come back today after work. I can't miss another day 'cause I'll get fired, okay? So I can't go with you now."

"Okay. What time so that we can make sure we're back at the station?" Sharpe asked.

"Six o'clock. I get off at five, but I gotta take the bus down there."

"Thank you, Raquel. We know how hard this will be for you, but you're doing a good thing," Kate said.

"You don't know shit, lady. I said I'd come and I will—later. Now please leave." She closed the door.

The two began walking back to the car.

"Looks like me being a woman didn't help as much as you thought."

"You got her to open the door."

AGENT VASQUEZ HAD COME THROUGH WITH A FEW JUICY DETAILS, Dwight saw as he read her email. "My agent in D.C. got back to me with a few things." He made his way to Sergeant Moore's desk. "Looks like we got a few bad guys on there, but nothing that makes me think they're anyone worth looking at."

Moore reached for the sheet of paper in Dwight's hand. "Why not?" He began to review the names.

"They're in the system for robbery homicide. Two were paroled a couple years back and one just went back inside. Used a disguise to hold up a jewelry store. He was caught on surveillance. Wore a mask too but ended up killing one of the employees. Anyway, no other sheets on anyone else."

"That doesn't mean he's not on here."

"No, it doesn't. Just means we're going to have to look a little deeper. Anything on your end?"

"No. Most of these were purchased around Halloween. Guess blonde male wigs are popular for costumes."

"Should we consider cash buyers? It'd make sense. Guys like this—blatantly displaying their handiwork—they don't make mistakes like using credit cards."

"Maybe you're right, but we need to keep looking. At least until Sharpe can get to that girl. Get her to give us a better description. We need that to compare to any surveillance videos we get from the stores. Otherwise, we're still shooting in the dark."

"We're shooting in the dark with these names. Without a face, any one of these people, male at least, could be the guy we're looking for."

"Yep. We're just hoping it's someone with a record to make it easier on us."

"Worst case, Sharpe doesn't get anywhere with the girl, we're gonna be knocking on some doors to see for ourselves. I need to check in with my team. I'll be back in ten."

Moore nodded and Dwight went on his way, back through the impressive building and over to Sharpe's office.

"Dwight, hey." Kate had just emerged from beyond the corridor. "I was just coming to see how things were going. We just got back."

"Any luck with the girl?"

"I think so. She's coming in around six, after her shift, to talk."

"Good. We need her to give us more to go on."

"Not much luck with the names?"

"Not yet. It's a hell of a long list, but we're working through it. Good guys over here."

"They are. Have you seen Nick?"

"Not since this morning." Dwight scanned the area. "Last I heard, he was with the captain, trying to appease the beast."

Kate chuckled. "I saw him briefly as we were leaving, but that was about an hour ago. Wonder if I should try to track him down?"

Dwight regarded Kate with skepticism.

"What?"

"What's going on with you two?"

She turned her sights to the floor. "Nothing—I don't know."

"Kate." He shook his head. "This isn't the time to be hashing up whatever it is you guys have going on. People are dying out there, being put on display like some kind of freak art show."

A flash of heat rose beneath her collar. "I know that. You think I don't know that? What the hell, Dwight? I thought we were friends."

"Calm down. We are friends. But I'm telling you, Nick is messed up, okay?"

"And that's my fault?"

"Don't pretend that the relationship between the two of you hasn't been contentious. I work with both of you, remember? I've seen how he reacts to you and vice versa. Shit's gotta end, Kate. One way or another. Both of you are stringing the other along and it's not right and it's not fair. To you guys or me. And I'm sure Vasquez has picked up on it too." He held her gaze, which seemed to grow darker by the moment. "Look, don't get pissed at me. You know I'm right."

"Yeah, well, looks like he's not going to be around much longer anyway. So problem solved." Kate turned her back on him and walked away.

"Kate. Agent Reid, hold up." Dwight waited for her to respond, but she didn't. She just kept walking. "God damn it."

RAQUEL CHECKED THE TIME. "OH SHIT. I GOTTA PUNCH OUT." SHE approached her manager. "It's time for me to go."

"Okay, Rocky. Have a good night."

She removed her hat and walked through the kitchen toward the employee locker room. With her fingers on the combination lock, she turned it until it popped open. Inside, she reached for her purse and then placed her hat on the hook. A quick change back into her regular clothes and she was ready to leave. But she'd begun to reconsider her plans.

Raquel stood still for a moment, staring at the inside of her locker. "If I don't go, they'll come back. They can't come back." She took a deep breath, closed the metal door, and walked through the employee exit out of the back of the restaurant. It was always nice when her head cleared from the scent of fried chicken and she could actually start smelling other things, like car exhaust and smog.

She walked around to the front of the building and headed south to the nearest bus stop that would take her back to the station. As she waited, Raquel began to feel as though she was being watched. A subtle turn of her head, just enough that her eyes could see to her left. No one. Another turn to her right and a man who was twenty feet ahead pushed off the building he was leaning on and flicked his cigarette to the ground.

He began to approach.

Raquel's heart jumped into her throat. She was alone at the stop and considered bolting but would still have to go home eventually. She looked at his wrist; he had the same mark she did on her thumb. A casual step to the left, slow and calm. And then another one.

"Hey, Rocky, where you going?"

She looked at the guy and smiled as if unaware he'd been heading her way. "Omar, what the fuck you doing here? I just got off work. I'm going home."

"Really?" He moved to within inches of her face.

She could smell the cigarette still on his breath. "Yeah."

"What the fuck you doing at this stop, then? You can't get home from this bus. This bus takes you downtown."

"I have to stop and pick up something for my moms. She has to work late and then I have to get my little brother."

"Oh." He nodded. "'Cause it looks like you're going to go see them fucking cops that came to your house today."

"What the fuck are you talking about?" She rolled her eyes and tossed her head. "Ain't no cops come to *my* house."

Omar smirked. "I fucking saw them, Rocky. What business you got with them, huh? Is it about your ex? You got some kind of beef with your ex?"

"No, I fucking told you, Omar. I gotta get some shit for my mom, okay? Shit. What's wrong with you?"

He grabbed her arm and began to pull her alongside him. "Don't fucking lie to me. This ain't no fucking joke. You know the rules."

"I swear, Omar. I'm not talking to no cops. Let me go. You're hurting me."

"I'll make sure of that." He continued to pull her along until they reached a faded red Pontiac Grand Am. "Get in."

"No." She tried to wriggle from his grip.

Omar pulled a gun from his waistband and pushed it into her ribs. "Get in the fucking car, Rocky. Now!" He shoved her into the front passenger seat.

Tears began to stream down her face as she waited for him to get behind the wheel. What choice did she have now? If she tried to get out and managed to get away from him, he'd only wait at her house. He'd hurt her mom and maybe her little brother. "Fucking cops," she cried under her breath.

Sharpe walked into the communication room where Kate remained alone, still searching for the owner of the car.

She checked the time. "Is she here?"

"No. I called the number, but no one answered." He shoved his hands into the front pockets of his jeans.

"It's only 6:20. She's probably just running late. Buses." Kate noticed the look on Sharpe's face. "You don't think she's coming. You think we should go back?"

"No. We'll give it until 7:00. She doesn't show, I might have one of the task force drive by her house. We can't go back there."

"Okay. I understand." Kate watched as he backed out and closed the door behind him. There was something in his eyes that brought her concern.

Within minutes, she couldn't take it any longer. He was thinking something and it was eating away at her. She left the room and walked toward his office, but he wasn't there. Kate continued to the captain's office, where she spotted Nick still working inside. "I'm sorry to interrupt, but have either of you seen Detective Sharpe?"

"'Fraid not," the captain replied.

"Neither have I. You need something?"

"No. I'll track him down. I just saw him a few minutes ago. Sorry for the interruption." She continued on and checked a few other areas, but still no luck. Finally, an officer stopped her. "You looking for Sharpe?"

"Yes."

"He's with the Gang Unit."

"Thank you." Kate remembered where that was located and continued to walk for a few more minutes until she finally reached the unit. She spotted him speaking with another officer whom she didn't know by name but had seen earlier in the day.

"Excuse me, Detective Sharpe?"

He turned to her and Kate knew. "She's not coming, is she?"

"No, Agent Reid. She's dead."

The other officer turned his attention to Kate. "One of my patrols got a call. She was shot in the head and tossed out of a car.

Her body was found about a mile from her house lying in the street."

"Oh my God." Kate stumbled back a step and covered her mouth.

"Agent Reid, don't blame yourself." The officer said. "It's the nature of the business. Happens all the time around here. She was associated with a gang. Once you're in, it's not easy to get out."

"Someone saw us there today." She looked to Sharpe.

"Probably." He walked away.

"You might be used to dealing with serial killers, Agent Reid," the officer began. "But what we deal with around here? Might not be serial killers, but they are killers and there are a lot of them."

15

The death of the girl, and only known witness, was a blow to the investigation as much as it was to Kate, herself. Every word she'd spoken to Raquel Garcia faced fresh scrutiny in her mind. Could she have said something differently to change the outcome? Second-guessing her actions, however, wasn't going to bring Raquel back, nor would it find her killer. That would now fall into the hands of the LAPD. So Kate did the only thing she could do and that was to bury herself deeper into the search for the person ultimately responsible.

Alone in the makeshift command center, Kate continued the task of finding the owner of the green car. It was their only real lead now, and a poor one at that. The door opened and Sharpe entered. "Agent Reid, you should call it a night. It's getting late."

"Are you calling it a night, detective?" She noted his expression. "I didn't think so."

"Look, I appreciate the work you and your team are doing to help us, but it's time to focus our efforts on another avenue. I don't know how much farther you'll get trying to find the owner of a car without a plate, without a location. We're starting to chase our tails here. I think you and your team, myself, and the captain should meet and discuss our options."

"Sure. That's probably a good idea." She met him at the door. "Agent Jameson is still with Sergeant Moore, and Scarborough, I think, might still be with the captain. He said they had a conference call with the mayor."

"Let's round them up and have a talk." Sharpe waited for Kate to walk into the hall. "I know what you're thinking Agent Reid, because I've been thinking the same thing sitting in my office for the past hour. There's nothing either of us could've done to change what happened to Raquel Garcia."

"You sure about that?" Kate eyed him as he let the door fall shut.

"I have to be."

"I HEARD WHAT HAPPENED TO MISS. GARCIA," THE CAPTAIN BEGAN. "I'm very sorry and I'm certain Ray and Agent Reid feel they are to blame, but as Detective Sharpe is acutely aware, this is the sort of thing that often happens around here. It was no one's fault. This young woman tried to do the right thing and it cost her her life. But we still have a case to solve. It's been two days since the killer has acted. I'm afraid he's probably due, given what we know of him." The captain folded his arms across his chest. "So I'd like to ask all of you, with only a vague description of this man, minor physical evidence that has yet to prove beneficial, and now no witness; what are our options here?"

"The only good thing to come from all of this," Sharpe began, "is that we know who Raquel Garcia was. I think we now need to find out who her friends are. Find out if she confided to any of them about our killer. It's highly probable she wasn't alone when they crossed paths. Whoever she was with when it happened is the only one who can help us now."

"I'll search her online profiles: Facebook, Snapchat, Twitter. Anywhere I can find her and see who she communicated with the most," Kate said.

"The problem I see now is that we have conflicting information." Dwight pointed to the forensics report. "Miss. Garcia's account doesn't coincide with the blonde wig; an indisputable piece of evidence. We have to be certain about what this guy looks like."

"Do you think it's possible then that the wig belonged to the victim?" Kate asked.

"I don't think so. Not in speaking with the family and not from what I read in the report." Sharpe began to pace around the front of the captain's office. "He has to be using multiple disguises. I like your idea of examining social media. She most likely wasn't alone at the time, or she might well have been his next victim. Whoever was with her that night, that's who we need to find. And until we do, I think we're at a standstill."

"Unless our unsub is getting restless and strikes again," Nick said. "If your plan doesn't pan out, we may not get anywhere until he does."

DINA WALKED DOWN THE STAIRS AND RETURNED TO THE LIVING room, where Andre watched the ten o'clock news. "They're finally down." She sat next to him. "I'll tell you what, Andre, we need to crack the whip on those two. Fighting us for an hour before they finally get to bed. It's getting ridiculous."

"I know, honey. We'll figure something out." He continued to keep his eyes glued to the screen.

She pursed her lips. "Mmm, hmmm. Sure. I can see you're wanting to jump right on that. What's going on with you lately? It's like you're completely preoccupied. Work going okay?"

After a moment or two, he pulled his eyes from the TV and turned to her. "What? Nothing's wrong. Work's work. No changes there."

"Then what is it?"

"I told you, it's nothing. You look tired. You should go to bed. I'll be up in a little while, okay?" He kissed her cheek.

"Fine. I can see I'm not going to get anywhere tonight." She pushed up from the sofa. "I'll see you in the morning. Don't forget, Ty has practice before school so he'll need a ride early. You said you'd take him, remember?"

"I remember. Goodnight, babe."

"Goodnight." She slogged up the stairs again.

Andre looked toward the ceiling and listened for their bedroom door to close. After waiting several minutes to be sure no one would be getting back out of bed, he retrieved his laptop, which he'd placed on the side table after dinner.

He began to log on to the site after ensuring sufficient concealment of his online identity. What he'd hoped to find was an update as to when to expect the next video performance and if he was lucky, maybe a reply to his comment.

Andre noticed the growing numbers of visitors to the site and he began to worry about the increase in popularity that could result in exposure of the man behind the camera. But all indications still pointed to the man's continuing forward movement of his art form. And, he did spot something that raised not only his hopes but also elevated his status as something more than merely a follower. "Oh, my God." Andre read the comment posted below his own.

"I'm so sorry I didn't offer advanced notice as to my next performance. I apologize and completely understand your need for the build-up. I feel it too and from this point forward, including a new blog post that you'll find here, you'll see that I've been generous with my narrative, and if you look carefully enough, you might find something useful."

A new blog had been posted and Andre began to devour it in search of when the next show would begin. "Tonight?" he whispered. "Shit." The man behind the camera had gone so far as to apologize for the lack of previous warning, but now it seemed he was intentional in his deception. How could Andre possibly make it there in time? A timer had been posted on the site that counted down until midnight. That was when it would happen. Midnight. And now Andre had to figure a way to get out of the house.

He began to study the clues. The man behind the camera, who seemed to always leave hints as to his locations, was more obvious than usual. This time, he'd made reference to the place once called the black Greenwich Village. Andre began searching for this reference and discovered the answer. A former resident and filmmaker once called Leimert Park this because of its cultural arts scene.

Andre smiled because, of course, he would choose this location. He was performing art himself and so this would be the perfect place. He considered, however, that this was also a highly populated area. Though less so during the week, which was perhaps why he'd decided to do it tonight. Still, it was a large area. The community itself was over a mile radius, but Andre had to assume the man behind the camera was referencing the park in and of itself. So that was where he would go.

Perhaps this time, the man behind the camera would ask Andre to join him. It seemed he'd left enough information in which to find him, but wondered too who else might pick up on the clues. Andre couldn't risk someone else getting there before he did and spoiling it for everyone. He'd almost regretted not revealing his presence at the events sooner. The invitation was clear and Andre wouldn't miss out on this one.

Within minutes, he'd slipped on his kicks, and a hoodie, and grabbed his keys. It would be about a twenty-minute drive, maybe less this time of night. Once he arrived, he'd have to put on his disguise, just like the man behind the camera. His excitement soared higher than he'd ever imagined. The prospect of participating. It was too much to hope for.

Andre did consider what might happen if Dina woke up, but his desire to partake in the show outweighed the consequences of her discovering he'd slipped out of the house. Besides, he could always make up a story. He was good at that.

The lamp on the side table flickered off as Andre flipped the switch and made his way to the front door. With a careful turn of the handle, he pulled it open just enough to slide out. He secured the deadbolt and walked to his car.

The small engine hardly made a sound as he turned the ignition. Leaving the headlights off, he reversed out of the driveway and onto the road and only when he was a block away did he turn on the lights.

Andre considered himself lucky that he lived nearby and knew the city well enough to decipher the clues. His intellect hadn't gone unnoticed either. The man behind the camera gave him even more clues. Yes, he was sure he would be allowed to at the very least watch the performance, and if he was lucky enough—no, he couldn't get ahead of himself. Not yet.

Ahead was the park and so he killed the lights again in case the man was already there, plotting, staging his area. He was about to catch a glimpse of greatness. Of an art pure in form. It was adrenaline-charged, titillating at the highest level his body and mind could feel. Total and absolute gratification the likes of which he'd never experienced before.

He parked on a paved area that was shadowed by trees and stepped out of the car. In the back was where he kept his disguise. Again, he pulled on the wig and baseball cap, this time pulling his hoodie over it to further obscure his identity.

Andre began to walk around the park, working to identify the most secluded location because that was where it would be done. He was certain of it. The park was closed, with A-frame gates blocking the entrances to the parking lots. A few people were dotted around, but most were either drug addicts shooting up or drunk and making their way out of the park. That was when he spotted the location. The final clue on the website.

Ahead he spied a pedestrian overpass, a concrete bridge held up by large storm-drain-type culverts. Not that he could ever recall a flood in the area, but he supposed it must have been possible. But he knew inside those enormous round concrete pipes, that was where the man would perform. Outside of the overpass were a few benches. He would choose one of them in which to place the artwork. A perfect location.

He began to traverse the park lawn and found that most of this area had already been deserted. With his hands in the pockets of his hooded fleece, he continued with careful and quiet steps to the location he was sure was where the performance would take place. Andre was good at solving clues and he was confident he was right this time, as he had been before.

The night sky was partially obscured by clouds. A slight breeze cooled his exposed face and Andre continued, his excitement growing with each step. A sound from the west reached his ears. He stopped cold and turned to listen, but it ended. Must've been a raccoon or some other night creature that roamed the park in search of scraps.

Andre stepped again, his shoes crunching the fallen leaves, making him wince out of fear of being discovered. But nothing could stop him now. He was much too close to what he longed to see. The beauty of fear and terror that embedded itself in their eyes and in their faces. Their flawlessly made-up faces, complete with red lips, soft pink cheeks, and smoky eyes. As though they were ready to adorn the cover of a magazine. They were the embodiment of perfection. Beautiful, lifeless perfection.

Only a few feet ahead lay the overpass with its concrete ducts. That was where he needed to go and that was the direction he continued. Again, his eyes shifted left, then right. Still, no one could be seen.

Something just on the inside of the culvert caught his eyes. "It's him." Andre darted for cover against one of the large pipes. Soon, he peered out again. There he was. Andre swallowed hard as he watched the man behind the camera plunge the knife into her gut. He could hear the woman try to scream, but her mouth was covered. It was too dark to see much more than two figures struggling against one another and there was no doubt the man was winning.

Again, he thrust the knife and when she finally collapsed,

sliding down against the curve of the concrete pipe, he reached for a box. Andre couldn't be sure, but it looked like a small case. He'd become so engrossed in the act that he no longer felt the cold breeze or heard the noise of the night creatures around him. For a moment, he considered making himself seen, hoping he might be invited to join. Instead, he watched.

The beam of a dimmed flashlight shone on her and it was the first time Andre could see the damage. Even from that distance, he saw the blood, but he quickly pulled back. Fear prevented him from taking the steps needed.

The time had come for the man behind the camera to set her up and record his art. He packed up the small case and turned off the light, slipping each one beneath the flaps of his hooded jacket; large pockets he must've sewn in.

Andre watched as the man peered out of the culvert in search of people. When he was confident of his seclusion, he raised the woman in his arms and carried her like a groom carrying his bride over the threshold. He was a large man, which made Andre even more fearful of exposing himself. But he wanted to; more than anything in this world, he wanted to.

Within moments, Andre began walking through the culvert. Dark stains adorned the walls that could only be one thing and that thought brought him even greater cravings. His lips began to part just enough to reveal a thin smile as he drew nearer. From where he stood, he could see the man already had her in place and had begun to film her with his cell phone.

Andre peered at his feet. He was about to step outside the culvert, exposing himself to the man. Was that what he'd wanted all along? Andre couldn't be sure and so he froze in place.

When the recording was finished, the man looked around and

when his eyes landed on Andre, he smiled and ran his index finger beneath the woman's shirt and raised it to his lips. He licked off of his finger what Andre could only assume was blood.

That was his invitation, but Andre waited too long. The man fled from view and he wondered if someone had spotted him. When he was sure the man was gone, Andre continued out of the culvert. He could see the woman's flowing dark hair, perfectly coifed and cascading over the back of the bench.

Only a few more feet and he would witness the art for himself. He couldn't contain his excitement and began to move quicker, with a wider stride. He checked again for any sight of other people that could squash his plans. He knew it would only be a matter of time so he would have to relish what he was given and not squander it, concerned for the arrival of others.

Finally, there she was. Legs crossed, one arm behind the bench, the other resting in her lap. Her hand on one knee. Her head slightly tilted to the right. A string around her neck was tied to the back of the bench to keep her in place. A larger, thicker rope bound her waist and was pulled between the slats on the bench. It was partially obscured by her blouse, which hung open just enough to view her perfectly smooth and caramel-colored décolletage. Below, blood seeped through her shirt.

Andre placed his hand gently on her hair and slowly caressed it. The soft and silky texture made his pulse race even more. He devoured her with his eyes. It was too risky to touch her body, though he wanted nothing more. Her eyes were closed making her appear as though she was merely napping. No blood on her face, no marks on her exposed skin. But it did make him wonder how he'd done it so cleanly.

Andre pulled back at the startling feeling that crawled up his spine. He whipped his head around and he saw a man some forty feet away. His eyes widened and his heart raced. He looked at her again and knew he had to go, no matter how badly he'd wanted to stay.

"Hey?" the man shouted. "Hey! What are you doing?"

When Andre turned around again, the unwelcome guest began to jog closer.

"What the fuck are you doing here, man?"

Andre began to run. Back through the culvert, back toward his car. When he felt he had a comfortable lead, he turned back and noticed he was no longer being followed. The man must've stopped for the woman. He continued again until he reached his car and jumped inside, keying the ignition with speed. A moment later, he pulled away from the curb that fronted the park and roared out onto the street.

The man who'd been chasing Andre now stood over the woman, but when he heard the sound of squealing tires, he turned and saw the car. A white Honda CRV, but it was too dark to see the plates.

"Lady? Lady, are you okay?" He shook her. "Oh shit. Oh shit. What the fuck?" He reached for his cell phone and began to dial 911. As it rang, the woman's eyes flicked open and she began to cough.

"Holy shit. You're alive? Jesus."

The 911 operator answered.

"There's a woman. She's hurt, but she's alive. You have to get an ambulance here now!"

"Sir, where are you?"

"Leimert Park. By the bridge."

The woman continued to cough and tried to bring her hand down from the back of the bench.

"She's fucking tied up, she's bleeding. Man, you gotta get down here now!" He dropped his phone to the soft ground. "Lady, what happened? Are you okay?" He began to untie her from the bench. "Jesus, Jesus, what the fuck?"

Tears streamed down her face, ruining her perfect makeup.

"It's okay. Help's coming. Just, just hang on."

16

Sergeant Moore hurried into Sharpe's office where he was meeting with the BAU team. "Dispatch just got a call. A woman was found in Leimert Park. She was tied to a bench like a prop. Good news is...she's alive."

"It's him." Sharpe bolted upright in his chair.

"A man found her, apparently after he chased someone off," Moore said.

"Has she been transferred to a hospital?" Kate asked.

"EMTs just arrived on scene. They're loading her up now." Moore looked to Sharpe. "We have a witness."

"We're on our way." Sharpe pushed up from his desk. "You guys coming?"

"You bet," Dwight said. "I'd like to talk to the man who found her and who chased off what we can only assume was our guy. With your approval, detective, Agent Reid should probably get the first crack at talking to the victim. How do you want to divvy this up? We've got a lot of ground to cover in a short period of time if we stand any chance of finding the killer."

Sharpe seemed to consider the proposal. "Agent Reid and I will go to the hospital. You, Moore, and Scarborough should get on scene and talk to our witness. Reid, you good with that?"

"I'm ready when you are."

As they entered the parking garage, Sharpe pressed the remote and the lights on his car flashed.

"What hospital? How far away is it?" Kate asked, stepping inside the car.

"County. Won't take long." He fired up the engine. "I want to thank you and your team. It's one o'clock in the damn morning and you all are still here. That means something. That holds water with me."

"We want to catch this guy as much as you do. We're glad to help. I'm sure as hell glad the victim is still alive. The bystander must've caught him before he was finished."

"Once those three assess the scene and talk to the witness, we should know more. Between that guy and the victim, I hope to hell we can get a description and catch the son of a bitch."

With sirens blaring along the streets of South LA, Sharpe's unmarked SUV rolled into the emergency area of the hospital. "Go on and find out where she is. I'll park up. See you inside in a minute."

Kate stepped out and walked through the automatic glass doors of the Emergency Room. She approached the information desk. "I'm Special Agent Reid. LAPD Detective Sharpe will be here in a minute. We need to know the status of the woman brought in from Leimert Park."

"Of course." The volunteer began to type on her keyboard. "EMTs brought in a woman by the name of Kimberly Johnson a few minutes ago. I believe she's the one you're looking for." She pointed down the hall. "Right through there, you'll find the nurses' station. I'll send the detective back there when he arrives."

Kate was already steps away, heading in that direction but glanced over her shoulder. "Thank you." She jogged until spotting the nurses' station. "I'm here to see Kimberly Johnson. I was told she was just brought in." Kate retrieved her credentials. "Agent Reid, helping out the LAPD." She glanced down the hall. "Detective Sharpe should be here any moment."

"Follow me." The nurse stepped out from behind the station. "She's still in triage. They're waiting for imaging results."

By the time she reached the victim, footsteps sounded in the distance. Kate turned and spotted the detective. The doctor who was treating the young woman emerged from behind the curtain at the nurse's insistence.

"This is Dr. Rush. Doctor, this is FBI Agent Reid."

Kate turned back and Sharpe had almost reached them. "Detective Sharpe is right here. How is she?"

"We're waiting on the CT results, but it appears as though she suffered several lacerations to her upper thighs and torso. She could have some internal bleeding from the knife wounds and the force of the rope that was pulled around her waist."

"No gunshot wounds?" Sharpe asked on approach.

"No. Knife wounds mostly, and there's no way to tell yet what sort of damage it did to her internally. Not until we get those imaging results."

"For God's sake. I can't believe she survived." He returned his attention to the doctor. "Is there any way she's in good enough shape to talk to? We've got a killer out there, Dr. Rush. Time is critical."

"She's conscious but heavily sedated. I don't think you'd get much out of her. And to be honest, as soon as I get the CT results, I may have to get her into surgery."

"Could we just try, doctor?" Kate began. "I'm sure you can understand what's at stake here."

The doctor seemed to consider their plight and finally stepped aside for a moment, raising the curtain behind him. He turned to the woman. "Kimberly? It's Dr. Rush. There are police officers who'd like to speak with you. You think you can talk?"

Her glassy eyes, stained from running mascara, turned to him and blinked slowly.

"Go easy on her. I need to see what's taking so long on the scan." The doctor stepped away.

Kate and the detective slowly approached the frightened and sedated young woman. He looked at Kate and nodded.

"Hi, Kimberly. I'm Agent Reid with the FBI. I know how difficult this will be for you, but do you think you can answer a couple of questions for us?"

She blinked her eyes once again and her lips parted. "I'll try." Her voice was barely above a whisper.

"Did you see the person who attacked you?"

The young woman nodded.

"Would you be able to give us a description of him?"

Her eyes floated between Kate and Sharpe. "Yes."

At that moment, the doctor pushed his way inside. "I'm sorry. I need to get her on an operating table right now!" He looked at Kimberly. "We're going to take you into surgery now, okay?"

Two nurses arrived to assist the doctor in moving the gurney and began to roll her out into the corridor.

"What's wrong with her?" Kate asked.

"He got her spleen. She's bleeding internally." The doctor

moved to the front end of the gurney and helped get her into the hall and they rushed Kimberly into the operating room.

"God damn it." Sharpe shook his head. "If she dies, he's going to get away." He slammed his fist on the metal tray table. "Fuck!"

"We should see if the others have had any luck with the man who found her. He'll be able to give us something. We don't know what he saw yet," Kate said. "Besides, she's going to be in surgery for a while, I imagine. We can come back when she pulls through. Because she will pull through." Kate placed her hand on the detective's shoulder.

THEY ARRIVED AT LEIMERT PARK, WHERE LIGHTS FLASHED, PATROL cars lined the street, and yellow tape surrounded just about the entire northern boundary of the park.

"I see them over there." Kate stepped out of the car and began walking toward them.

"Hey." Sharpe followed behind her. "What I said back there, at the hospital? I didn't mean to sound..."

"I know you didn't."

"What are you doing here?" Nick asked. "I thought you were at the hospital with the victim."

"She's in surgery. Right now, they aren't sure if she'll make it. It's too early to tell," Kate replied.

"You talk to our witness?" Sharpe moved in.

"Yeah. He's sitting over at the ambo." Nick tossed a glance over his shoulder. "He didn't see much. Saw a guy in a grey hoodie and ball cap."

Sergeant Moore and Dwight soon approached.

"Any luck with the victim?" Dwight asked.

"She's in surgery. Don't know how it'll pan out," Sharpe replied. "So our guy over there, could he give us any more details? Height, weight, hair color? Is he blonde?"

"Says it was too dark," Moore began. "He mostly saw him from the backside. I guess the suspect did turn for a moment, but he didn't get a good look at the guy. He took off in a shot."

"One good piece of news, though; he saw the car the guy was driving," Dwight replied.

"Plates?" Sharpe seemed to have a glimmer in his eye.

"No. Says he took off like a bat out of hell. Just saw that it was an older Honda CRV, white."

"Better than nothing," Moore said.

"Okay. Moore, stay here and see if you can get him to give us anything else. Try to get him to nail down a height and approximate weight. And help CSI with whatever they need. I think it's best if we all head back to the hospital and wait for Kimberly to get out of surgery," Sharpe said.

"Sounds like a plan. Thanks for getting us out here, Sergeant," Nick replied.

"No problem. Glad to have the help." Moore began walking toward the ambulance where the witness remained, sheathed in a light blanket.

"I got room for you both. Hop on in." Sharpe pulled open the driver's side door and stepped in.

Kate soon followed and Nick and Dwight slipped into the back seat.

He pulled away from the curb and turned around, heading back toward the hospital. "I should probably take you all back to the station so you can get your things and go get some rest."

"We're staying here with you," Kate said. "We can be of some use if we can just talk to her."

"You've got yourself a pretty damn good team, Agent Scarborough." Sharpe peered through the rearview mirror.

"Tell me something I don't know."

Kate glanced through the sideview mirror and raised her lips into a thin smile. What the detective didn't know was that the team, their perfect little well-oiled machine, was about to be disassembled for parts. And a man whom she loved, but didn't know if she loved enough, or in the right way, was going to leave. And everything was about to change whether she was ready for it or not.

THEY RETURNED TO THE HOSPITAL AND, UPON FURTHER INQUIRY, discovered Kimberly was still in surgery.

"How much longer?" Sharpe asked the nurse.

"I can check with the doctor. I don't know."

"Please. If it wouldn't be any trouble."

The nurse nodded and left them standing in the waiting room.

"She has to pull through," Kate said. "For her sake and the sake of God knows how many other potential victims."

"I don't know about you guys, but I need a coffee," Nick said. "Kate, you want to come with me?"

"I'll take one," Dwight replied.

"Same here, please," Sharpe added. "Thanks."

The two disappeared from view as they made their way to a kiosk that sold coffee and light snacks.

"You want anything to eat?" Nick stared at the items inside the glass case. "None of us have had any dinner."

"I should eat something. Just to keep up my energy." Kate peered inside the case. "Maybe the giant cookie."

Nick smiled. "Really?"

"Yeah. You got a problem with that?"

"No, ma'am." He turned his attention to the cashier. "Four coffees, a banana muffin, and one of those giant chocolate chip cookies." Nick retrieved his wallet. "I'll let the Bureau pick this one up."

A few minutes later, the coffees were placed on the pick-up table along with the food.

"Thank you." The cashier handed Nick his receipt.

"Let's sit down a minute so you can get a head start on that cookie." Nick walked over to a few chairs that lined the wall. "How you holding up?"

"All right. Just tired. But we're all tired." She bit into the cookie.

"It was a good idea coming here. You made the right call. Even if it was at Aguilar's suggestion. By the way, have you heard from him? I half-expected to see him at the news conference the captain held earlier today."

"He texted me and said he was coming but couldn't get out here before the conference. I expect him here first thing in the morning."

"Great. Haven't seen him in a while."

"Now you're just being facetious." She patted his knee.

Nick looked upon her face, her eyes, her hair. He appeared to marvel at her mere existence. "I'm so sorry I've made a mess of things."

She pulled the cookie from her mouth just as she was about to take another bite and met his gaze. "You didn't. If anyone did, it was me. I made decisions that affected not just me, but you too.

And I failed to see what those decisions did to you and us until it was too late."

Nick raised an index finger and pressed it gently against the corner of her lip. "Cookie crumb."

Her eyes brightened for a moment. "Thanks. That would've been embarrassing. We should probably get these guys their coffees." Kate stood up.

"Yep." Nick pressed his hands against the arms of the chair and rose to his feet. "Don't want them to get cold."

As they emerged from around the corner, Kate spotted the doctor speaking with Dwight and Detective Sharpe. She cast a worried glance at Nick and they both hurried their steps.

"You're back. The doctor here was just telling us that Kimberly pulled through." Sharpe's tone was much lighter than when they had arrived. "She's still in recovery, but we can talk to her when she wakes up." He turned back to the doctor. "Thank you. We appreciate the update. More than you know." After the doctor left, Sharpe continued, "Doc said it'll be a couple of hours before she wakes. You guys should really try to get some shuteye. You all don't need to stay here. I can stay. Your hotel isn't too far and when she wakes, I'll give you a shout. There's nothing more for us to do right now. I've already put out a BOLO on the white Honda."

"Without a plate number?" Kate asked.

"We had to do something. It's all we've got right now. Go on. Get some rest. All of you. It's been a shit day and I know damn well you're tired. I'm going to stretch out here on the sofa and catch a few z's myself until she wakes." He reached for the drink. "Thanks for the coffee." He waited a moment longer when it seemed they still hadn't made up their minds. "Well? What the hell you waiting for? Get the hell out of here and get some sleep.

None of you will be any good if you can't keep your eyes open after she wakes up. Now I'll see you in a couple hours."

It seemed that was the last Sharpe would say on the matter as he walked toward the two-seater sofa in the waiting area and proceeded to lie down, but not before gulping down all of his coffee.

"I guess we've just been handed our orders," Dwight said. "There's a cab outside."

17

The doctor hovered over Sharpe, who was still curled up on the utilitarian sofa in the waiting room. It took a moment for the detective to realize he was being watched and soon opened his eyes.

"Detective? You asked me to let you know when Kimberly was awake. She is and you can talk to her now."

Sharpe pulled upright and placed his feet on the floor. Still feeling groggy, he looked at the doctor. "She's awake?"

"Yes. All I ask is that you keep your questions brief. She needs to rest."

Just as the doctor was about to leave, Sharpe stopped him. "Doc?" He stood up and walked toward him. "Did you do a rape kit?"

He nodded. "No results yet."

"Thank you."

"She's in room 368."

A final nod and Sharpe retrieved his cell phone. "Agent Reid? I know it's still early, but Kimberly's awake. Can you and your team head back now?" He started down the hall. "Great. See you in a few."

Sharpe walked to the nearby kiosk for another coffee. He wanted a clear and alert mind and, right now, his mind was neither of those things. The time had just passed five a.m. and the sun still sat below the horizon, but its grey morning light shone through the hospital windows.

After finishing his drink, Sharpe walked into the men's room to splash water on his face. Upon his return to the waiting area, he spotted the feds' approach. "You made good time."

"I don't think any of us were actually sleeping," Kate said. "How is she?"

"I haven't been in to see her yet. Just grabbed a quick coffee. But I'm ready to go back when you are."

"Agent Jameson and I will wait here," Nick said. "I think it would be too much for all of us to go in there."

"I agree. We'll keep it brief," Kate said.

"Doc said the same thing. Let's go see what she knows." Sharpe led Kate beyond the doors and toward Kimberly's room.

"Do we know if sexual assault took place?" Kate asked as they approached the victim's door.

"They used a rape kit. It'll be days before we know if he left behind DNA." Sharpe pushed open the door and carefully stepped inside. "Kimberly? It's Detective Sharpe. We spoke earlier?"

As they entered the room, the young woman turned her head slowly in their direction.

"Hi, Kimberly. You remember me? This is Agent Reid; she was with me as well just before you went into surgery. Would it be all right if we asked you a few questions?"

Her eyes closed and her head bowed.

"I don't want you to have to rehash all of the events. For right now, we would just like for you to tell us what your attacker looked like," Sharpe said. "Did you see his face clearly?"

Kimberly nodded and in a soft, hoarse voice, she spoke, "I saw his eyes. Brown."

"Can you give us an idea of how tall he was? Would you say under six feet?" Sharpe pressed on.

She nodded.

"Was he white?"

Another nod.

"Hair?"

"Brown. Long and curly." Kimberly paused. "That's all I remember."

"That's good enough," Kate said. "You should get some rest." She placed her hand on top of the young woman's. "I'm so sorry this has happened to you. We're going to do everything in our power to find the man who did this, okay?"

A thin smile appeared on Kimberly's face. "Thank you."

"I'll be back later after you've had a chance to rest and hopefully start to feel a little better. I'd like to see if you can talk to our forensics artist. He can put your description into a sketch so we can get it out there and have a better chance at finding this person." Sharpe held her gaze. "Thank you, Kimberly." He nodded to Kate and the two left the room.

"What do you think?" Kate said as they stood in the hall outside the girl's room.

"Her description matches the one Raquel Garcia gave."

"But not the blonde synthetic fiber found on one of the victims."

"No."

"I'd like to get back to the station and start taking a look at Raquel's online presence. We should be able to glean some information from that. At least give this young woman a chance to rest for a while."

"And we still have a description of the car from our witness. We can pull CCTV surveillance video from the area and try to get a plate number," Sharpe said.

The two reemerged in the waiting area where Dwight and Nick remained.

"How'd it go? How's she doing?" Nick asked.

"She's shaken up, but she described the same person as Raquel Garcia," Sharpe said. "We'll get a sketch artist down here later and see if we can get something on paper."

DINA TURNED TOWARD THE CLOCK ON HER NIGHTSTAND AND SHUT off the alarm minutes before it was set to go off. She'd been awake for the past several hours since Andre had come up to bed. The sound of the front door opening awoke her and she walked to the front window and spotted Andre's car in the drive. But who had come in? She had contemplated going downstairs, but only moments later, Andre entered the room and she pretended to be asleep.

Her mind raced with theories. Had he been gone and, if so, why? Where did he go? But rather than confront him, she continued to feign sleeping and thought of the possibilities of why she had heard the door open. There were a host of reasons and yet, none would settle her mind on the matter. Andre had been acting strangely in recent weeks. Distant, unattached, and unaffected. She'd inquired about his behavior, but he merely shrugged it off as work distractions.

With a heavy sigh, Dina rolled quietly out of bed. She had the early shift today and it was four a.m. The rest of the house wouldn't awaken for at least another two hours. Her scrubs lay folded in a dresser drawer and she retrieved them on her way to the shower. It was there that she tried to consider what it was Andre had been doing at night, after work, and any chance he could get to be alone. Had he been seeing someone? Someone from work?

She tried to shake the thoughts from her mind as she pressed the towel against her wet skin and stepped out of the shower and onto the cold vinyl floor. Her wet hair was pulled back into a tight bun, and she pulled on her dark green scrubs. Dina emerged from the bathroom and switched off the light. Andre still slept and so she quietly padded across the room and through the doors.

She felt along the banister and walked down the stairs, assisted by the light of the moon that still shone in the sky and a street lamp that burned across the street from their house. Once she reached the bottom step, Dina turned toward the family room. She noticed Andre's computer resting on the side table. Walking into the room, she approached his laptop and placed a hand on top of it. Nothing. She peered at the lights in front and it only showed that it was charging. It didn't appear as though it had been in use. Then again, he'd come up to bed at least two hours ago, so what had she expected? Still, she couldn't bring herself to open it. Something stopped her. Perhaps there was still trust there, or perhaps she had been afraid of what she might find just beneath the surface.

In the end, deciding against probing further, she made her way into the kitchen to get a cup of coffee and make a quick couple of slices of toast. Sitting at the dining table with her breakfast prepared, Dina reached for her cell phone to catch up on the news. That was when she saw it. Another attack. Only this time, the woman had survived and was in the hospital. And someone had witnessed a car drive away from the scene.

Dina's face appeared stunned as she set her mug on the table and continued reading. *"A white older model Honda CRV was found leaving the scene,"* the article read. "Oh my God." She stood up, walked to the front window, and peered through to see Andre's car on the driveway. A 2004 white Honda CRV. "No. No, no, no. No way." She dropped the blind and stepped back in a daze. "It's a coincidence," she continued to whisper.

Dina walked toward the staircase and held the railing as though it was there solely to support her weight while she considered the impossible.

INSIDE THE 77TH STREET PRECINCT, SEVERAL REPORTERS WAITED. Among them was the man who'd been an acquaintance of Marc Aguilar. The man who'd ultimately been responsible for Kate offering assistance to Sharpe. As she approached from a rear entrance, she looked for Marc, whom she'd expected to also be here, but had yet to see him.

"There you are."

Kate whipped around. "Marc, you're here. I was beginning to think you were skipping out on this."

"Not a chance." He glanced at his former colleague. "Have you talked to him yet?"

"No. We just got back from the hospital."

"I heard about the woman. Thank God she's alive."

"We still have a lot of work to do to find this man. I assume you're here for the update from the captain?"

"Yes. And to see if I could do anything for you. Anything at all."

"I don't think so, Marc. We're just the B-team right now and it doesn't appear that that's going to change."

Nick soon approached. "Aguilar. Long time no see." He offered a greeting. "How's New York treating you?"

"Like the runt of the litter, struggling to suckle at the teat of its mama."

"So—good, then?"

"It's nice to see you too, Agent Scarborough." After shaking hands, Marc looked into the lobby where more reporters had gathered. "Any news you can share? You know—exclusive?"

"Afraid not. You'll have to talk to the captain. BAU is consulting. That's all."

"Uh-huh. Got it. I'd better go have a word with my old buddy. He'll be anxious to see what CBN said about the story."

"I caught it yesterday morning, by the way," Nick continued. "Probably should have steered clear of perpetuating the local press' notoriety they've already granted this killer."

"You've never liked us much, have you, Agent Scarborough?"

"You mean the press in general, or just you?"

Marc smiled and returned his attention to Kate. "I'll catch up with you later." He began to walk away.

"You didn't have to be such an ass, you know. Marc's a good guy. He stood by me when others didn't."

"Right. I remember." Nick placed his hand on her shoulder. "Sharpe's looking for you."

They walked back through the corridor in search of the detective and Agent Jameson. Upon reaching the communications room, they found both were inside.

"Found her," Nick said. "There's a horde of reporters gathering in the lobby. Your witness has been talking to the media and whipped up a storm."

"I'm aware. Captain's getting ready to talk to them in a few minutes." He turned to Kate. "You mentioned earlier about digging into Raquel Garcia's social media. How are you going to gain access?"

Kate took a seat next to him. "I'll start with anything public that she had posted. Most of the things younger people post are public. Not so with the older generations using Facebook and the like. The youth want their posts to go viral—gain as much attention as they can get. So that's where I'll start. Then, if I don't find anything of use, I'd like to reach out to her family and ask permission for access to her accounts."

"You think they'll comply?" Dwight asked. "They lost her likely as a result of reaching out to the police. Chances are you won't get far with any of them."

"He's right," Sharpe said. "She's dead because of me. My team, my people." He pushed up from the chair. "I've got to get with the captain before he briefs the press. Get started on what you can and we'll go from there." He walked toward the door. "I think this thing's about to blow up on us and we'll need all hands on deck."

Kate waited until he closed the door. "What do you guys think? What's our best chance right now to find this guy?"

"I'd still like to pursue the origins of the synthetic fiber. It means something. I just haven't found the connection to the descriptions we're getting right now," Dwight said.

"You're right. It could still lead us to our guy," Nick replied. "I'll go see what help I can be in gathering CCTV video from the scene. See if we can find the car." He stood up to leave. "Kate, get what you can on social media. I hope Raquel Garcia wasn't alone that night she saw him. You find out who she was with, you'll probably find the green car."

"And we'll have ourselves another witness," Kate replied. "Got it." She began to search Facebook for Raquel's profile. She was confident she could find a friend who had known where Raquel went that night and with whom. But as she began, several profiles appeared. Kate would need to whittle down the field of prospects and typed in the location she needed. From there, she narrowed it down further by age, eliminating anyone who popped up who was over thirty. While she didn't know the exact age, she was quite sure Raquel wasn't older than her mid-twenties.

Before her now were roughly twenty profiles. Now she had something she could work with. A brunette, slender Hispanic. Kate managed to eliminate another ten in the search. She continued to view each of the remaining profiles that fit her criteria.

Moments later, a text appeared on her phone. She glanced at it and noted Marc had informed her that the captain was about to brief the press. He'd wanted her to be there, but she thought that could only create confusion. It was up to the captain to let the media know of the FBI's involvement. She needed to stay in the background until otherwise required. She began to type a reply. *"Can't make it. Working on something else. Talk later."*

Upon return to her task at hand, Kate continued to peruse the Facebook pages of the young women whose names and appearance matched the young woman who ended up dying trying to help find the killer.

And then she found it. Raquel Garcia's public profile. Several photos had been uploaded and set to public. Some appeared to be friends of hers, others perhaps family. A young boy, maybe her little brother, sat next to her on some steps of a home.

She continued to view the images, desperate to find a friend they could track down to speak to. Somebody who could corroborate her description. She did note that someone who had access to her account posted that Raquel had died and a Go Fund Me page had been set up to help with funeral arrangements. Kate studied the message. Her heart broke for that young woman's family. With a click of a button, she donated a small amount to help. It would be completely against the Bureau's policy, but she wasn't about to tell anyone.

It was when she returned to Raquel's profile page that she spotted it. Kate leaned in for a closer look, but the image was still difficult to see. She clicked on it and a new window popped up, giving her a better view of the picture.

Raquel and another woman, probably a friend, were in front of a nightclub. But what interested Kate was what she saw on the street opposite the club. The photo had been taken almost a month ago, but there it was. What she'd been searching for over the past few days. A green car, a Honda Civic. "That's it." Kate zoomed in on the image. "That's the car."

She looked again at the post. Raquel had tagged the friend in the photo. "Vanessa Ruiz." Kate quickly grabbed the laptop and left the room in a hurry. She quick-stepped through the hall and toward Detective Sharpe's office. "I found the car."

Sharpe looked up at her. "Where? Whose is it?" He stood up to meet her halfway.

"Look." She turned the laptop. "I think it might belong to this girl with her, Vanessa Ruiz."

"Then she was there. She had to have seen him too. We need to find this girl. Now."

18

It was the morning light that spilled into the bedroom and not the alarm clock that awoke Andre from what had been a disturbing and restless sleep. Images of the woman, tied to the bench; the man yelling questions at him, charging after him. Now he felt more exhausted than ever, even snuffing out the exhilaration of the act he'd witnessed prior.

But he lay in bed, knowing it would be another few minutes before Dina would have to leave for work. He had to avoid her at all costs. With a clouded head, he might slip up. He'd been caught at the scene, his car spotted as clear as day. And Andre half-expected the police to knock down his door at any moment.

This had gone horribly wrong. The woman was alive and he wondered if she had seen him in the precious few moments he had to examine her. It was only when the man stopped to help her did he look back and notice she had moved on her own—confirmation that she was very much alive. His stare burned into the bedroom ceiling, wondering what Dina had known if anything.

They were going to think he did it. He wasn't the killer, but he was there, watching it all and doing nothing about it.

Andre rubbed his face hard as though that might wipe away the images that swam through his mind. He listened as the garage door opened. With relief, he exhaled. Dina was leaving for work as if it was any other day, which meant she hadn't known; not yet.

He ripped off the covers and sat upright with his hands pressed against his knees. The kids needed to get ready for school and he had to drive them in a car that, who knew if the police were looking for. And he would have to pretend that this nightmare wasn't actually happening. That he hadn't done the unthinkable. If he'd had his wits about him, he could've stayed there and told the man who approached that he only happened upon the woman and was about to call for help. After all, he hadn't done the deed. Instead, he panicked and ran. "Damn it!" His tone was loud, too loud, and he had to check himself because if he couldn't get his shit together, he wasn't going to get out of this.

Andre jumped as his alarm rang out, playing a loud, insufferable tune. He slammed his hand down to stop the horrific noise. The time had come to make a decision.

"Daddy?" A knock sounded on his door. "You awake?" His daughter pushed it open. "Morning, Daddy. Can I go downstairs and pour my own cereal?"

"Go ahead, baby. I'll be down in a minute. Where's your brother?"

"Still asleep."

"Okay. Go downstairs. I'll get him up." Andre waited for her to leave. He hung his head low and breathed slowly to appease his nerves. A moment later, he stood. It seemed he could find no other choice but to continue on as normal. Get the kids to school, go to work, come home, and hope his face wasn't all over the news. Or his car. Because if it was, Dina would know. And he couldn't let that happen.

～

DWIGHT PEERED AT HIS MONITOR. "HEY, SERG, I THINK I GOT something here. You want to take a look at this?"

Moore stepped toward him. "What is it?"

"That's the white car."

"Right. I see it."

Dwight zoomed in on the video image. "This is his plate." He smiled. "We got the son of a bitch."

Moore offered a laudatory slap on his back. "Hell, yeah. I'll run the plate now."

As they waited, Dwight noticed Kate enter. "Hey. We got the plate off the white car."

She continued toward them. "That's great. Maybe we don't need this information then."

"What'd you find?"

"I found Raquel's Facebook page and, from there, I looked into her friends." She placed a piece of paper on Dwight's desk. "This picture was posted about a month ago in front of a nightclub." Kate guided her index finger toward the car in the background. "That's the green car. And this is her friend, Vanessa Ruiz."

"You think it's her friend's car?"

"I do. And I think she was with Raquel that night they crossed paths with our killer. I just met with Sharpe. They're tracking Vanessa down now. But, with what you've got, we may not need a statement from her."

"I don't want to dismiss anything right now," Dwight said.

"I got a name." Moore walked toward them. "Andre Knight. Lives in South Park. Let's get Sharpe and head over there now."

"Keep looking for Vanessa Ruiz, Agent Reid. We might still need her testimony." Dwight followed the sergeant out.

"I'm right behind you. I'd like to see what Sharpe wants to do," Kate replied.

As they reached the detective's office, they found that Nick was inside.

"Good. You're both here," Dwight began. "We got the owner of the white Honda CRV."

Sharpe stood in surprise. "No shit? Let's get after him."

"Agent Scarborough and I will keep working to track down Vanessa Ruiz," Kate said.

A rare conviction masked the detective's face. "We might just get this son of a bitch after all."

It was the first time since Kate had arrived that she'd seen his spirit rise to the level of near-elation. She returned her attention to Nick. "According to Vanessa's profile page, she works at H&M, not far from here. I say we go there first."

ANDRE LABORED TO SUSTAIN FOCUS ON HIS JOB. A MULTITUDE OF scenarios played out in his mind and each one ended badly for him. He needed to get on the site and find out if the man behind the camera knew what had happened. That he hadn't killed the woman and now she was a witness. In a burst of acuity, it dawned on him. Could this have been his plan all along? Guide Andre down the primrose path, allow him to watch, and then set him up to take the fall?

There was no way to know until he could access the site, but from work, that would be impossible. He would have to leave. Andre glanced at the time. "Lunch. I can go to lunch."

Reaching for his carrier bag, Andre walked out of his cubicle and toward the breakroom, where he would punch out.

"You going to lunch already?" A woman he never spoke to except through email sat in the room, drinking a coffee.

"I've got some errands. See you later." He inserted his punch card into the electronic timer and stamped it. It was 11:25 and he had exactly one hour.

Andre walked to the employee parking lot at the back of the building and tossed his laptop bag onto the passenger seat. He gripped the steering wheel firmly and inhaled a deep breath. He had to find a way out of this because it was going to cost him everything he had and everyone he loved.

Turning the ignition, he pulled out of the lot and onto the main road. He needed to go to a café or a fast food place that offered Wi-Fi so he could connect via an IP address completely unassociated with him.

Within a few minutes, he'd found a suitable place. A McDonald's café. It would do. Andre parked up and walked inside. The lunch crowd was just getting started, so he found a seat and ordered a soda. His appetite was nowhere to be found.

Immediately, he used his proxy server and logged into the site. The video had been posted of the girl on the bench and the events leading up to her staging. The man behind the camera had again captured his victim with exquisite beauty and Andre admired it— for a moment.

As he scrolled down to see the comments, some knew what had happened. Who'd known the girl was still alive and that someone had seen him? But by "him," had they meant the man behind the camera?

Andre continued searching the post for any signs of a reply from the man himself. Perhaps he hadn't looked at it, but Andre didn't think that was likely. From what he knew of this person, he lived for the feedback. The praise of his work. And yet there were so many comments about her being alive. "He's gone," Andre whispered. "He has to be gone."

It wasn't until he reached the bottom of the page that he spotted a reply to his initial comment. *"Did you enjoy the show? I saw you watching. And if they don't catch you, I will."*

Andre slammed his laptop shut. His heart leaped into his throat and his pulse quickened enough to make the back of his neck turn hot and clammy. Now he had to worry not just about the police, but also about the man behind the camera.

THEY'D ARRIVED AT THE HOME OF ANDRE KNIGHT, BUT THERE WERE no signs of a white car. Not on the driveway, not parked along the front. Detective Sharpe was the first to approach, followed by Sergeant Moore and Agent Jameson.

Sharpe knocked on the door. "LAPD. Open the door, please."

No answer.

He knocked again. "I'm looking for Andre Knight. This is Detective Sharpe with the LAPD."

Dwight surveyed the exterior of the home. The blinds were closed, no open windows, no signs of life. "I don't think he's here."

"The car was also registered to a Dina Knight. I assume that's his wife. She might be here," Sharpe replied.

Dwight stepped back to get a view of the second floor. "I don't know. I'm not seeing indications anyone is home."

The deadbolt on the front door clicked and the sound brought them to the door again when it finally opened.

Sharpe moved in. "Dina Knight?"

Only partially exposed from behind the door, she nodded. Her distressed appearance was not without notice.

"Mrs. Knight, is your husband, Andre, here?"

"He's at work."

Dwight noted she was dressed in scrubs. "Did you just get home from work, ma'am?" He paused. "I'm sorry. I'm Agent Jameson, FBI. I'm here to help these gentlemen."

"I got home a little while ago."

"Ma'am, could we ask you a few questions about your husband? We won't take up much of your time," Sharpe continued.

Dina stepped back, pulled the door open a little more, and waited.

The men walked inside and began to survey the home.

"Where does your husband work, Mrs. Knight?" Moore asked.

"At the Corecom building downtown. He works in Accounting."

As Sharpe made his way into the living room, he pressed on. "When do you expect him home?"

"Around six. I worked the early shift today and that's why I'm home. My kids will be home soon too. Can you tell me what this is about?"

Dwight eyed her expression and figured she already knew the answer to that question. "Do you and your husband own a 2004 white Honda CRV?"

She closed her eyes and nodded.

"Did he drive it to work today?"

She nodded again.

"Ma'am, was your husband home with you last night?" Sharpe asked.

"Yes."

"Okay. And what time did you both go to bed? I'm sorry for the personal questions, but we're trying to find out if maybe someone had his car, because it was spotted near Leimert Park in the early hours of this morning. And I don't know if you heard..."

"I did." She looked at Sharpe with resolve. "He was here with me, like I said. We went to bed after the ten o'clock news, just like always."

"Okay." Sharpe nodded. "I hate to ask you this, but do you think we could have a look around?"

"Do you have a warrant?"

"No, ma'am, we don't."

"Then you're welcome to look around when you do. Now, if you don't mind, I'd like you to not be here when my children get home from school."

"Of course, we understand, but this is a very serious matter and we'd simply like to clear up any confusion as to your husband's whereabouts last night," Sharpe said.

"Like I said, he was here with me."

"Maybe it's best if we discuss this with your husband. You said he works at Corecom?"

"You can't—you can't go to his work. He doesn't need any trouble at work."

"Then maybe you'd like to reconsider allowing us just a quick look around?" Sharpe continued.

They all knew that without a warrant, anything they found in the house wouldn't be admissible, but it would at least get them a step closer to knowing if Andre Knight was the man who attacked Kimberly Johnson.

"Please, just make it quick. I can't have you here when my kids get home."

"Thank you. We won't make a mess. Just need a few minutes. We really appreciate your cooperation." Sharpe turned to the others. "Let's just have a quick look around. Agent Jameson, you want to check out the kitchen? Moore, you can take the living room and I'll have a look upstairs."

Dwight began to walk into the kitchen, but not before Dina stopped him. "Why are you here? I mean, why is the FBI here?"

"The LAPD has asked for our help."

"Help with what?"

"Finding the person responsible for killing four women and assaulting another, who remains in the hospital as we speak."

"Oh my God." Dina placed her hand over her mouth. "You think my husband killed those women?"

"He's just a person of interest right now, ma'am. His car was spotted near the area where the latest victim was found—alive, thank God. We just really need to speak with him. I'm sure there's a perfectly reasonable explanation for this." He began to look around.

"What are you looking for?"

Dwight stopped and turned toward her again. "Has your husband been behaving in an unusual manner lately? Working late or anything like that?"

"Well, yes, but his boss makes him work late."

Dwight noticed she didn't answer the first part of that question. "Of course." The sound of footsteps on the staircase caught his attention and he spotted Sharpe approaching.

"We won't take up any more of your time, ma'am. Thank you so much for allowing us to look around. Your cooperation is very much appreciated." He pulled out a business card from his wallet. "Please call me if you need anything or have any questions."

"What about my husband?"

"I'm afraid we're going to have to make a visit to his office. We'll keep it discreet, I promise you." He motioned for Dwight to follow him back into the entryway. "Sergeant Moore?"

Moore reappeared from the back corner of the room.

"We're heading out." He turned to Dina once again. "Remember, if you need anything, please don't hesitate to call."

The three walked outside and stood just steps from the door, waiting for her to close it.

"Did you find something?" Dwight asked.

"No. Nothing. I just wanted her to know this was serious. We'd better make a trip to Corecom."

"You think she'll warn him?" Moore asked.

"I guess we'll find out. I'll have a patrol stay around here in case he shows up."

Inside, Dina peered through the front window while the police and FBI pulled away from her home and disappeared. Terrified at the prospect of what her husband had done, she called him. No answer. At the end of his voicemail message, with a tremor in her voice, she began, "What did you do, Andre?" Her eyes welled with tears. "What the hell did you do? They're coming for you. You'd better clear this shit up."

19

With his car idling in the McDonald's parking lot, Andre listened to his voicemail. Guilt and shame that Dina had now known what he'd been involved with surged through him. But he had to remind himself of his innocence. He wasn't a killer; someone else was. He just watched it happen.

There was an explanation for him being at the park, and that was what he had to focus on now as he drove back to the office. That was how he had to play this. Go back and just talk to them, convince them that he was merely a bystander who feared repercussions. Why he was there, why he took off. It all had a straightforward explanation.

On his return, he noticed a black SUV parked along the front of the building that could certainly be an unmarked police car. And in his present state of mind, that was an easy deduction to make. He continued around to the back lot, parked, and made his way inside the building.

"Yo, Andre?" Miguel stopped him in the hall. "Dude, you got people waiting up front to see you. Boss has been looking for you for the past ten minutes. You're late from lunch."

"I know. Fuck off, Miguel." Andre brushed by him and continued to the lobby.

"Fuck you too, man." Miguel twisted his face in disgust. "Just trying to help a brother out."

As Andre entered the lobby, the eyes of the men, who were undoubtedly law enforcement, fell upon him and one of them began his approach.

"Mr. Knight? I'm Detective Ray Sharpe, LAPD. Do you have a minute? We'd like to ask you a few questions."

"What's this about?" He tried to suppress the urge to bolt, and the flood of adrenaline that coursed through him made his heart feel as though it would explode if he didn't.

Sharpe placed his hand on Andre's shoulder. "We should probably discuss this in private. Is there somewhere we can talk?"

By this time, Sergeant Moore and Agent Jameson had caught up to them.

Andre gestured toward the exit. "Outside?" He maintained his composure as he followed them out. A few employees who had been passing through stopped and followed their every move.

"We appreciate your willingness to speak to us." Sharpe opened the door, allowing Andre to exit before him. "This will only take a minute of your time."

Under the concrete canopy of the building's exterior, Sharpe halted and was now flanked by Moore and Jameson. "Your white Honda CRV was spotted leaving the scene of a pretty gruesome assault last night. And it appears someone matching your description was witnessed running from that same location. Can you tell me, Mr. Knight, what it was you were doing at Leimert Park at one o'clock this morning?"

"I don't know what you're talking about. I was at home with my wife and children."

"We stopped by your house a short while ago and talked to your wife."

"I'm sure then that she told you the same thing. Because that's where I was." Andre seemed defiant now and had shifted his initial stance of pleading innocent as to his whereabouts.

"Mr. Knight, I'm Agent Jameson. I'm sure you realize the simple fact of my being here must allude to the severity of the situation. A young woman was found in Leimert Park around the time your car was seen, and a man similar to your build was also seen fleeing from that woman, who'd been injured and still lies in the hospital as we speak. Are you saying that your car was taken without your permission for the sole purpose of going to the park and then it was returned to your home while you slept?" Dwight paused to allow for maximum effect. "Don't make this more difficult than it needs to be. It is a fact that your car was there. We have it on closed-circuit television and were able to get your license plate number from that video."

Andre opened his mouth and inhaled deeply as if preparing to confess. Instead, it was his fight or flight instinct that finally took over and he considered making a run for it. Backtracking to his original plan was out of the question now. It was too late. They'd want to know how he knew about the woman, how he happened to come across her. The man behind the camera had already issued a threat and now he was caught between the police and a killer who'd likely set all this up for him.

His chest began to heave and his mouth grew dry. Admitting the truth now would land him in jail. He'd have to confess to Dina.

He would lose everything. "Look, can we do this someplace else?" Andre peered through the glass doors at the gathering of people eyeing him as though he was already guilty.

"You want to come down to the station?" Sharpe asked.

Andre nodded.

"Then it will have to be now. And we're going to have to impound your vehicle. It was caught on tape leaving the scene of a crime. It's evidence now." Sharpe turned his attention to Sergeant Moore. "You want to call it in and have it towed out of here ASAP?"

Moore nodded and stepped away to radio it in.

"Do you need to get anything inside? Cell phone or keys? You'll need to turn the keys over to Sergeant Moore."

"I have everything with me. I just need to get out of here." With sweat now forming at the hairline on his neck, Andre again looked inside the lobby.

"Follow me. My car is right here."

Jameson waited for Moore to finish calling the impound lot to send a truck. "Hey, what are the chances we can take a look right now before it gets caught up in the system?"

Moore glimpsed Sharpe helping Andre into the back of his SUV and considered the suggestion.

"Otherwise, we might not get a look inside it for a while. We're short on time as it is."

"Yeah. Let me get the keys." Moore approached the detective. "Agent Jameson and I would like to take a look inside the car before it's impounded."

"Mr. Knight?" Sharpe held his hand out for the keys.

"Don't you need a warrant or something?"

"Your car is already evidence, Andre. You don't want to fight us on this one."

Andre reached into his pocket. "Here. I told you, I didn't do anything wrong. Go ahead and look. You won't find anything." He was reasonably confident of his words. He'd never had any of those women near his car and so to tie him to any of it would prove impossible.

"Thank you. Your cooperation is duly noted." Sharpe handed the keys to Moore. "Catch a ride back to the station from the tow truck."

Moore made his way back to Dwight. "Got 'em."

"Let's go see what we can find." Dwight pushed back through the doors and approached the lobby desk. "Excuse me, where is the employee parking lot?"

"Head straight through the hall here and at the end is the employee exit. That'll take you to the lot."

"Thank you."

Word must've already spread because as they walked through the building, it appeared that the entire staff lined the corridor to see them pass. Outside, the lot was heaving with cars.

"Just press on the remote. Hopefully, we'll see the lights flash and hear the horn," Dwight said.

"There it is." Moore began to approach with Dwight closely behind. "What are you hoping to find in there?"

"Not sure yet. We didn't get a good look around the house, although I suspect after today, we'll easily get a warrant for that. I'm just looking for anything that might tie him to the murders."

"Forensics will check for prints, blood, and any DNA," Moore added.

"I know. I'd like to get a jump on it. Bearing in mind, we'll need to take care not to destroy anything. I just want to take a cursory look."

"Sure." Moore examined the handle on the driver's side door. "I've got some gloves. Hang on a second." Inserting the key, he unlocked the door and pulled it open to reveal a strikingly clean interior.

Dwight began to examine the seats and the flooring from the other side. "Hey, you see a latch for the rear swing door?"

"Yep. Here it is." He pulled it open.

"Thanks." Dwight walked around to the back of the car. "How long before the tow truck gets here?"

"Probably twenty minutes, maybe less."

Dwight used his suit jacket to open the swing door and flashed the light from his phone inside. "Looks like he might have vacuumed back here recently. For a man with two kids, I'm not seeing any crumbs or dirt or anything like that."

"Yeah. It looks like the whole damn car was just detailed."

Dwight retrieved a pen from his shirt pocket and used it to lift the bottom cover where the spare wheel was located. "There's a bag back here."

Moore walked toward the rear of the car. "What kind of bag?"

Dwight shone his light on the grocery bag. "See that? You want to take that out since you have gloves."

Moore reached inside and carefully lifted the bag from where it had been tucked next to the spare tire. He waited for Dwight to lower the cover again and set it down. With a gentle touch, he pulled the handles of the plastic bag away to reveal its contents. "Looks like clothes. T-shirt..." He continued to glance inside. "Holy shit."

"What is it?"

"There's a baseball cap in here and..." Moore lifted the cap away from what lay beneath it. "Oh my God. It's a wig. A blonde wig. I think we found our Pretty Face Killer."

~

THE BUILDING AHEAD WAS WHERE NICK AND KATE WOULD FIND Vanessa Ruiz and, hopefully, the green car.

"This is it," Kate said. "This is where she works."

Nick parked the car and stopped the engine. "Let's go see if she's inside." He stepped out and waited for Kate to appear before locking the car. "We'll need to take caution on our approach. She knows what happened to her friend after talking to the cops."

"Yeah, but we don't know if she's involved in the same group of people."

"Maybe not, but I doubt she'll be a willing participant in the conversation."

"All we can do is try and see if she'll talk to us." Kate continued inside the store, maneuvering between the racks of clothing, accessories, and costume jewelry. As they approached the check-out, Kate began, "Hi. Can you tell me if Vanessa is working today?"

The young woman behind the counter eyed the two of them with apprehension. "Vanessa who?"

"Ruiz," Kate replied.

"Who are you?"

"We're investigating the death of her friend and would like to ask her a couple of questions."

And with that, the girl's expression softened. "Oh, right. Yeah, she's in the back on her lunch break."

"Would it be all right if we went back there?"

She nodded.

"Thank you for your help." Kate motioned to Nick and the two walked toward the back of the store and stood in the doorway of the breakroom.

Inside were three employees and the smell of microwaved frozen meals wafted through the opened door. Kate recognized one of them. "Excuse me? Vanessa?" She walked inside. "Sorry to bother you. We were told we could find you in here."

The other employees looked them up and down and then at Vanessa, who remained quiet but kept her eyes glued to them.

"We're here to talk to you about your friend, Raquel Garcia. It won't take long, but could we trouble you with just a quick word?" Kate moved in, still masked in sincerity and concern. "This is my partner, FBI Agent Scarborough, and I'm Agent Reid."

"FBI? What do you have to do with Raquel? Some gang banger killed my friend. I didn't know that was FBI stuff."

"Well," Kate pulled out a chair next to her, "it isn't exactly, but we are working with the LAPD. We can talk somewhere else if you'd prefer."

Vanessa scrutinized her colleagues until they got the hint and left the room. "No. This is fine. I don't have much time left on my lunch break, so you'll have to be fast."

"First, I'd like to tell you how sorry we are that your friend has passed away."

"Yeah, well. Shit happens all the time around here."

Kate could see the girl's pain even as she tried hard to hide it. "Can you tell me, were you with her the night of November 10th near Vermont Avenue at around one or two in the morning?"

"I don't know. I don't remember."

"Vanessa, it's very important that you try. Another young woman was killed later that same night. She worked at a bakery. Do you remember hearing about that last week?"

Vanessa shrugged. "I don't watch the news. It's depressing as shit."

"I agree with you about that," Kate said. "But, I'm asking because, well, do you own a small green car, a Civic, I believe?"

"No."

Kate glanced at Nick and both picked up on the fact that she was not being truthful. "You don't have a green car? You know, in helping the LAPD find Raquel's killer, I was asked to take a look at her social media profiles. And what I found was, on Facebook, a photo of you and her that was taken outside a nightclub some weeks ago. In that photo was a green Honda. It was the same car that was seen in a surveillance video not far from the bakery."

Vanessa averted her eyes for a moment. "It's my mom's car. She lets me take it sometimes when we go out. When we *went* out, I mean since my friend is dead and all."

"So, did she let you borrow it that night when the other girl was murdered?"

"No. I asked her to come pick us up. But we didn't see nothing about a girl who got killed. We didn't go to no bakery or nothing. My mom just came and got us 'cause Rocky hurt her foot and couldn't walk the rest of the way home. We only live a few blocks from that club and so we walked 'cause we was drunk. And my moms would've been pissed at me. She was anyways when I called 'cause it was so late."

"So neither you nor Raquel saw anyone in the area? A man or anyone else walking by?"

Vanessa again looked away.

"Vanessa, it's very important that you tell me if you saw anyone that night. Anyone at all. You were very near where that young girl was murdered and we think the person who did it might have been in your area prior to the attack."

"Rocky wanted to tell the cops, but I told her not to. I told her it would only be trouble for her and now she's dead."

"Vanessa, I understand how you must feel."

"Do you?" Her voice rose in anger. "You know what it's like

living with this shit day in and day out? Your friends getting killed?"

"As a matter of fact, I do," Kate replied.

Vanessa rolled her eyes and clicked her tongue. "Sure. Looks like you live a real hard life, lady." She paused for a moment and took a breath. "We saw some freak who stopped to talk to us, but then he left."

"Can you tell me what he looked like? We only have a vague description and we need someone with a first-hand account who can meet with one of the forensics artists to get a sketch drawn. We're hoping you can do that for us."

"Oh, hell no. I ain't going to the police station. No way. Are you fucking crazy?"

"Are you mixed up with similar people as your friend?" Nick asked.

"No. I ain't that stupid, but it don't mean I don't know people who get locked up and get pulled over for shit all the time. I ain't risking that. No way."

"What if we could bring the artist here for you? Or somewhere you feel would be safe?"

Vanessa began shaking her head. "I don't know. Shit, man. I didn't want none of this." Her eyes began to well. "Now Rocky's dead."

Kate reached for her hand. "They'll find whoever killed your friend, Vanessa. And right now, you can help find the man responsible for killing at least four women and severely injuring another."

"You mean you have someone who didn't get killed?"

Kate nodded.

"Then why can't you talk to her? She's going to know more than me."

"She only remembers a few details about the attack and a hazy description of her attacker. But what we need from you, is a description that we're hoping will match that man she remembered."

"It won't take long and we can have the artist meet you at a coffee shop or a comparable place," Nick said.

Another moment passed with Vanessa in silence, but then she pursed her lips and held Kate's gaze. "Fine. I didn't pay much attention to him, but I'll tell you what I remember."

"You think you can get the rest of the day off and we'll make the arrangements? I'm afraid timing is vital, Vanessa."

"You want to pay me for my missed hours?"

"We can help you with that," Kate said.

20

Andre Knight entered the 77th Street precinct, ushered in by Detective Sharpe. He'd spared him the embarrassment of handcuffs but kept a firm grip on his left arm as they walked inside and into an interrogation room.

"Right through here, please." Sharpe opened the door and led Andre to a chair tucked beneath the table. With deliberate steps, highlighting with each one the gravity of the situation, he walked to the other side of the table and sat down. Sharpe leaned in and stared, a final action to ensure Knight understood who was in charge.

After an agonizing silence, Andre began, "Am I being charged with something?"

"You did come down voluntarily; however, it remains to be seen whether you can explain your whereabouts last night. We both know you were there, so you can drop the story that you were home with your wife. She might be defending you now, but I bet she has no idea what you've done."

"I haven't done anything."

"Then tell me why you were at Leimert Park at one a.m. this morning? We have a witness who saw you run from the woman you assaulted and, of course, there's the issue of your car on closed circuit."

"Okay. I was there, but I didn't hurt that woman."

"Then why did you run?"

"I was scared."

"Of what? You saw an injured woman and you didn't think to call 911?"

"I was scared people would think I hurt her. I didn't, though. I swear it."

"You haven't answered my question as to why you were there. If you only saw the woman and then took off because you were afraid, why were you there at all? Scoring drugs?"

Andre averted his eyes and whispered, "No."

"Were you meeting someone? Can you give us a name so we can verify your story?"

"I was alone. I wasn't there to get drugs or meet with anyone."

"Andre, you're running out of options here. Four other women have died; all staged, all made up like they were at some sort of modeling shoot. Only this last one survived. Was it because someone saw you? Was that why you took off? Couldn't finish the job?"

"No!"

"Then you'd better tell me what the hell you were doing there because with what we have, it's enough to bring charges against you. Do you know what that means, Andre?"

Andre was silent for several moments and then looked at Sharpe. "I was following him."

Sharpe rubbed his face with both hands, appearing frustrated. "You were following who, Andre?"

"I don't know his name. I follow him on a blog and he said he was going to be there. I didn't know why, though. I just wanted to meet him."

"A guy who writes a blog was supposed to be at Leimert Park." Sharpe began to nod. "And you wanted to meet him? Who is he? Does this blog of his have a name?"

Andre was silent but soon continued. "If I tell you, he'll come after me. I think he might already be coming. I think he planned all of this."

"I'll tell you what, you think this guy is going to cause you some problems if you talk? If you don't talk, I'm going to throw your ass in jail and no judge will grant bail on a case like this."

"He's an artist, sort of," Andre said. "He does like performance art and stuff."

Sharpe's brow furrowed as he listened.

"He makes them up after—you know—then he puts them on display and films them."

"The fuck? Films them?"

"Yeah. And that's what he puts on his blog. They're his performance pieces." Andre wiped away a tear that traced his cheek.

"You're telling me you wanted to meet this guy and that's why you were there? You knew what he was going to do and didn't bother to call the cops? Well, I'll tell you, Andre, if what you're saying is true, you're still going to prison."

"But I didn't..."

The two of them stopped cold when they spotted Agent Jameson and Sergeant Moore enter the room.

Sharpe noticed they appeared to have some news. "The car here?"

"Yes," Jameson said.

"We found something. Something we've been looking for," Moore added.

Sharpe stood up while holding Andre's gaze. "What is it?"

Moore held in his hand an evidence bag. Sharpe knew immediately what it was and reached out to grab it. "You found this in his car?"

"Yes, sir. Jameson and I searched the vehicle, careful not to contaminate it, and he found this in a bag shoved behind the spare wheel."

"What else was in the bag?"

"A t-shirt and a baseball cap," Jameson replied.

Sharpe's expression immediately masked in triumph and he turned to Andre. "This your blonde wig?"

Andre shrugged.

"It was in your car, along with the shirt and ball cap." Sharpe dropped the contents in front of Andre.

"It's mine. So what?"

"So what?" Sharpe smiled. "That wig there, I'd wager that it will match a fiber we found on one of the victims. We've been looking for this wig, Andre, and what do you know? Here it is. So you want to rethink that tale you just spun?"

THE SUN LOWERED IN THE SKY AND ITS RAYS BURNED THROUGH THE windshield as Nick drove to a nearby café with Kate in the passenger seat and Vanessa Ruiz in the back.

"I see it, just ahead." Kate pointed to the right. "He should be here by now."

Nick pulled curbside and glanced over his shoulder. "Okay,

Vanessa. This is the place. It won't take more than ten, maybe fifteen minutes at the outside to give him the description and then we'll have you back at your store."

She rolled her eyes and stepped out onto the sidewalk.

Kate led the way into the coffee shop. She spotted the LAPD forensics artist at the far end and raised a hand to confirm he was the right guy.

"Officer Phillips? I'm Agent Reid and this is Agent Scarborough. Thank you for meeting us here."

"Pleasure. Detective Sharpe said this was urgent. And this is Ms. Ruiz?" He offered a greeting, but when she didn't accept, he pulled his hand away. "Okay, then. Guess we should get started. Why don't you all take a seat?" He waited a moment for the three to settle in. "Ms. Ruiz, the person you saw, can you tell me what his eyes looked like? Were they round or almond shape or large or small?"

"Um, kinda almond-like, not too big. Brown, I think. Dark at least."

"Great, and what about his hair? Color and style?"

"It was weird, like curly and dark, and laid on his shoulders, I guess."

"When you say weird, what do you mean exactly?"

"I mean, like it didn't look real."

"Like he was wearing a wig or something?"

"Yeah, something like that. A wig. It was just like all Jheri-curled and shit. I mean, what white guy wears a Jheri curl?"

"Right. Okay." Phillips glanced at the agents and quickly returned his attention to Vanessa. "Can you tell me a little bit about his facial features? What kind of nose did he have?"

Vanessa placed her hand on her own nose. "Sort of like, you know, wide and shit. Um, like the tip of it was wide."

"Like this?" Phillips began to sketch. "Kinda bulbous, you mean?"

"Yeah, just like that. And you got the hair right too and his eyes, except one thing."

"What's that?"

"He was wearing a Chicago Bulls baseball hat."

"You remember that it was the Chicago Bulls?"

"Yeah, of course. I mean, we're in LA, right? This guy's wearing a Chicago hat. I knew he wasn't from around here."

"Okay. We're getting somewhere now. Ms. Ruiz, what about his cheeks? Were they really high and sharp, or were his cheeks fuller, kinda fat, you know?"

"I think they were, um, kinda like normal. I mean, like I don't remember them being anything special like all cut, you know?"

"Okay." He continued to sketch.

"And finally, you're confident he was white?"

"He was white. Definitely a white guy." She paused. "Well, I mean, maybe he coulda been Latino, but if he was, he was really light-skinned."

"Any facial hair?"

"No. no beard or anything like that."

Officer Phillips was quiet for a moment longer while he put the finishing touches on this sketch. "Did he look like this?" He turned his pad of paper for her to see.

"Oh my God. You're really good. Yeah, that's him. I'm sure that's him. Holy shit." She looked at Kate. "That's really good."

Kate smiled. "The fact that you remembered as much as you did was what helped him to be as accurate as possible. Thank you for your help, Vanessa. I know your friend would've been proud of you."

"I remembered a lot about him 'cause he was so strange.

Creepy and shit, you know? Even Rocky thought so." She began to fidget with her hands. "I wish she would've done it like this, you know? I mean, not go to the police station. She might still be here."

Kate pressed her hand against Vanessa's shoulder. "Come on, we'll take you back to work."

Nick walked back to the car while Kate waited there for his return. He slid into the driver's seat. "I tried to give her fifty bucks, but she refused. Said she did it for Raquel." He keyed the ignition.

"I feel bad for her, for her friend too. What a sad thing to have to live in fear and worry about who you talk to and where you go," Kate said. "Must make you feel like some sort of prisoner."

"I'm sure it does." He pulled away from the store. "We'd better get this sketch to Sharpe. He said he's got the guy in custody who owns the white Honda. Guess we'll find out if he matches Vanessa's description."

It had reached the full height of rush hour and traffic back to the station moved at a snail's pace. When they returned, both seemed equally hurried to get inside and show the sketch to Detective Sharpe.

Nick handed it to Kate. "You made this happen. You might as well show him what you got."

"Thanks." Kate continued to walk along the hall toward Sharpe's office. "Detective?"

"Agents Reid and Scarborough. Glad you could finally make it." He stood up from behind his desk and walked around to meet them.

"Traffic was a nightmare. Sorry we were delayed," Kate replied. "But we have the sketch from Vanessa Ruiz. This was what Raquel Garcia wanted to show us, but we couldn't help her in time."

Sharpe took hold of the sketch. "You make copies of this yet?"

"No, but Officer Phillips had a carbon copy, or whatever that paper is that he uses. I don't know, do they use carbon anymore?"

"I don't think so. Most of them use a tablet they can draw on so they have it electronically," Sharpe said. "But I think Phillips is a little old school."

That phrase coming from him seemed ironic. "So, what do you think? This look like Andre Knight to you?"

Sharpe walked back to his desk to retrieve his glasses and slid them onto his face. He held up the paper and began to study it.

It was when his expression dropped that Kate realized something was wrong. She regarded Nick with concern and he noticed it too.

"This isn't him." He began to walk by them and into the hall. "Come on; I'll show you." He led them to the viewing room adjacent to where they held Andre Knight. "Look for yourself."

Nick and Kate stood in front of the monitors and looked at Andre Knight, who still sat at the table, sipping on a cup of coffee. He sat in the direction of the camera but hadn't looked up for confirmation.

Sharpe leaned in and pressed a button. "Mr. Knight, someone will be with you in a moment." His voice sounded over the speaker in the other room.

Knight then looked up at the camera and they both saw his face clearly.

"It's not him." Kate turned. "I don't understand. How can this not be him?"

"He's not wearing the wig," Nick began.

"No, but look closer." Sharpe pointed to the sketch. "This shows his eyes are narrower. Take a look at that guy. His eyes are round, his cheeks and jawbone, more squared off." He began to shake his head. "Son of a bitch. He was telling the truth."

"What do you mean?" Kate asked.

"He started on some cockamamie story about how he was following this guy who had a blog or some shit and he wanted to meet him. But get this, whoever the guy is, Knight says he was putting the girls in these positions and then filming them for his website."

"For God's sake." Kate recalled her own conclusion that whoever this was could have been uploading the images to the web. Turned out, she was right and she regretted not pursuing the idea further.

"That's not the worst of it." Sharpe turned to face the monitors again and peered at Knight. "He said the guy put the videos on his blog and has a shitload of followers. Knight was one of them."

"He knew what was happening?" Kate said.

"And didn't do shit about it. Yep," Sharpe replied.

"I don't know. I can't believe a bunch of people would watch these videos and not one reported the crime?" Nick said.

"Agent Scarborough, you work in BAU. I thought you'd have seen far worse than that."

"I guess I have, but we're usually dealing with one unsub, with few exceptions." Nick glanced at Kate in brief recollection of Edward Shalot and how he manipulated so many people; his followers. "To have his crimes playing out on a blog." Nick trailed off. "Wait a second. Did he give you the name of this website? Have you looked into it?"

"No. He's scared shitless of the 'man behind the camera,' he calls him. Hasn't given us anything to go on yet."

"What if he's lying about that too?" Nick continued. "What if he's working with this other guy? Helping him out? Maybe that was why he was at Leimert Park. And this whole website blog bull-shit could just be a lie. This supports the initial theory that there could be more than one. Either way, we know he's involved in this."

"How do we get him to talk?" Kate asked.

Sharpe placed his hands on his hips. "His family. I think the only way this guy gives us the truth is by using his family. I highly doubt his wife knows about any of this. At least, it sure didn't seem like she did when we paid her a visit. And he's got kids."

"Okay. We'll play that card. He's either going to tell us he was involved, or he'll have no choice but to give us the name of this so-called 'man behind the camera' and his website." Nick said.

"And if that is true," Kate began. "Then we'll have a whole lot of accomplices."

21

The door handle turned and caught Andre's attention. Detective Sharpe and two people he didn't know entered the interrogation room. He pushed his shoulders back and sat up tall as though awaiting a verdict.

"Andre, I'd like for you to meet FBI Agents Scarborough and Reid. They've been working with my team to help us find you."

"I didn't do it. I didn't kill those women."

"That's what you keep saying, Andre, but from our standpoint, we have physical evidence of your being at the crime scene, evidence you left on a previous victim, and videotape showing your car." Sharpe sat down across from him. "You have to admit; it's looking pretty bad for you right now."

"I need to call my wife. She'll be worried."

"You'll get the chance to speak with her, although it seems doubtful she'll want to speak to you," Sharpe continued.

"You mentioned to Detective Sharpe something about a website," Nick began, "but refused to show him. Why is that? If what you claim is true, then why not allow us to find the person who did commit these horrific murders?" Nick leaned against a back wall and folded his arms in front of him.

"Because he'll kill me."

"So, you're willing to go to prison for multiple homicides, sexual assault, and whatever else we can throw your way because you're afraid this person will come after you?" Kate said. "Seems counterintuitive to me. If you tell us who he is, we can make sure he pays for his crimes. Think of what this will do to your family, Andre, and your children. Think of what they'll face when they go to school and kids taunt them because their dad is a killer or worse. The best thing you can do is get us to this website so we can track this person down before he kills again."

"He might have taken the site down already," Andre said.

"That's a chance we'll have to take." Sharpe stood up. "I'm going to have someone set up a laptop in here so we can take a look."

After he walked out of the room, Nick continued, "How did you come across this site, Andre? How many people follow this 'man behind the camera'?"

"Look, I know my rights. I don't have to tell you anything. Are you going to press charges? Because I'm allowed a lawyer."

"You are, and we can provide you with one if that's the route you wish to take," Nick added. "Or you can work with us to find this man."

"The detective said I'll still face charges of aiding and abetting, so I'm going to jail no matter what."

Nick tossed a glance to Kate and the two left Andre in the room alone. "We're going to have to get this guy a lawyer. We need to let Sharpe know he won't talk without one."

"You know what's going to happen," Kate said.

"I do, but he asked for one and we don't have a choice now." Nick proceeded along the hall toward Sharpe's office. "Hey. Knight wants a lawyer."

Sharpe was on his way out of his office when Nick and Kate appeared. "Are you serious? God dammit. What did you tell him?"

"That he has that right," Kate began. "What else could we say?"

"You and I both know what's going to happen now. He'll clam up and we won't get the name of that website."

"That's not necessarily true," Nick said. "If the lawyer is worth his salt, he'll get Knight to cooperate, assuming his story pans out."

"And if he's lying?" Kate asked.

"Then we'll have our answer pretty damn quick because he won't say a word until he's charged," Nick said.

"All right. We don't have a choice." Sharpe pushed his way between the two of them. "I'll get him a damn lawyer."

Kate watched as Sharpe walked away. "We're going to need to keep this from the press. They get wind that we have a suspect in custody, and this mysterious man behind the camera is still out there, he'll run, especially if what Knight says is true; that he thinks he was framed."

"You think Aguilar can pull some strings?" Nick asked.

"With his help and whatever strings we can pull, we can probably keep it under wraps for twenty-four, maybe forty-eight hours. The problem we'll have is our witness in the park and our victim."

"I think she'll cooperate and she's still in pretty bad shape and won't be released any time soon. It's the park witness we might have trouble with," Nick said. "I'll see if Jameson and Moore can find him and give him an incentive to keep quiet, for a little while." He began to walk away.

"What kind of incentive?"

"Whatever will work." He disappeared around the corner.

Kate retrieved her cell. "Marc, it's Kate. Can I meet up with you?" She waited. "Now, if that's okay. Great, I'll see you there in just a few minutes."

THE REFINED ESTABLISHMENT WITH ITS STEEL-GREY WALLS, HANGING drum lights, and sleek furnishings was tucked behind the lobby of Marc's hotel. Turned out, CBN had a bigger travel budget than the Bureau. He sat at the bar, swirling the ice in his vodka. Kate spotted him as she walked inside.

She perched atop the barstool next to him. "Don't take this the wrong way, but you look like you just lost your dog."

Marc turned his attention to her. "My producer told me I needed to come back. That this story was a non-event and hadn't gained any real traction with the other news outlets."

"Seriously? A guy who's killed four women and brutally assaulted another? Wow."

"Yeah, go figure." He tossed back the rest of his drink.

"I'm sorry to hear that. However, it does bode well for us who are out looking for this man. And that brings me to why I'm here."

Marc nodded to the bartender for another drink. "You want anything?"

"I'll take an iced tea."

"You're kidding, right?"

"I'm on duty, Marc."

"Oh yeah. How's that going, by the way?"

"I'm going to tell you something because I know how much you want to help us."

With a sideways glance, he revealed a half-cocked smile. "You need my help?"

"Yes, actually, I do. We've got someone in custody, but he just lawyered up. However, before he did, he gave us something of an unusual story that, if it's true, might mean he's innocent—of the murders, at least." She waited while the bartender placed their drinks down. "This guy, well, we don't know if he's telling us the truth or not and we need time to look into it."

"Why? What's his story? You guys don't think he's the killer?"

"Honestly, we don't know. Evidence points to yes, but there's something in his story that isn't sitting right. Something that is so far out there that it just might be true."

"Okay, you've got my attention."

"First of all, I'm telling you this because we're friends and I need for this not to get out. The media can't know we have someone in custody. It could jeopardize the rest of the investigation."

"Well, I'm not going to say anything. My bosses could care less." He took another swig of his drink.

"What can you do with the local press? Your friend at KTLA. Any other connections you or he might have? You think you can prod them on their take on the story? Dispel any rumors of a suspect in custody. What are the chances we can keep this quiet for another twenty-four to forty-eight hours?"

"That's a tall order. You'd have to keep this guy's family quiet too. And the captain has already had a couple of press briefings. They'll only continue asking questions."

"So far, he has yet to include the fact that we have a person of interest and he doesn't plan to disclose that any time soon."

"The problem I see with your plan is if LAPD charges this guy.

Those charges would be public and very easy to track down. And believe me, the media is waiting—and watching for that to happen."

"Okay, that's something we can control on our end. The detective in charge wants what we want."

"Good. Then you'll have to ensure, as I said, that the family, wife, or whatever, keeps quiet."

"I think we can do that, considering it will only help her husband if she does. We've got a witness we'll have to work with too, but I can't imagine he'd want to risk the investigation. He seems a stand-up guy."

"Don't overestimate the morals of upstanding men," Marc said.

"What I'm mostly concerned with is your friend who's been pushing you to run with this story for his own gains."

"You could say the same thing about me."

"I could," Kate smiled. "But I won't."

"I can talk to him. Let him know there could be a bigger story that comes out of it without revealing too much information on the matter. He'll prod me because he knows I have an in with the feds. But hell, if that is the case, I might be able to sway my producer after all." A sheepish look masked his face. "I'm sorry. I don't mean to make light of the fact that people are dead and there's a killer still out there. I know it's more than a story."

Kate placed her hand on his shoulder. "I know you do, Marc. I'd better get back to the station." She glanced at her phone while downing the last drink of tea. "Where the hell did this day go? It's already eight?"

"Have you eaten anything today?"

She reached into her purse for a five. "I've had a snack or two —Dad."

"Keep your money. I think I can spare a few bucks for an iced tea. Come see me when you can have a real drink."

"Goodnight, Marc. And thanks for your help. It means a lot."

Marc watched Kate walk away and then tossed back the rest of his drink. "Can I get the tab, please?" he asked the bartender. "Thanks." He left thirty bucks on the table and walked out of the bar and into the hotel lobby. The skies had grown much darker than when he arrived and now were nearing black, except for streetlights and cars that drove by, leaving yellow and red streaks in their wake.

Marc pressed the contact button on his phone and waited for the line to pick up. "Hey, Vince, it's Marc. Listen, can I meet up with you? I wanted to talk to you about something." He stepped outside into the fresh night air. "Great. I'll come over. You still up in Calabasas?" He hailed a cab. "See you there. Thanks."

The cab driver pulled alongside the curb of the hotel and Marc opened the door. "Calabasas, please."

Within seconds, he was on his way to meet with his former colleague from his short time in LA, just prior to moving to New York. He didn't consider him a close friend, but he was more than an acquaintance and so Marc felt fairly confident he'd agree to keep things quiet for a day or two while the feds and LAPD lined up their case. It didn't mean there weren't others who would want the story, but it was a small industry and everyone knew everyone else. No one would want the risk of letting a killer go because they spouted off after the feds asked them to keep it quiet.

"That's it, up on the left." Marc retrieved his credit card and swiped it into the payment device. "Thank you." He slipped out and walked toward the front door of the moderate home in the respectable neighborhood. It took a lot of money to live in

Calabasas, so it was no surprise the home was somewhat modest. However, in New York, it would be considered positively enormous. That was the one thing about being a transplant. People thought it was expensive to live in L.A. They had no idea what expensive was until they tried to get a place in New York.

Marc stood beneath the sheltered entrance and knocked on the door. Within moments, his old colleague opened it. "Vince, how's it going, man? Thanks for meeting with me." He offered his hand.

"Pleasure. Come on in." Vince closed the door behind him. "Can I get you a drink?"

"Sure. I'll take a vodka on the rocks if you got it."

"Go and have a seat in the living room. I'll be right back with the drinks."

Marc's shoes on the slate floor broadcast his entry into a room that could only be described as a formal living area, which appeared to be rarely utilized. He hoisted his trousers and sat down on the high-back leather chair.

Vince soon approached with drinks in hand. "Here you are. Vodka rocks. So, what brings you over here? Thought you were hanging close to the station?" He took a seat.

"I am. I just had a quick word with a friend of mine about the Pretty Face Killer investigation."

"Did I miss a conference?"

"No, no. It's nothing like that. I've got a friend who works for the FBI. She's here helping LAPD."

"Right, I talked to her about the tipster lead. LAPD must be lacking confidence to involve the feds."

"Maybe, but the reason I'm here, actually, is that my friend needs *our* help."

"Our help?" Vince took a sip of his drink and placed it on the coffee table. "What can we do?"

"They've got a theory that sort of flies in the face of what they know of the investigation so far. And they've asked us to keep things quiet for a day or two until they can see if it pans out."

"Can you elaborate? What do they have? What do they think is going on?"

Marc ran his finger around the rim of the glass. "Look, I know you have a lot of friends in the business. And I know you have some pull with them."

"Not as much as you might think."

"Regardless, we need to keep quiet that they've got someone in custody. You're going to find out about it sooner rather than later and that's why I'm here."

"That's a good thing, isn't it? That they've got a suspect?"

"Yes, but until they know for sure it's the guy they're looking for, they don't want the press to mention it."

"Because if this guy isn't the killer, then the killer might jump ship."

"Something like that. Can you help? I mean, I know you can only do so much. But right now, anything will help. They need some time. Just a little bit of time."

"I'll do what I can, buddy, but like I say, this is a cut-throat business. You know that as well, if not better than I do. I'll push the story down. I'll talk to a few friends who will listen. That's about the best I can do. There's always that rogue reporter trying to make a name for himself."

"I understand that. But those are the guys who, if they don't play the game, won't get very far in this business."

"That's a fact. Not many will want to risk being blackballed for going against the grain. So, what can I expect in return?"

"You'll be the first—well, second—to know if they have the right guy. I'll take the story upstream, get my people interested again. But I guess that depends on the result of the investigation. Locally, I'll make sure you get the exclusive and I'll interview you on my show about it."

"I can work with that." Vince smiled. "Sounds like a plan."

"Good." Marc tossed back another swig. "Hey, you got a restroom around here?"

"Down the hall, first door on your right."

"Thanks." Marc pushed from the chair and made his way down the short hall and into the powder room. With a flip of the switch, the room illuminated and he admired the masculine décor, soon recalling that Vince had recently divorced. "Must've had the place redecorated."

After using the facilities, he ran his hands under the faucet and glanced around the small bathroom until his eyes landed on the shelf on the back wall. He turned off the water and dried his hands, opening the door to leave.

His shoes continued to click and clack on the grey slate floor until he returned to the living room where his friend was perusing his cell phone. "I'd better head back to the hotel."

"You need me to call you a cab?"

"Nah. I'll Uber it." He placed the request on his phone. "There's one nearby." Marc picked up his glass and finished off his drink. "Thanks for the drink."

"I'll walk you out."

The two walked toward the front door and Vince pulled it open. "It was great seeing you, Marc. I'm sure we'll be in touch."

Marc shook his hand. "Absolutely." He stepped out onto the porch and stopped, turning back to him. "Hey, since when are you a Bulls fan?"

"What's that?" Vince furrowed his brow.

"In your bathroom. I saw a Chicago Bulls baseball hat on your shelf. I thought you were Lakers all the way?"

"Oh, that. Yeah, I think a friend of mine left it here last week. Looks like your ride's here. Take care, man."

Marc waved goodbye as he walked toward the car.

22

Robert Grainger walked into the lobby of the precinct at nine p.m. after receiving a call requesting his presence. He approached the officer at the information desk. "I'm here for Andre Knight, a suspect who invoked his right to have an attorney present during questioning." Robert laid his business card on the table.

"I'll let Detective Sharpe know you're here. Please have a seat." The officer placed the call while Grainger stepped aside.

He noted a few reporters hanging around and because he didn't live under a rock, figured it was because of the Pretty Face Killer investigation—a story he'd been following closely, but one which seemed to be at a standstill while victims continued to surface.

Sharpe appeared from beyond the corridor and offered his hand. "Rob, thanks for coming down."

"Who've you got?" Grainger wasn't a man to mince words and he knew Sharpe was the same. He'd been working this area for the better part of ten years and they'd crossed paths several times before.

Sharpe cast a glance at the onlookers, mostly reporters who seemed keen to listen in on the conversation. "Why don't you come back to my office and I'll fill you in." He led Grainger to his office where the BAU team waited along with Sergeant Moore.

"Why do I get a bad feeling about this?" Grainger said upon entering the overcrowded office.

"Rob, this is the FBI's BAU team. Agents Scarborough, Jameson, and Reid. They've been consulting with us on the investigation. And you already know Sergeant Moore."

"I do; nice to see you again." Robert turned his attention to the agents. "BAU? Let me guess, the serial killer? What are you guys calling him? The Pretty Face Killer?"

"Yes," Sharpe replied.

"You have a suspect in custody?" Grainger continued.

"We do, but he's got a very unusual story."

"You've been talking to him? Without a lawyer?" Grainger shook his head. "You understand what that means?"

"I think we all know what it means, Rob," Sharpe sat down at his desk. "He decided to exercise his right to have an attorney present and so here you are. But there's something you should know before I send you back there to talk to him. This needs to stay quiet, which is why I brought you back here and didn't say anything up front."

"Why is that? I thought the LAPD would be thrilled to announce they had someone in custody—unless you aren't sure he's the guy." Grainger noted the faces of those present and a half-cocked smile formed on his lips. "Why don't you just take me back there so I can have a word with my client?"

Sharpe led Grainger to the interrogation room and opened the door.

"We'll need a more private place to converse," Grainger said.

The officer standing watch looked to Sharpe, who nodded. He approached Knight, proceeded to help him from the chair, and kept his hand on his shoulders. "Where to?"

"They can take holding cell 2b. No one else is back there right now." He turned to Grainger. "Follow them."

Grainger waited until the officer started down the hall and followed closely behind.

"Are you my lawyer?" Knight asked.

"Yes. Wait until we can speak in private."

"Right through here." The officer held the door open. "I'll be here when you're ready."

"Thank you, officer." Grainger closed the door behind them. "Take a seat, Mr. Knight. I'm Robert Grainger. Why don't you tell me why you're here?"

"They think I killed those women. I didn't do it and now they want me to help them."

"Help them do what?"

"Find the real killer."

"It's a good thing, Mr. Knight—may I call you Andre?"

He nodded.

"It's a good thing, Andre, that they don't think you're responsible. However, the simple fact that you're here suggests they suspect your involvement somehow. Is that right?"

"Yes."

"Why don't you tell me how you came to be here, then?"

Kate leaned back against the wall in Sharpe's office. "We're wasting time here, detective. The longer we wait, the more likely it is that this website will disappear completely."

"You believe him?"

"There is reason to. We've got a description from a witness that doesn't match our guy, but we've got physical evidence on at least one victim that did belong to Knight."

"You don't think the possibility exists that he could be working with an accomplice?" Sharpe continued.

"It's possible. But that would mean we're still wasting time. If he can get us closer to whoever he knows or who he could be working with, then we need to move on that."

"I know this is frustrating, but you've been able to help them keep this quiet," Nick began. "That buys us time."

"She's right," Dwight said. "We are wasting time. What can we do right now? Can we see how the most recent victim is doing? See if she remembers more?"

"My officers have been checking in on her all day and from what I gather, it seems pretty clear she didn't get a good enough look at her attacker, just what she told us. He took her into the drainage culvert. It was too dark, and she'd lost a lot of blood. No. We need to talk to Knight."

Kate's phone vibrated in her pocket and, upon retrieving it, she noted the caller ID. "I need to take this." She stepped outside of Sharpe's office. "Marc? Hang on a second; I'm walking outside." She emerged through the main entrance and stood at the top of the stone steps, peering at the lights on the surrounding high-rise buildings. "I didn't expect to hear from you tonight. You already talk to your friend?"

"I did. That's why I'm calling. Sorry it's a little late."

"Don't be. I'm still here at the station. Our suspect is with his lawyer now."

"I won't keep you then. I just wanted to let you know that I think my message was well received. I don't think you'll have any problems, at least, not for the next day or two. After that, I make no promises."

"I appreciate that, Marc. Thank you." The temperature dropped substantially since she'd last stepped foot outside and her breath drifted before her eyes. "What are you going to do? Go back to New York?"

"That's what I'm supposed to do. Someone's filling in for me on the show. I don't know if I can convince them to give me a couple more days."

"Don't risk all you've worked for on this case, Marc. I know you wanted something to sink your teeth into and help out your friend, but it sounds like they want you back home."

"Is there anything at all you can tell me that I can entice my producer with?"

"I'm just not sure. I don't think so. I mean, hell, I don't know. This case is getting more bizarre by the moment."

"Apart from the obvious, what makes you say that?"

Kate knew he was digging around for something more now.

"You said you weren't sure if you got the right guy. Why?"

"I'll give you this much, and I swear to God if you quote me or mention an anonymous source, we're through. You understand?"

"Of course, Kate. I'd never do that to you. I just want to know if it's worth my time to come up with an excuse as to why I need to stay here."

She hesitated but finally continued, "We're either dealing with two men working together, or we're dealing with one and our guy was a witness. The problem lies in the fact that the man we have in custody left physical evidence on a previous victim. And we have a discrepancy in the descriptions."

"Really?"

"Yeah. Funny thing is, we think both of these guys, whether collaborators or not, were wearing disguises when they approached the victims."

"Like a mask or something?"

"No. Luckily, no masks. Just wigs and baseball hats. But it appears as though they're different."

"I see. Sounds like you've got your hands full sorting through this heap of crap."

"We just need to figure out if we're looking for a Chicago Bulls fan or an Oakland As fan."

"Sorry?"

"Those were the baseball caps described by the surviving victim and a witness. So, you see what we're dealing with."

"Okay. I'll let you get back to it, then. Let me know how things go tomorrow if you get a chance. Goodnight, Kate."

"Night, Marc." Kate walked back inside, but before she made it to the hallway, Nick appeared.

"Hey. We can talk to Knight now. He and his attorney are in the interrogation room." Nick turned on his heel and headed back.

"Sharpe already back there?" Kate asked.

"Yeah." Nick approached the door. "You ready?"

She nodded and walked inside. Sharpe was already seated and Kate realized they'd stopped the show on their arrival. "Please excuse the interruption."

"So, Andre, you were saying about this website?" Sharpe continued.

"I found this website and, I don't know, I guess I was curious." He cast his eyes down.

"How did you find this site? I find it hard to believe something like that would exist and no one would say anything to the authorities about it, or it wouldn't have been flagged by an ISP provider or something of that nature."

"It's on the dark web."

"You know how to access the dark web?"

"Yes. It's not that hard, actually."

"Just answer the questions, Andre," Grainger said.

"And that's where you found these--what did you call them--performance pieces?"

"Uh-huh."

"And you didn't think it was at all necessary to let the police know what was happening?"

"You don't have to answer that." Grainger looked to Sharpe. "Detective, let's keep this conversation on point."

"Okay, then." Sharpe placed a laptop on the desk. "Take us there. Show us this site."

Andre looked at Grainger.

"We talked about this. You need to help them if they're to help you. That's the arrangement."

Andre opened the laptop and began to type, continuing for several minutes.

"Are you just yanking our chain, here, Andre, because this seems to be taking a long time," Sharpe said.

"I said it wasn't that hard to get into the dark web. I didn't say it was quick." He turned the screen toward Sharpe. "Anyway, this is it. This is the site. I guess it's still up and running."

The team moved in for a closer look.

"Where are the videos?" Kate asked.

Sharpe tried to navigate the site and looked at Andre. "Where do you find the videos?" He turned the screen back. "Show us."

Andre began to search the site, checking each page. He looked to Grainger. "I don't see them anymore. They used to be right here. Now all it says is 'more to come.'"

Grainger turned his attention to Sharpe. "Doesn't seem to be anything here. Just a blog. No videos."

Sharpe reached for the laptop and spun it around. "Andre, you'd better not be screwing around with us."

"I'm not. They were there. I swear it. He even threatened me because he knew I was—watching."

"That's right. You said he was coming after you." Sharpe cast a stern eye on Andre. "How was he planning on doing that, exactly? Does he know where you live?"

"I don't know. He tricked me into following him. Left me clues. And at Leimert Park, I know he saw me. That's why I was afraid to say anything. And now it looks like he got rid of the videos."

"I don't see any threatening posts either, Andre. Nothing mentioning any threats to you personally. You sure you aren't just playing us?"

"I'm not. Please, you have to believe me. It's probably because he saw your news conferences. He knows you're onto him."

"We made no mention of you or any possible suspect. He would have no idea except for what we've already stated about the previous victims," Sharpe continued.

"Hang on. Take a look at some of the most recent comments." Kate pointed to the screen. "'Where are the videos? When is your next performance?' And take a look here. This one says, 'I heard someone saw you. Does that mean this is it?'"

"Christ. How many fans did this guy have?" Nick stood in disbelief.

"A lot," Andre replied.

"That's enough. My client has assisted you as you've asked. I think it's time we talk about that deal you promised," Grainger said.

"There's nothing here, Robert. Your client has done nothing more than show us a website he says will give us the man behind the camera. I see no such evidence," Sharpe said.

"How could I know he was going to pull the videos? I did what you said. You can't charge me with these murders. I didn't do it."

"You sure as hell enjoyed watching them happen, didn't you? How the hell do we know you aren't in it with him, huh?" Sharpe pounded his fist on the table.

"Okay," Nick pressed his hand on the detective's shoulder. "Maybe you should step outside for a minute to cool off."

Sharpe thrust the chair from beneath him, knocking it over, and marched out of the room.

"What am I supposed to do?" Andre pleaded with his attorney. "I can't help it if it's not there now."

"We'll be right back." Nick motioned to his team and the three stepped outside.

"What now?" Dwight asked. "You guys think what Knight's saying is true?"

"I do." Kate turned to Nick.

"So do I."

"Okay. I'll reach out to Vasquez. Have her work on identifying an IP address or ISP for this website. Anything she can find," Dwight said.

"If it's on the dark web, it won't be easy to trace," Kate said.

"I know, but it's worth a shot. You want me to have her get it taken down?" he asked Nick.

"I think that would be a mistake," Kate replied. "We don't want this guy to know we're onto him."

"He might already know," Nick said.

"I don't think so, or the site would be down. He removed the videos, but I think he craves the attention too much. He'll lose his followers if he stops posting. What if we use Knight? Have him post a reply to the supposed threat he received?"

Nick considered the idea. "To what end?"

"Bait, pure and simple. This guy is clearly an egomaniac. He needs people to watch him, and admire him. We'll use Andre to bait him. Have him apologize. Tell him how much he admires his work and that he couldn't help but follow him to see him in action. And that he must continue on. Then we'll have him. We'll know where and when he's going to act because he's so damn arrogant that he posts everything he's about to do before he does it. That's how Knight was able to track him down."

"That could work," Dwight began.

"I agree. Let's get Sharpe on board." Nick began to walk back inside.

"Agent Reid had a suggestion." He turned to Kate. "You want to let everyone in on your thoughts?"

Sharpe had reentered after a moment to settle his temper. "What's going on?"

"Agent Reid was about to lay out a plan that should help us find our 'man behind the camera,'" Dwight said.

All eyes turned to Kate. "Andre, we'd like you to communicate with him. You said he threatened you. Even going so far as to frame you for the latest attack. Answer him by lavishing compliments on his talents. Beg him to continue."

"What do you hope to accomplish with that, Agent Reid?" Grainger asked.

"First of all, if you want that deal, you have to help us because what you've given us here isn't enough."

"Agreed," Sharpe said.

"Our hope is that this person won't be able to ignore the pleas. Andre, you'll call for him to continue his work. The man we're dealing with is a narcissist. Why else would he be so bold? Because he thinks he can get away with it. And his fans have let him so far."

"And then what?" Andre asked.

"We'll follow him and stop him before it happens. Can you do that, Andre? Remember your family. You'll want to keep them from knowing the worst of this, right?"

Resigned to his fate, Andre nodded. "Yes. I can do it."

23

The late model BMW had begun to draw unwanted attention. The luxury vehicle shimmered beneath the glow of the parking lot lamppost and could not have appeared more out of place, particularly in this part of town. But Vince Sanchez had made the desperate call and now waited in the parking lot of a grocery store. It was Aguilar's visit that prompted the drive and the impending meeting. However, his cohort had yet to arrive.

Vince checked the time again. The man was late and the hour had become even later. He worked the morning news for KTLA and would have to be there in just three short hours. Time was running out and this issue needed to be put to bed. He'd begun to regret the deal they'd made.

He peered through the windshield at what looked to be a car approaching, except its headlights were not shining. "That better be you, you son of a bitch. You're a half-hour late."

An old black Chevy Malibu pulled alongside Vince. He waited

for the driver to kill the engine and roll down his window. When he did, Vince began, "Where the hell you been? You're late."

"You think I got nothing better to do than meet with you, Vince? I got my own shit to deal with. What do you want anyway? Pulling me away at this time of night."

"I thought you preferred working at night," Vince replied. "We need to cool things off for a while."

"Why? Because of that moronic fan who followed me? I already put him in his place."

"You know that girl is still alive, right? How long you think it'll be before they find you?"

"They aren't going to find me. She didn't see my face and even if she did, I had my disguise. Besides, I think the cops have enough evidence to find that little shit who thought he could take part in my plan. That buys me more time to continue my work."

"Oh, and hey, thanks for leaving your hat at my place. A friend of mine found it and I had to play it off."

"Did you bring it? It's my favorite one."

Vince tossed it out the window and into the man's car. "There. You'd better keep track of your shit. So, like I said, we have to put the kibosh on this for a while."

The man stepped out of his car, and while there were only a few feet between them to begin with, he stood directly in front of Vince's driver's side door and squatted down. With his elbows resting on the door, he firmly held Vince's gaze. "You think you're in control here? I'm the one who tells you when and where. I'm the one who makes sure you get the scoop. You don't tell me when we're done. Do I make myself clear?"

Vince didn't flinch. "You're forgetting one thing here, I can always tell the cops about you."

The man smiled. "Don't threaten me with something you have

no intention of following through with. You're in this too, Mr. Sanchez, and don't you forget that." He pushed back up to his feet. "Now, I have things to do. And as usual, you'll be the first to know."

"What about the witness?" Vince asked.

"He didn't see me. He saw the fan who's been following me for a week. Don't worry, he won't be a problem for much longer." The man slid back into his car, keyed the ignition, and began to pull away from the BMW, but not before revealing a brutish smile. "You worry too much, Vince."

Vince watched the monster that he helped create drive away and began to realize whatever illusion of control he thought he had over him had all but vanished by way of his black car in the night. Perhaps it was time to call it. Tell the authorities that he knew who the killer was. Who would believe that man over him? A man whose smiling face graced the television screen every morning in millions of Californian homes. He had the upper hand here, not that monster.

KATE APPROACHED DETECTIVE SHARPE, WHO WAS STILL PROCESSING Andre Knight's paperwork. "So, you're keeping him here?"

"I don't have a choice. He was seen running from a sexual assault and attempted murder victim. Whether or not he did it remains to be seen, but I have to keep him here."

"I agree with you. Given the chance, he'd be gone in a heartbeat. I don't know how someone can stand by and watch something like that. Someone being killed. I've seen my share of horrific crimes, but to me, that's almost worse than the crime itself."

"That it is, Agent Reid. That it is." Sharpe turned away from his monitor. "When do we want him to leave the comment on the website?"

"The sooner the þetter. We need to keep him interested. Let him know his fans still need him."

"Then we'd better get Knight in front of a computer." He stood and began to leave his office, but stopped and turned back. "You want to be in on this, right?"

"Yeah, let me grab the rest of my team. I think they're with Sergeant Moore."

"Meet me back there as soon as you can."

Kate made her way to Robbery Homicide where Moore worked and found Nick and Dwight nearby. "Sharpe is ready to get Andre Knight in front of a computer. We need to get back there and oversee this." She began to study what was on Moore's screen. "What are you guys looking at?"

"We're reviewing the closed circuit video from the area surrounding Leimert Park at midnight last night till around two a.m.," Moore replied.

"We wanted to see if any other images surfaced that might show us Knight in the background," Nick added.

"And what did you find? Anything?"

"Show her," Nick said to Moore.

"You see that car on the far left corner of the screen?"

"Yes."

"Watch what happens when I forward the video to the time when our witness catches Knight with the victim." He began to fast forward the video and stopped. "You see the car now?"

"Its headlights just came on, and it looks like it's about to pull away."

"Right." Moore continued to forward. "And here, we see the car leaving."

"It's pretty far out of range from where the incident occurred. What are you thinking?"

"That there could be more than one 'watcher,'" Nick said. "That maybe this guy, because he posted where he would be, had more followers than just Knight."

"Maybe there are more witnesses," Dwight said. "Or that could be his ride."

"Whose? Knight's?" Kate asked.

"No, he had a car. I'm thinking it could be, assuming we all believe his story about the videos on the website, the actual killer's ride."

"You're thinking he has an accomplice?"

"Seems a little too coincidental that that car leaves around the time our witness runs toward Knight," Dwight continued.

"So the killer did see him and possibly could've been waiting for him to see what Andre would do. Knight said he threatened him. That he saw him there. Maybe that was him waiting?" Kate added.

"That's a possibility too, but what we need to do, then, is to identify that vehicle," Nick said. "That's what we're working on now. As you can see, it's difficult to decipher the make and model."

Dwight stepped away from the desk. "I think we can leave the rest of it in Sergeant Moore's capable hands. Sounds like we need to get with Knight and hang him on the fishing line." He rapped his knuckles on Moore's desk. "We'll catch up with you afterward."

Kate led the way back to the holding cell where Sharpe was about to transfer Knight to another interrogation room with his attorney's approval. The three met him in the hall and Kate began, "We ready to do this?"

Sharpe nodded. "Indeed we are." He opened the door to the room. "Have a seat, Andre. This won't take long."

THE KEYS IN HIS POCKET JINGLED WHEN HE REACHED FOR THEM TO open the door of his apartment. The night had grown increasingly cooler and, as he inserted the key, he noticed goosebumps on his arms. The unexpected call, or rather, demand from Vince Sanchez to meet meant he left his place without a coat. And now he regretted going out at all.

Sanchez had pulled at a string that ought not to have been pulled. Who the fuck did he think he was? He switched on the light and locked the door behind him. "That fucker will be famous because of me. He'd do well to remember that." A nearby card table was where he set down the laptop bag. He was careful never to leave it unattended, even in his secured apartment. His artwork was never far from his side.

A drink was what he needed now and so he continued to the kitchenette and retrieved a glass from the cabinet and a bottle of bourbon. Now all he had to do was check his site to see if he got a response from the jackass who followed him. He almost jeopardized the whole thing. For now, though, he needed to know if the jackass was going to be a problem. He already had Sanchez and he didn't need another problem. All of these people were getting in the way of his work and that was unacceptable.

With the bottle and glass in his hand, he walked back to the table and booted up his laptop. A few swift keystrokes and he was on his site. Taking down the videos was a must. Couldn't risk the jackass spouting off to anyone, especially the cops, although he'd only incriminate himself, so he felt pretty comfortable the guy would keep his mouth shut. While he sat in Sanchez's car last night, after the fact, he'd seen the guy well enough, but tracking him down would be another story, one he hoped wouldn't need to be told.

The first shot of bourbon went down easily as he continued to scroll along the page. And that was when he found it. The reply he'd been waiting for from Dre1995.

"I only wanted to admire your work. I don't have the courage you do. I am a follower and you are the leader, an artist ahead of his time. I haven't and won't go to the cops. I await your next masterpiece and will not follow without your permission."

He leaned back and laced his fingers behind his head. Maybe he'd overreacted. This guy was a true admirer of his work. Perhaps he'd been looking at this all wrong. If his fans wanted him to continue, then why shouldn't he? Fuck Vince Sanchez. What did he know of art? He began to craft his reply.

A CALL RANG THROUGH ON KATE'S CELL WHILE SHE SLEPT, STILL fully clothed, in the hotel. She raised to answer it. "Reid speaking."

"It's Sharpe. We got a reply. Can you meet me at the station in half an hour?"

"Of course. I'll wake the guys and we'll head over." She ended the call and checked the time. Two a.m. and they'd only been in their rooms since midnight. Still, two hours was better than nothing.

Kate pressed Nick's contact. "It's me. Sharpe got a reply and wants us back down at the station." She paused while his fuzzy mind tried to focus on her words. "Okay. I'll see you in the lobby in fifteen. Please tell Dwight."

She moved to the edge of the bed in the pitch-black room and stood. Her careful steps with arms outstretched in front of her ensured she didn't run into a wall until finally, she reached a light switch. The bright light burned her eyes, but she soon recovered and began to splash water on her face and smooth down her disheveled hair, pulling it back into a ponytail.

Within minutes, she was in the lobby, waiting for Nick and Dwight. They emerged from the elevators.

"I expected to be the last one down," she said. "You two look like death warmed over."

"We're not as young as you, but your time's coming." Dwight patted her on the back. "Let's get down there and see what we've got."

A short drive later, they arrived at the station inside the half-hour time frame. Sharpe appeared to be waiting for them in the lobby. "Good. You're here. Follow me." He led the way, dismissing pleasantries, and headed back to the interrogation room where the computer had been set up.

"Where's Knight?" Nick asked.

"Sleeping in his cell. I wanted to show this to you three before we decide whether or not he needs to be up for this."

"Well, we know how to get onto the website now," Kate began. "I'm not sure we need him at all for this part anyway." She pulled up a chair. "When did this come in?"

"Not long before I called you. One of my officers had been monitoring the site all night and called me first. I came straight down and had a look. That was when I knew you should be here to see it." Sharpe began scrolling down to the comment. "You were right, Agent Reid. The killer is an egomaniac. He wants admiration from his followers."

"Based on what we've seen so far, it was the logical conclusion, in my mind." She glanced at Nick. "You agree?"

"Definitely. He's wanted attention on this from Day One. Why else would he have posted his so-called performance pieces online?"

"And why would he have told his followers where he would be?"

"Arrogance. A feeling that he's above the law." Dwight pulled up a chair at the end of the table.

"This is it." Sharpe turned the monitor toward them. "What do you think?"

Kate smiled and looked to her team for confirmation. "This was exactly what we wanted. Have Knight play to his ego. Beg for him to continue." She paused while they studied the killer's words. "So now that we've reeled him in, it's time to get the net. Detective Sharpe, we'll need to stay logged on to this site, and continually monitor it for the killer's next announcement."

"How long you think before he'll act again?" Sharpe asked.

"Best guess, inside of twenty-four hours. He won't want the fans to be disappointed. I think they might mean more to him than his victims. That may not have been the way it started, but with Knight essentially pleading with him to continue, I think his ego will drive the decision to perform again."

"And until then?"

"We can start getting a team in place," Nick began. "Get all the players ready because once he decides to pull the trigger, we won't have time to screw around."

"What about Andre Knight?" Sharpe said.

"Charge him. You have enough. He'll continue to cooperate if needed because he wants that deal. But I think we'll only need him if the killer insists he be there when the act takes place."

"We need to consider keeping the latest victim under protection," Dwight began. "This guy may feel the need to finish the job and she's due to be released from the hospital this afternoon, last I heard."

"We'll get her someplace safe until we catch the son of a bitch," Sharpe replied.

24

In a rush of immediate perception, Marc Aguilar shot upright in his bed. The time showed six a.m. and perhaps it was his ringing alarm that brought him awake, or was it the fact that he had understood the relevance in his spotting the baseball hat in his former colleague's home. Whatever tricks his mind played to bring forth the conclusion didn't matter at this moment. What mattered was that he had to speak with Kate.

Marc tossed his legs from the bed and onto the floor, standing up with a speed that often accompanied one who was in desperate need of a wee. But this desire far exceeded any physiological yearning. He reached for his phone and called his friend.

"Kate, it's Marc. Listen, I have to talk to you about something. I know it's early, but..."

"I'm sorry, Marc, but this is a bad time. I'm right in the middle of something. Can I call you back later?"

"This is important. Really important. Kate, I need to talk to you."

"Okay. Just give me a second. I'm sitting in the detective's office at the moment."

Marc's anxiety was reaching frantic levels as he waited for Kate to continue.

"I'm outside. What is it? What's so urgent?"

"You told me that your suspect wore a baseball cap, right?"

"Yeah."

He began to pace his hotel room, which was still bathed in darkness, though light spilled around the seams of the curtains. "I went to my friend's place last night. Vince Sanchez? The guy who..."

"Who brought you the story. Yeah, I remember."

"Right. Well, I was about to leave after we'd had a drink and talked for a while, and I went to use his bathroom." He paused to gather the right words. "Kate, I saw a Chicago Bulls baseball hat in the bathroom on a shelf."

Kate was silent, except for the sound of her breathing.

"I asked him about it because I know him to be a lifelong Lakers fan. He said it belonged to a friend of his. Didn't give me a name. Anyway, I didn't think twice about it after that. Even when you and I spoke yesterday and you mentioned the hat. It just hadn't occurred to me. Jesus. Some reporter I am, right?"

"I understand your urgency here, Marc, but a lot of people own a Chicago Bulls hat. That hardly makes him a killer. I appreciate your concern, but we have the killer on the hook right now. It's only a matter of time."

Marc exhaled through his nose, making a whistling sound. "I'm not saying I think Vince Sanchez is the killer. I don't believe he is. What I do believe, is that he would do anything for a story. I'm not saying I'm much different, but this guy. Kate, you don't know the lengths I've seen him go to get a scoop."

"What are you saying, Marc? Are you saying he's involved? That he knows the killer?"

"I think so—yes. I think he knows and that maybe he's working with him."

Kate fell silent again and Marc waited for her to reply. "What do you think? Don't go quiet on me now. I'm onto something, aren't I?"

"Look, um, can you come down to the station? I don't know if you're on to anything or not, but there's something I haven't told you yet, and I don't think I should until we meet with Detective Sharpe."

"I can be there in twenty. I'll see you soon." Marc ended the call and tossed his phone onto the nightstand. "That son of a bitch. He knows this guy. I'm sure of it." He walked toward the bathroom and turned on the shower. "I just have to convince them of it."

KATE RETURNED TO SHARPE'S OFFICE BUT SAID NOTHING OF THE conversation she'd just had with Marc Aguilar. Sufficient intrigue wasn't enough to mention the topic and Marc would need to be here to field the questions. But while the others continued to speculate as to when the killer would act, this single thought stirred through her mind.

"Kate?" Nick nudged her arm. "Did you hear what I said?"

"Sorry, no. I was thinking about something else."

"Seems like it. You all right?"

"Yeah. Fine. A little tired, like everyone else. Sorry. What was it you said?"

"I was saying to Sharpe that the killer might choose a more public place to display his work."

"More public than Leimert Park?" she asked.

"It's possible," Sharpe added. "Look at how easy it was to bait him. He's going to want to create a superior performance after listening to his fans."

"So where are you thinking?"

"There's no shortage of landmarks around here, but we also need to consider that he's chosen to stay around the South LA area."

"Why do you suppose that is?" Dwight asked.

"I think it's because he thinks it's easier to pick them off here," Kate said. "More people taking to the streets. Using mass transit, buses, and the like. Simply walking because of the close proximity of many establishments. Leimert Park is the perfect example. Several communities in and around the park. Easily accessible public transportation. So, given that, Detective Sharpe, this is your town. Where's the most likely location?"

Sharpe appeared ready to answer but stopped short when a man appeared in his doorway.

Kate immediately shifted to see that it was Marc.

"What are you doing here, Mr. Aguilar? I have nothing to say to the press right now," Sharpe said.

"I asked him to come down." Kate walked toward him. "Thanks for coming, Marc." She returned her attention to the others. "I spoke with him a short while ago and I believe he has some information that could be of use to us. I didn't want to mention it because, well frankly, it's a little out there, but I don't believe we can dismiss it. Marc, please, tell them what you told me."

He proceeded to share his account of his visit with Vince

Sanchez, concluding with the discovery of the baseball hat. "Now, I realize, and Kate did tell me, that obviously, a lot of people are going to own that ball cap, but, I'm telling you, I've known Vince a long time. I know the type of person he is, the type of reporter, and what I'm saying to you is conceivable with a man like him. As much as I'm disgusted to admit it."

"Let me get this straight," Sharpe began. "You don't think he's the killer; you just think he's involved with him."

"Yes. I truly believe that is the case."

Nick turned his attention to Sharpe. "The car at the park. We have no idea who that belonged to." He turned again to Marc. "Do you happen to know what type of vehicle he drives?"

"Um, yeah. I saw what I'm sure was his car parked in the driveway of his house. It was a BMW, a sedan, I believe. Yes. It was a sedan, big. I just remember the emblem on the hood."

"Can you pull up that video again, Sharpe?" Nick asked.

The detective turned to his computer and inserted the USB drive. A moment later, he had retrieved the image. "This is it here." He rolled back in his chair. "Come take a look, Aguilar."

Marc walked around the agents and met Sharpe behind his desk.

"You see that car off in the corner over there."

"Yeah."

"Does that look like Sanchez's car?"

Marc leaned in and squinted his eyes. "Jesus. It's hard as hell to see it at all."

"Let me see if I can zoom it in a little and try to catch a glimpse of the hood." Sharpe began to manipulate the image and managed to get it pulled in a little tighter. "What about now?"

"Well, I can't see the emblem clearly, but I can tell by the shape of the front end, the headlights, and the grill, yeah, I think that could be it."

"Marc, we need something more than that," Kate said.

"I'm trying. It's just hard to see. I can't even tell what color it is."

"What color is his car?" Sharpe asked.

"I'd say it's a dark grey, charcoal, maybe."

"Take another look. Here." Sharpe stood up and stepped away from his desk. "Sit down. You can get a better view."

Marc sat down and studied the image and began to shake his head. "Shit, I just don't." His brow furrowed and he tilted his head a fraction of an inch to the right. "Wait. Can you zoom in on the tires?"

Sharpe leaned over him and again altered the image. "How's that?"

"Yeah. I think," he studied it even more closely, "that is his car. Oh my God. The wheels. I remember seeing them in his car. They looked custom, high-end, you know? I'm sure of it. That's Vince's car."

"Okay, we can't jump to conclusions here," Nick began. "First of all, we figured we had another watcher or someone who was following this guy. I mean, shit, he posted all of his activity online. So Vince Sanchez could've been one of those people. There's only one guy in that car."

"Is there?" Sharpe reviewed the footage again; this time, more closely than before. "No."

"What is it? What are you looking for?" Kate asked.

"I was hoping to see if anyone else got inside the car. But if they did, it was when the car was already out of view. Still, Agent Scarborough, I don't see the harm in checking this out. What have we got to lose? We're waiting for the killer to post his next moves. We don't know when or where that will be. And now we have the possible owner of this vehicle. Now, whether or not he's involved in this remains to be seen, but I'd say Aguilar has some very compelling evidence."

"I got to agree with him, Nick," Kate said. "Sanchez could be an accomplice. It sure as hell would explain why he was so anxious for Marc to reach out to me to get me involved in this investigation."

"Was that how you ended up here?" Sharpe asked.

"Yes. Marc brought the story to my attention and asked that I offer assistance from the BAU."

"Shit, all this time I thought it was the captain who insisted the feds get involved. Doesn't matter now, but anyway, I'm glad as hell you all are here."

"Sanchez wanted the story to go national," Dwight said. "Why did he need Marc to do that?"

"Because he's at a local station. To get his bosses to pitch it to the networks, cable, or otherwise would have been unlikely. Unless and until it became a larger story, which it has now, in my opinion," Marc said.

"I'd like to make a visit to Sanchez." Sharpe pulled his leather jacket off the back of his chair. "Agent Reid, I think it would be a good idea for you to come with me. This was your lead."

"Marc's lead, but I'll go with you."

"He'll be at the station," Marc began. "I can help you spot his car in the parking lot."

Marc was working hard to stay relevant to the story, but Kate didn't mind. He had the right to go, so long as he didn't overstep his bounds. "Just remember, this is Sharpe's investigation. You follow his rules."

"Let me know what you find," Nick said. "I'll keep you posted on our end."

SHARPE PULLED INTO THE KTLA PARKING LOT AND BEGAN TO DRIVE through slowly. "Shout out when you see it, Aguilar."

The daylight had broken through and was now shining well above the horizon. However, the shadow cast by the tall building gave off the appearance of a dusky early morning.

"We're looking for a BMW, four-door sedan. Dark grey," Marc said as he pulled himself forward between the headrests of the front seats.

"Right." Kate peered through the windshield and her passenger side window, but nothing popped out. "And you're sure he's working today."

"Pretty sure. He's on the morning news program. Even if he's in the field, his car should still be here."

"Try pulling around to the back lot," Marc said. "I bet most of the on-air talent park back there."

Sharpe began to drive around to the back of the building. "There are some nicer cars over here. This might be the place."

"I see it!" Marc pointed at Kate's window. "Right over there. Go right, go right!"

"Okay, okay, hold your horses. I can't exactly go barreling through here."

"That's the car. That row just ahead, fourth car in."

"I see it too," Kate said.

"I'm on it." Sharpe continued until he pulled up just behind the vehicle in question. "BMW 535. Dark grey. Nice car."

"Take a look at the wheels," Marc said. "Those are what drew my attention."

"Okay, so what now? We've found the car that was spotted at

the scene of an attempted murder. How do you want to handle this, detective?" Kate said.

Sharpe kept his attention on the vehicle. "Son of a bitch. We gotta bring him in. He's either a follower or he knows our killer. Let's go inside and get it done." He pulled into an empty spot and turned off the engine. "You want to come with us?" He looked to Marc. "He's going to know it was you who gave him up one way or another."

"Doesn't matter. I brought this to your doorstep. I'm in it now."

Sharpe stepped out of his car and waited for the others to emerge. "We'll do this quietly. No sense in disrupting the entire studio."

Kate fell in behind Sharpe as he led the way toward the building's entrance. Once they were inside, a security officer quickly approached.

"Morning. Can I help you?"

Sharpe reached for his badge. "Detective Ray Sharpe, LAPD. These two are with me. We'd like to have a word with Vince Sanchez, please."

"May I tell him what this is regarding?"

Sharpe looked at Kate.

"He might," she answered, reading Sharpe's concern that Sanchez might make a run for it. "Is he on air right now?"

"No, ma'am."

She turned back to Sharpe. "Then I think you should go back. No point in the three of us going. It'll only make him jumpy."

"I'd like to just go on back if I could. It's very important that I speak with him regarding an ongoing investigation."

"Of course. I'll take you back myself."

Kate waited with Marc in the lobby while Sharpe disappeared with the security guard. "You think he'll flip?"

"I don't know. I guess that depends on how deeply he's involved, if at all," Marc replied.

"Are you second-guessing yourself?"

"No. No, I'm not. I guess it would be too much to assume his car being at Leimert Park and the hat I found in his house were a coincidence."

"Yes, it would."

Moments later, Sharpe returned with Sanchez walking next to him. He wasn't cuffed and didn't seem distressed at all. It wasn't until he saw Marc that Sanchez's face masked in worry.

"Oh shit," Kate whispered. "If he didn't know what was up, he does now." She palmed her holstered gun and eyed Sharpe.

Sharpe quickly picked up on the signal and tried to grab Sanchez, but it was too late; he'd begun to sprint through the lobby.

"He's heading toward the door!" Kate withdrew her weapon. "FBI! Stop now or I'll shoot!"

Sanchez continued to run and was nearing the exit.

Sharpe pulled out his weapon and sprinted after him but didn't fire.

Sanchez pushed through the doors and stood outside, seemingly trying to decide which way to run, but the time he wasted with indecision was enough for Sharpe to catch up to him and tackle him to the ground.

Out of breath and surging with adrenaline, he pressed down on Sanchez's arms. "Why you running, man? Why you running?" He cuffed him and soon pulled him back to his feet.

Kate and Marc reached the outside.

"What did you do, Vince?" Marc began. "What the hell did you do?"

25

It was up to Detective Sharpe to keep Vince Sanchez's arrest under wraps while they figured out what role he played in the killings. A task that was mounting in difficulty as they returned to the station and noted the slew of media vans fronting the building. He pulled into the parking garage and entered through a secure door, one which was used for the transfer of detainees to other facilities.

Sharpe opened the rear passenger door of his Tahoe where Kate watched over Sanchez. "Get out."

The reporter shuffled out while Kate and Marc waited next to the vehicle.

"What's going to happen now?" Marc asked her.

"Depends on what he's done. How involved he is, but no doubt, he'll be charged."

"But what does it mean as to how we're going to get the killer? We now have two people who've seen him, possibly even worked with him. He has to be able to give us something."

"That's something we need to find out."

As they entered the rear of the building, Nick met them near the back. "Kate, are you all right?"

"I'm fine."

"Sharpe said you had to draw your sidearm."

"I did, but I didn't use it. Sharpe tackled him to the ground just as he made it outside."

"Jesus. I can't believe this shit. Only in LA." Nick shook his head as they followed Sharpe once again through the halls and toward the interrogation rooms. "Sanchez lawyer up yet?"

"Not that I'm aware of, but I imagine it'll only be a matter of time. So, nothing new posted from our unsub?"

"No. It's still early, though. Now that we've got these two guys, maybe we won't need to bait him any longer. I have to think Sanchez can give us something."

"I hope so." Kate continued walking alongside him. "My concern now is that he's going to figure out we have Sanchez. He'll either pull up roots and we'll never hear from him again, or he'll go all out, figuring he's going to get caught anyway, so why not take down another victim or two before the inevitable."

Nick stopped her in the hall. "I've underestimated your ability to get into their heads. I mean, I knew you were good, don't get me wrong, but your assumptions have proven to be right. You know how I've always told you that you've got some sort of sixth sense when it comes to the minutia of a case? Never letting anything be overlooked, seeing what others have missed, including me? Well, I think that talent of yours has carried. You understand their motivations. More so than ever before. I think you would rival Georgia's abilities and might even surpass them in years to come."

"Thank you, Nick. I'm not sure if it's a gift or not. Sometimes I see things in my sleep. I wouldn't say nightmares. Not anymore.

But more like ideas than clues. I don't know. Most of my life, I've been affected in one way or another by men like him. Shaped by their actions. I guess they've rubbed off on me—in a manner of speaking."

BENJAMIN PATRICK, THE MAN BEHIND THE CAMERA, SAT DOWN ON HIS couch with a coffee in hand and pressed the remote to turn on the television. His favorite newscaster was on and he had to know what it was he would say, feeling fairly confident it would be business as usual. But as he watched, and the story cut back to the anchors, he realized his buddy wasn't on air today.

Ben, as he preferred to be called, began to consider that he'd been too hard on his companion. That his threats had been taken too close to heart. It left him to ponder, though, if could there be another reason for his absence. Vince Sanchez never missed an opportunity to be on TV and unless he was ill, which Ben was certain he was not, then there had to be another explanation.

If Sanchez had talked to the police, chances were better than fair that Ben wouldn't be sitting here right now. While Sanchez couldn't lead them directly to Ben's home, he could lead them to his former place of employment and it wouldn't be a difficult leap from there.

Ben Patrick, a master in his field, had once been a name with which to be reckoned. The top makeup artist in Hollywood, he'd been admired and even coveted by some of his colleagues. But that was a long time ago. His reputation began to get in his way. His demands, and his vision for the films he worked on interfered with others who had far more pull. Soon, Ben found himself without work or taking jobs far beneath his standards.

Now he found himself living in a one-bed in Burbank, working on off-off-Broadway shows, where he could get it. That was when Ben's visions became his desires. He didn't need Hollywood or those who pulled the strings. He could bring to life the characters in his head, and their beauty, as he designed their faces to perfection. Ben could again be a force, only this time, he pulled the strings; he decided when and to whom his performances would be shown.

And for the past few months, he worked to plan all the necessary arrangements. But it wasn't until after his first work of art that he happened to cross paths with Vince Sanchez. He'd watched the coverage of the story and admired Sanchez's artful delivery. His feigned sympathy, his tragic expression. Ben knew then that Sanchez could be an ally. He'd seen through the falsehood and needed him to help bring his art to the masses.

The website was only the first step in his plan and, much to his surprise, the site had grown exponentially. He'd underestimated the depravity of these creatures called human beings. Their desire to consume the pain of others, and watch as if they themselves were participants in the brutal freak show. Once Ben realized this, his audience behaviors, the way they fed into his own needs, the more he posted, the more they commented, the more praise he received. That same praise was what he needed from the reports Sanchez had delivered. But somehow, he hadn't yet seen the same impact as his followers on his website. People were repulsed, but there was a beauty in that too.

Ben saw beauty in death and destruction and that very same depravity. He'd left a message for Vince Sanchez before the next art piece. And Sanchez responded with an enthusiasm Ben hadn't expected.

But now Sanchez was gone. He had to fear Sanchez no longer

had the stomach to continue. And could now bring about his downfall.

The time had come for him to go into hiding, exile himself as many great artists before him had done. The work must continue, though, with or without the support of Sanchez. Time, however, was running out because if Sanchez had turned against him, his discovery was inevitable.

"Where are you, Vince? I thought you had the balls to handle this, but it seems you don't." Ben stood from his sofa and switched off the television. "The show must still go on, with or without your help."

WITH A FEVERISH STRIDE, DWIGHT ENTERED THE INTERROGATION room where Sharpe and the others had begun talking to Vince Sanchez. "He posted an update."

Kate pushed up from her chair, almost knocking it over. "I'll go," she said to Nick and followed Dwight back out into the hall.

"You can help us put an end to this, Vince," Sharpe said. "They were talking about a post your friend made on his website. You knew about the website, right?"

"I told you, I have nothing to do with this."

"Then why did you run from Detective Sharpe?" Nick asked.

"I don't know. I was scared, I guess."

"If you didn't do anything, then there's nothing for you to run from," Sharpe replied. "Now I'm going to ask you again, why was your car there the other night at Leimert Park? Did you know that was where he was going to be? Do you know where he's at now?"

"Mr. Sanchez, you're a public personality. Cooperating with us now will go a long way, especially if it leads to the capture of a killer the people of LA have been in fear of for almost a month," Nick said.

"It was a tip. That's all it was. Just a tip from an anonymous source. That's why I was there at the park."

"Why didn't you call the police?" Sharpe asked.

"Because I wanted to keep running on the story. And how the hell did I know the guy would follow through? I wanted to get it on CBN and Marc Aguilar said he would help because he wanted the story too."

"Are you saying Marc Aguilar suggested you not contact the police when you received this tip?"

"No. He—he didn't know about it. I was going to send him the video."

"Wait," Sharpe began. "You have video of the crime?"

Sanchez was quiet as his head sank to his chest.

"Holy shit. You have video." Sharpe pressed hard against the table and took to his feet. "You captured this son of a bitch on tape. Now we can confirm, unequivocally, what he looks like." He turned his attention to Nick. "We can run it through recognition software to see if we get a positive ID."

Nick regarded Sanchez before answering. "I think he has more than video. I think he knows how to find him. Don't you, Mr. Sanchez?"

"I don't know where he lives if that's what you think."

"But you know something. You know how we can track him down," Nick pressed on.

"I know where he works—worked. I don't think he's done anything for them for a while, but he used to do make-up for a small theater on Vine Street in Hollywood."

"And how do you know this? You must've gotten real chummy with him," Sharpe said.

"He likes to talk about himself. You'd know that if you looked at his website." Sanchez cast his gaze between the two of them. "I know what you must think. That I had knowledge of all this and I should've called the cops. Well, I didn't know anything for sure. Just that he said things and told me where I could find the..."

"Victims?" Nick said.

"Yes. He fed me information, but I didn't really think he was responsible for it. I would've called the cops if I did."

"Even if that were true, which I highly doubt, you knew what was happening and did nothing about it, except make sure it hit your morning broadcast." Sharpe paced the room. "Where is this theater? What's the name of it?" He turned to Nick again. "We can try to get employment records from them and see if they have a last known address."

KATE FOLLOWED DWIGHT UPSTAIRS TO SERGEANT MOORE'S department. His team had been observing the site and finally received what they had all been waiting for.

"Is it up right now?" Kate made her way toward Moore's desk.

"Jameson's got it up."

"Here, take a look." Dwight sat down at the desk and turned the screen toward her.

Kate began to view the page that had been updated. A video began to play with an elaborate, movie-style introduction. "This must've taken some time to put together."

"He's nothing if not a showman."

The video continued to pan down from high above and zoomed in toward a street.

"Where is that? Anyone know yet?" Kate asked.

"We're trying to locate it as we speak," Moore said.

She continued to view the movie when a voice sounded over the images.

"In a world where art no longer exists in its purest form, but instead is watered down, and made to appeal to the masses whose only care is to be entertained at their deepest and most primal levels, comes a new era in filmmaking."

"Is this guy serious?" Kate asked.

"Tonight is the night you've all been waiting so patiently for. This will be my most extravagant performance piece yet. One I'm sure will haunt your dreams and stay with you for all eternity. Stay tuned because, at exactly midnight, you will see my final masterpiece. And for those of you who choose to continue to follow me, this will be the last word. And maybe, if you're smart enough, you will find the clues I have left."

The music swelled and the screen faded to black.

"That's it?" Kate asked. "He didn't say where he was going to be."

"No. But he's hoping Andre will study the clues, meaning we'll have to decipher them ourselves if we want to capture him before he finishes his masterpiece," Dwight added.

"We'll have to identify any landmarks captured in this video and work to triangulate a location. And, it appeared that he used satellite imagery in his opening scene. It isn't much, but it'll have to be enough to help establish a position."

"He made specific reference to his follower," Dwight said. "Meaning, Andre might know this location already. I can only speculate, but I'd say our killer is smart enough to have done some research on his follower. Possibly even traced his IP address."

"That would be difficult, considering his use of a proxy server," Moore said.

"Difficult, but not impossible. I'm willing to bet Andre knows something and we need to show him this video to see if he can pinpoint a location. That might be faster than our process of elimination."

"Let's show him the video, then," Kate said.

Dwight stood up and began to follow Kate. "Moore, you coming?"

"I'm just getting screenshots of as much of this as possible in the event he decides to pull the video. Give me a few minutes and I'll meet you down there."

Dwight followed Kate toward the elevators as the two stepped inside. "What's going on with the reporter? Any information that'll help us find this guy?"

"They're working on him now. He knows where the killer worked, but has no idea where he lives. I still think he knows more than he's letting on. I mean, Marc found the baseball cap he wears as a part of his disguise."

"Any DNA on it?"

The elevator doors parted on the bottom floor and they stepped off.

"He gave it back to the killer. He doesn't have it anymore."

"Jeez. Does this guy realize he's going to prison for being an accessory to murder?" Dwight continued.

"Honestly, I don't think he realizes what he's done. He wanted a story and it didn't seem to matter who got hurt in the process." Kate entered the holding cell area.

"You mean, killed?"

She turned her attention to the officer. "Agents Reid and Jameson. We need to talk to Andre Knight."

"I'll need approval from Detective Sharpe." The officer picked up the phone. "Sharpe, two FBI agents want to talk to Knight. Okay, thank you." He hung up the phone. "I'll let you through."

They followed the officer back to the holding cells and spotted Andre Knight sitting on the edge of his bed while his cellmate stood opposite him, leaning against the wall.

"Mr. Knight? We need you to take a look at something." Dwight raised the laptop into full view.

The officer opened the cell door and waited for Knight to step out. "Do I need to cuff you?"

"No, sir."

"Then go with these nice federal agents and do as they say."

Dwight reached for Knight's arm and pulled him alongside as they walked into a room adjacent to where Nick and Sharpe were still questioning the reporter. "Step inside, please." Dwight followed him in and waited for Kate to close the door behind him.

She set down the laptop and opened up the site. "Take a look at what your friend posted. We need to know where this is." She pressed play.

Knight watched it with mild interest and, when it was over, began, "I have no idea where this is."

"You sure about that? I believe he mentioned his follower would know if he looked at the clues. Why don't you take another look?" Dwight pressed play this time.

He watched again and a flicker of recognition seemed to spark in his eyes.

"You know the place, don't you, Andre?" Kate asked.

"Maybe. I'm not sure." He stared at the screen. "I think maybe it could be..." He paused and began to shake his head. "I think it's the open space, like a small park area, near..." He stopped. "Oh my God."

"What is it, Andre? Where is this place?" Kate continued.

"It's the park in my neighborhood." His eyes were imbued with panic as he looked at Kate. "Oh my God. He's going to go after my wife, isn't he? He found me. He found her."

26

B en Patrick leaned against the stucco column and pulled his baseball cap low on his head. He was not in full disguise and was on a reconnaissance mission, scouting his next victim. An unusual situation, as he'd been accustomed to taking days to plot, not hours. But this time was different. He knew who he needed to ensure this was his best performance yet. His magnum opus.

And it was his follower who gave him the idea. The man who fancied himself worthy enough to embark upon the adventure started by Patrick himself. He was certain this was the man who would ultimately need to pay for such an intrusion and demonstrate to his other followers that only Patrick could fulfill their desires. And with some work, he'd discovered much about the man's existence. His family, his place of employment, and even where he called home. It had been easy, really. A copy of the video provided to him by his partner in crime, Sanchez, caught the footage of the white car driving away from the scene at Leimert

Park. And from that vantage point, the car's plate was easy to read. Having dabbled inside the dark web long enough, Patrick was able to discover the owner of that white car, which had led him to this exact point in time.

And so now, he waited for confirmation. The woman was completely unaware of her husband's penchant for watching young women die and then be placed on display for all to see. That alone would likely be enough to bring about pain for the intruder. His wife's knowledge of his decadence would mean her departure.

Perhaps it hadn't been the watcher himself, but in combination with the news anchor, Ben knew his days were numbered and decided to take vengeance on those who would seek to turn against him. Vince Sanchez could still suffer, but Ben had to focus on completing this task first.

He knew she worked here, thanks to a social media post, a tweet, from the follower's account that mentioned a blood drive his wife's clinic was running. "Donate today," the tweet said. Funny how outside, the follower sought to have others view him as compassionate when he was entirely the opposite.

Ben checked the time. Two p.m. She was working the early shift today and would be getting off work right about now. A simple question posed to the information desk attendant was all he needed to get that little tidbit of information. Still, it had been much more work than any of his other performances.

The doors of the clinic opened and a woman stepped out, still wearing her scrubs, but carrying a purse and a water bottle. Ben examined her. Carmel-colored, shoulder-length hair, average build, and a decent rack. Yeah, that was her.

"Excuse me, ma'am?"

Dina Knight turned in the direction of the man who was speaking. "Yes?"

"You work at this clinic?" Ben suddenly reached for his left arm.

"I do." She began to approach, noting that the man appeared to be in some pain. "Are you okay, sir? Are you hurt?"

"It's just my left arm and I'm having some trouble breathing." He inhaled a deep breath.

"Sir, you should go inside. I think you need help right away." Dina touched his arm.

Ben immediately grabbed her hand and, with his right hand, pulled out a gun and pushed it into her ribs. "Don't scream or you'll be on the ground, you understand?"

Dina halted the scream that threatened to erupt and slowly nodded.

He stood upright and pulled her close, walking her toward his car. "You can thank your husband for this, ma'am. He brought this on himself." Ben opened the passenger door. "Get in."

Dina's eyes reddened and her heart must've been pounding fast because Ben could see her chest quickly rise and fall. He slipped into the driver's seat and kept his gun pointed at her. "Don't cry. It'll make your eyes swell up and I won't be able to make you look pretty."

"How do you know my husband?" Her voice cracked with fear.

"Oh, we hang out sometimes."

"What did he do to you?"

"You'll find out soon enough. He's made a real mess of things and this is the only way I can think to pay him back for the trouble he's caused me. He jeopardized all I've worked for and I'm afraid I can't forgive him for that."

"What do you mean? I don't understand. He's been in jail for the past twenty-four hours. He couldn't have hurt you."

Ben whipped his head around. "What did you say?"

Tears streamed down her face now. "He's in jail. He couldn't have done anything to you."

Ben returned his attention to the view from his windshield. "For the past day?" He knew the post had been made only the night before. "Then they must've made him do it."

"What are you talking about? I don't understand what Andre could've done to you. Please, I have children."

He turned his sights on Dina again. "Well, this does change things. Still, it doesn't mean I can't continue with my work. It just means I may have to make some adjustments."

THE TEAM WAITED INSIDE THE DETECTIVE'S OFFICE FOR HIS RETURN. The operation had to be authorized and resources allocated. When Kate informed Sharpe of the location and that Andre Knight's wife could be at risk, he wasted no time in getting the captain's ear to inform him of this latest development.

"Okay, we're going to send Moore along with his partner to Knight's house and get his wife and children to safety," Sharpe began on his return. "In the meantime, I'd like you three along with myself to track down the last known address of this man."

"We still don't have a name," Kate said. "How do you want us to approach this?"

"I don't imagine they use many make-up artists. It's a small theater in West Hollywood, not Broadway," Nick said. "We get their names and addresses, rule out the ones we can, and follow up on the ones we can't. It's the only way."

"That will take some time I'm not sure we have," Dwight replied.

"Right now, I don't see another choice. We can hope Moore finds the wife and children and gets them to safety, but that doesn't mean our killer won't seek another victim to fulfill the needs of his followers."

"And himself." Sharpe continued to walk toward his desk. "Agent Scarborough, would you and Agent Reid head down to the theater and get us the names? Agent Jameson and I can assist Moore until we hear back from you."

"Sounds good. I'll touch base as soon as we have names."

Kate trailed Nick and the two exited through the rear entrance as more and more media vans and reporters showed up at the station. Word had gotten out that Vince Sanchez hadn't been seen since leaving the station with Detective Sharpe and rumors were flying. It wasn't going to be long before Sharpe would have to say something, but he'd wanted to wait until they had confirmation that the family was safe. Ideally, until they had the man behind the camera behind bars.

"Sharpe said it'll take us about half an hour to get down there. Hopefully, we'll know by then if they've been able to track down the family and get them to safety." Nick pressed the remote on the car's entry and the two stepped inside.

"If he gets to her first and finds out Andre's been helping us, he might just kill her right then and there."

"Based on your profile of him, I'm not so sure. You said yourself that he's a showman. An attention-grabber. He won't want to disappoint his followers."

"I did say that. But at the very least, I suspect he'll alter his plans. Maybe a change of venue?"

"If he does that, then we're screwed." Nick studied her for a moment, then returned his attention to the road. "You look like you could use some sleep. You feeling all right?"

"I'm fine. I've gotten as much rest as you and Dwight, and probably Sharpe too, so if you all can handle it, then I certainly can."

"Didn't mean any offense. I know you can handle yourself. You don't need to wear that chip on your shoulder around me."

She wanted to refute him but knew he was right. Kate often felt the need to prove herself and she wondered when that would stop. How many cases did she need to have under her belt? How many awards or commendations did she need before they took her seriously? "You think I wear a chip on my shoulder?"

"Sometimes, yeah. But I understand. You've never felt like you deserved to be here, Kate. No matter how many times I've told you otherwise. Or ASAC Campbell or even Dwight."

"Is that why you're leaving the team?"

"What?" He shot her a glance.

"You think I'd do better if you were gone. That maybe I'd be more independent."

"No. I don't. You're missing my point. You've proven your independence time and again. Do I think that this complication between us could prevent you from becoming the type of agent you want to be? Possibly. But only time will tell."

"After you leave," she continued. "Only time will tell after you leave."

"Look, Kate, if you want to say something to me, maybe now is the time. If you're angry with me, then just say it. Tell me you think I'm abandoning you. Because that's what I'm doing, right?"

"I didn't say that. If that's what you think, then that's on you." Kate could feel the tension rising and this wasn't the time to get into an argument. "Look, we do need to talk about what's happening and what's about to happen. But we aren't going to resolve anything on the drive to Hollywood. I'm sorry I brought it up. We should focus on this investigation."

"I couldn't agree more."

Kate sighed at his final comment. She'd started a fight and now forced him to cut it off without resolution. "I'm sorry. Please don't be irritated with me. We need each other's backs right now."

"I've always had your back, Kate. Regardless of how I've felt." Nick turned right. "That's the place, up ahead."

"I see it. Says there's parking around back. You think anyone will be here?"

"We'll find out." Nick pulled into the parking lot around the back of the small theater where a few cars were dotted around. "Looks like there's a few people here anyway." He parked the car and cut the engine. "Let's go inside and have a chat."

They walked in through the door marked "employees and talent only." The corridor was dark and smelled of body odor and stale cigarettes.

"This place has seen better days, I'm sure," Nick said. "I assume someone's here since the door was unlocked."

Kate followed closely behind and noted the black-painted ceiling, the dirty white walls that were covered in handprints, scuff marks, and God knew what else. "I hope the house is nicer than backstage."

"I wouldn't count on it." Nick stopped at the T-junction in the hall. "Let's try going right."

They continued down the hall until they heard voices.

"I was beginning to think the place was abandoned," Kate said. "You hear that?"

"I do. We'll have to follow the sound."

Another several feet and they made it to the stage area where a few people appeared to be building a set.

"Excuse me?" Nick approached one of the men. "I was wondering if there was any office staff here today?"

The man with the hammer in his hand and a nail between his lips eyed Nick up and down before using his free hand to remove the nail. "I think Shirley's up front. She's the office manager. And you are?"

"Just needed to ask her about a former employee. Thank you for your time." He nudged Kate and the two walked through to the stage and into the auditorium. On the right was an exit. "Let's go this way. It should take us up front."

They made their way to the office and inside was a plump woman with big hair and too much makeup.

"Excuse me, ma'am?" Nick said. "Can I speak with you for a moment?" He presented his badge.

"FBI? What can I do for you two?"

"Are you Shirley? The office manager of the theater?"

"Yes, sir."

"I'm Agent Nick Scarborough and this is Agent Kate Reid. We're looking for a person who used to work here—a makeup artist. I'm afraid I don't have a name, but from what I understand, he worked here in the recent past."

"I assume this is a matter of some importance or else the FBI wouldn't be here."

"Yes, ma'am. It's very important we find this individual. People's lives are at stake."

"Well, let me have a look, then." The woman began typing on her outdated desktop computer whose monitor took up most of the desk space. "Don't suppose you know when this person worked here?"

"No. I'm afraid not. I would venture to guess inside the last year, though. And it is a male I'm looking for."

"Well, that should narrow it down substantially. I've seen plenty of female makeup people come through here, not many men." She continued to study her screen and began to shake her head. "Oh wait. Hang on a minute. I think, yeah, I think I remember this fella. Dark hair, slim but athletic, becoming in a weird sort of way."

"Can you give me his name?" Nick asked.

"Benjamin Patrick. Looks like he worked here up until, well, up until a month or so ago, by all accounts."

"Don't suppose you have an address for Benjamin?"

"Well, I most certainly do, young man." Shirley grabbed a yellow sticky note from her desk and began writing it down. "Here you go. Name and address. Will that do?"

"Oh yes, ma'am. That'll do just fine. Thank you so much for your help."

"Anytime. You two have a good day now."

They began to leave through the front entrance of the building and stopped under the awning.

"I don't know if this place is nearby, but we'd better let Sharpe know what we've got." Nick retrieved his cell from his pants pocket and dialed the number. "Detective Sharpe, this is Agent Scarborough. I'm here with Agent Reid at the theater and we just got a name and an address." He paused. "Yes, it's very good news. You have a pen?"

27

After weeks of tracking down the killer, Sharpe finally had what he needed to capture him. However, what he hadn't counted on was the involvement of a local reporter and a man who'd followed the killer's every move, even going so far as to approach the victims after their deaths. The problem now was the fact that the killer was about to take or had already taken his next victim. The where and when was established, but it seemed that could all change and Sharpe would find himself back at Square One.

The FBI agents had been of great help and, in fact, he'd admired the work Agent Reid had done on the investigation and now he wanted her help again. This time, to attempt a raid on the suspected killer's home before he struck again.

He'd met with the captain and both had agreed to split up as they had earlier in the day. One team to go to the suspect's home, the other to try to preempt his efforts to take another victim. And Sharpe couldn't be sure either one would pan out.

Inside the communications room where the FBI team had been temporarily set up, Agent Reid prepared to go with Sharpe to Ben Patrick's home while Agent Jameson along with his supervisor and Sergeant Moore would make a coordinated effort to find and protect Dina Knight, though their options were narrowing.

"Agent Reid, you ready to go? We need to get this show on the road."

"I'm ready, detective." Kate pulled on her FBI windbreaker and double-checked her sidearm before approaching Sharpe. "I'd like to check in with Agents Scarborough and Jameson to make sure we're on the same page before we head out."

"We can do that." Sharpe followed her into the corridor as they walked toward the others who were gathered around a map of the location of the probable victim's home.

"We can approach from here." Nick pointed to the map. "This will give us the vantage point with the least amount of visibility from the street. I don't want this guy sneaking up on us in the event he's not there."

"Understood. And if we encounter the suspect?" Sergeant Moore asked.

"Take him out, if necessary," a voice sounded in the distance.

Nick turned around at the interruption. "It's your call, Detective Sharpe. We'll do what we can to ensure the safety of the Knight family." He looked at Kate. "You heading out?"

"We are. Just wanted to get a sense of your game plan and what we're to do in the worst-case scenario."

"You mean if he's already got her and taken off?" Jameson said.

"Yes."

"In the unlikely event that happens, let's reconvene here and we'll have to come up with a new plan. But let's hope that's not the case." Sharpe turned to Kate. "We'd better go. Moore, we'll radio you when we've got him."

As they made it to Sharpe's car, Kate slid into the passenger seat and waited for the detective.

"You really think he's at his house? He has to know something's up. With Sanchez off the air, he's got to be onto us."

"Let's cross that bridge when we come to it." Sharpe started the engine and pulled out onto the road. "You don't think he's there, do you?"

"I think he's smart enough to know when he's been made. He can't think it's a coincidence that the reporter and his most avid follower have essentially fallen off the radar."

"Okay, so what do you propose?" Sharpe turned onto the highway. "You're the profiler. What's he going to do?"

"I don't know for sure, but I can almost guarantee he won't do what the video says. The time and place? I think that's out the window now and he's working on a new plan. I think the best we can do is get to his place and hope to find something that will give us an idea of what he's thinking. How desperate he is to prove he's smarter than us."

"The one thing to remember here, Agent Reid, is that this is a man who wants fame. That's what he's been seeking since the start of his career, probably. We know he's fallen out with the Hollywood-types, based on our background and employment check."

"Which was why he was working at a third-rate theater," Kate replied.

"Exactly. My guess is he'll prove his point with Dina Knight. I just hope the rest of your team and Moore find her before he gets the chance."

BEN PATRICK CONTINUED TO DRIVE AIMLESSLY THROUGH THE streets of South LA with Dina Knight still trembling and full of fear as she sat next to him. With Andre Knight in custody, he had no choice but to assume he'd told them everything, including where his next performance would be held. He was lucky to have been able to get Dina before the cops found her. Now he just needed a plan as to what to do with her. Where could he go that would still give the proper effect, it would need to be a place that would make it easy for him to get quickly out of town before they found her. He could still post his video, but there would be no returning to his home and LA would be history.

This did present a quandary, but then he recalled a place. He'd met Sanchez there once, early on in their peculiar relationship. And the more he thought about it, the more he realized it could be the perfect place.

Ben made a sharp left turn, forcing Dina to press hard into the passenger door.

"What are you doing? Where are we going?" Her face grew pale and her eyes reddened again. "Please let me go. I'm begging you. I have to get to my children."

"Shut up or I'll take them too." He continued on this new path. "You'll know where we're going when we get there. It's going to take some time to work on you. I can see that already."

His hostage stayed silent for the remainder of the drive and he soon arrived at the old KTLA studio that had been vacated earlier in the year. Vince Sanchez was the brilliant mind behind this location. And as Ben parked the car and peered through the windshield, he could see that much of the old furnishings had remained. Through the glass wall at the back of the studio, he noted the anchor desk was still in place. "What could be a better place than this for my final display?" He turned to Dina with delight. "Let's go inside and check it out."

Detective Sharpe was the first to approach the apartment door. He raised his palm to Kate, suggesting she stop while he knocked. "Benjamin Patrick? This is LAPD. Open the door."

Nothing. Sharpe pursed his lips and knocked again; this time, with more force. "LAPD, open up!" He waited but still nothing. Finally, he turned his attention to Kate. "He's not here."

"We still need to get inside."

"Yes. Yes, we do." Sharpe raised his elbow, which was clad in his favorite leather jacket, and pushed hard into the windowpane next to the door. The glass shattered on impact and he began to clear away the shards for ease of entry. With one leg in, he looked at Kate. "You're coming in too, right?"

"You're damn right I am."

"Well, at least he's a clean person." Sharpe assessed the small apartment as they stood inside the living room. "Here's your chance, Agent Reid. I heard you had a knack for finding clues. So have at it."

"Where did you hear that?" She began to walk around.

"In case you haven't noticed, I've been spending a fair amount of time with your colleagues. Particularly Agent Scarborough. He's mentioned a thing or two about you."

"Great. Well then, you know all about me." Her guard immediately shot up.

"No, that's not what I meant to say. Scarborough just mentioned how you've been instrumental in many instances where things had been overlooked. And you've had the ability to find them. Sorry, I didn't mean to offend you."

"That's okay. You didn't." She'd begun to regret her sudden jump to a conclusion. "Let's just take a look around and see what we can find." Kate moved down the short hall and entered Patrick's bedroom. "Holy hell." She placed her hands on her hips and let her eyes absorb the scene.

"Did you say something?" Sharpe appeared in the doorway.

"What do you think about this place?" Kate said. "He definitely has an interest in art."

The walls displayed posters that were in the vein of Andy Warhol. Bright colors are painted on the faces of celebrities. Black and whites with splashes of color on the eyes, cheeks, and lips.

"Look here." Kate pointed to one of the posters. "I bet that was one of the films he worked on."

"Probably so."

"What do you think made this guy flip?" Kate asked. "It seemed like he had a decent career."

"Isn't that your job to figure out?"

"I guess it is." Kate began to walk around again. "We'd better keep looking and hope we find something. We don't have all day to contemplate the mindset of a killer." Kate continued through the bedroom while Sharpe left her to it and searched the rest of the apartment. What she was looking for, as always, would remain elusive until it presented itself. And even then, she would need to put it into context. It was never as easy as Sharpe had made it sound, and perhaps that was the fault of her supervisor and the man she'd been sleeping with for the past week. He was of the mistaken impression that these things just came to her as if it was a gift. It wasn't, not really. It was the culmination of her circumstances, being in the right place at the right time, and sheer luck. And sometimes, on the odd occasion, help from above, which she gladly accepted. These were the things that made her talent special and unique.

Kate searched everywhere inside that room and nothing she noted could be of value. This was a man obsessed with creating art and beauty through makeup. That was his instrument of choice. Cover the imperfections; bring forth with light and shadows a false perception of outer beauty. It was all make-believe. Even the deaths of these victims she thought he also perceived as make-believe. All part of the illusion. Yet this brought her no closer to finding where he had chosen to make his presumed last stand.

She stepped back into the hall and walked inside the bathroom. It was sparkling clean, an anomaly to be certain, especially in a so-called bachelor pad. But again, this displayed his need for perfection in all aspects of his life. "Perfection." She considered the word. "Where could he achieve perfection in an imperfect environment?"

Kate turned on her heel and approached Sharpe. "Any luck?"

"Nothing yet. You?"

She folded her arms and furrowed her brow. "It's clear Ben Patrick is obsessed with perfection. We can see that in the way he keeps his home and the way he's taken care to make up his victims. Even going so far as to keep their wounds hidden beneath their clothing."

"Except for pooling blood, but I'm with you so far."

"So, where can he go now that will give him the perfect environment in which to achieve his goals?"

"Okay, maybe I'm not with you."

"The title of his video was 'Magnum Opus,' meaning a great work of art, or greatest work of art, right?"

"If you say so."

"I think it's safe to assume that he's disregarded the previous location, figuring we'll be there waiting for him, so what if he's found another, better place?"

"Like where?"

"A place like the theater Agent Scarborough and I were at earlier today. A place with lights, a stage, and..." She raised her index finger and turned back toward the bathroom, peeking inside before returning to Sharpe. "Makeup. He's a makeup artist, and I don't know about you, but I haven't seen a kit around here. Meaning..."

"Meaning he's got it with him."

She nodded.

"There are several theaters in Hollywood, even more if you include the rest of LA," Sharpe said.

"Maybe we need to search the ones that are closed, or empty, under renovations; things like that where he could slip in and out without being seen."

"It does seem like a place like that would be perfect for such a person." Sharpe considered her theory. "Well, this may all be moot if Scarborough and those guys have tracked down Dina Knight."

"Even if they have, it doesn't guarantee he won't get someone else. We have to consider that possibility."

"Agreed. Let's head back to the precinct, get in touch with the other team, and create a plan of attack."

THE REST OF THE TEAM WAS ALREADY BACK AT THE STATION, WAITING for the detective and Kate to return. Nick left a message on Kate's phone, revealing the devastating news that they were unable to find Dina Knight. He now stood in the back entrance, holding the door open as he spotted their return.

"No luck at the apartment?" he asked Kate.

"I wouldn't say we struck out completely."

Nick stood aside to let both of them in. "What do you mean?"

"Your agent here thinks our guy is going to look for an old theater or something like that. Similar to the place you two were at earlier today," Sharpe replied. "Thinks that's where he'll go and I have to say, she's probably right. Especially considering Dina Knight is now officially missing. Which, by the way, have you told Andre yet?"

"No. I wasn't sure how you wanted to handle that. I don't think he can be of much help now." Nick let the door fall closed as they walked through the hall.

"Let's hold off for the moment. I don't know how that'll play out and we don't need him going ballistic on us right now."

"He should know," Nick said.

"Yes, but I need a minute to figure this out. Right now, we have to assume Patrick has a hostage and her safety is our priority." He stopped in front of his office. "What about the kids?"

"Moore went to the school to get them. They're here and they're afraid."

"At least they're safe. They with Child Services?"

"Yes."

"Good. Let them deal with them for the moment." He looked around for Kate. "Where did Agent Reid go?"

Nick cast his eyes around before it appeared to dawn on him. "I bet she's already in the comm room searching for theaters."

"You weren't kidding about that gift of hers. She does have a certain knack," Sharpe replied.

"Told you." Nick opened the door and Kate was there, just as he predicted. "You looking for where he might've taken her?"

"Yep. We don't have much time." Kate stopped typing and turned her chair toward them. "I've also got the site open in case Patrick posts any updates."

Nick sat down next to her. "How many places have you come up with?"

"You know, I can get my team to jump in on this too. I bet there will be several locations that will need to be checked out," Sharpe said.

"Good. We're going to need all the help we can get right now."

28

Kate yanked the list from the printer and rushed back inside the communications room where Sharpe's team and her own had assembled. "This is it. We've got eight names on this list and locations that are spread out in nearly a twenty-mile radius. We're assuming he won't go farther out than that, considering he likes to stay close to home."

"It's a big assumption," Moore said.

"If we don't use some sort of search parameter, there's no chance in hell we'll find Dina Knight in time," Sharpe replied. "Okay, you all know your assigned locations. We need to find her, so let's do it." As they began to file out of the room, Sharpe held the door. "Remember, keep in constant radio contact. You see something, you get back up ASAP."

Moore nodded as he walked by.

Sharpe turned his attention to the feds still in the room. "Since Agent Reid's got a pretty good handle on where these places are, I think I should pair up with either one of you two." He looked to Nick and Dwight.

"Guess I'm with you, then," Dwight replied.

"Scarborough, you ready?" Kate asked.

"As I'll ever be." He followed her out of the room after Dwight and Sharpe left. "Between all of us, we should be able to cover this ground in less than an hour."

"I hope so. I don't think he'll wait until midnight to do this. He knows he's running out of time and it's already later than I'd hope it would be."

They jumped into a loaner squad car that was equipped with a radio for communication with the other three teams. Nick pulled out onto the road and headed in the direction of the first theater on their list.

"Hollywood Blvd, near Vine Street," Kate said. "Isn't that by the place we were at earlier?"

"I think so. Must be more than a few over that way." He glanced at her. "You got your vest?"

"Yes. You saw me put it on."

"Right. Just checking." He returned his attention to the road ahead. "Detective Sharpe thinks you got a pretty good mind for profiling. Says they wouldn't be this far without your insight."

"I haven't saved anyone yet and the fact that everyone's counting on me to be right makes this all the more difficult."

"It's all part of the deal, Kate. Besides, if it's any consolation, I think you're on the right track. I'd have said otherwise if I didn't."

"I know you would've."

"You talk to Aguilar about any of this yet?"

"No. Well, not about what we're doing. I just told him I'd be in touch when it was all over. He's hanging around the station till we get back."

"He must want this one pretty badly."

"He's not a bad guy, you know. He was the one who came to us and helped us identify this man. Can you at least give him some credit?"

"Sorry. I know he's your friend. I know he's helped you in the past. But, well, it doesn't matter."

"No, what were you about to say?"

"Nothing. It's all in the past anyway. It's not important anymore."

Kate peered through the passenger window. "I know what you're thinking. And I'll tell you something, Marc already thought the same thing. He's not responsible for what happened to Marshall. He knows he should've come to me sooner, but I think he's paid for the sins of his past. As we all have."

It seemed Nick decided he didn't want to pull at that thread and didn't reply.

"I'm sorry," she continued. "I'm just on edge. I feel like if I didn't get this right, I'm going to be the reason that woman dies. Whatever problems her husband has, they aren't hers and yet she's the one who will pay while he stays nice and safe inside a cell."

"I know. We'll find her, Kate." He made the final turn to the first theater on their list. "This is the place, right? Looks abandoned."

Kate double-checked the address. "This is it." She reached for the door handle and when he rolled to a stop, she opened it and stepped out.

"Hold back, Kate." Nick walked around to meet her. "Don't start without me."

Both unsnapped their holsters and withdrew their weapons.

Nick was the first to reach the entrance. He signaled for her to step behind him before he noticed the chain on the door.

"There has to be another way in," Kate whispered. "Let's check around back."

They walked along the side of the building toward the back. The theater had been closed down since last year and was still in decent shape. Some peeling paint and the sign was gone, but otherwise, it seemed all right.

Nick spotted the back door. "Lock's been taken out." He pointed to a hole where the deadbolt used to be and then proceeded to turn the handle. "It's open." He pushed his way in, pointing his weapon straight ahead.

Kate moved beside him, the weapon also at the ready.

The walls were a dark blue and the worn carpet appeared to have once been grey, but with little light to guide them, it was difficult to see. There was no electricity and when the door behind them closed, they were encased in darkness.

Nick retrieved his flashlight and rested it on top of his weapon. He nodded for her to do the same.

They continued through the maze of the backstage area. No voices, no lights. It had begun to seem that no one was inside but them.

As they reached the right side of the stage, Nick directed his light to get a glimpse of the vast space between the front and back. A curtain still hung high but was opened. Rafters appeared above in the glow of the flashlight and it appeared as though the rigging was still in place. Several large spotlights hung from the catwalk.

They began to move again and stopped at the sound. Nick shot a glance at Kate and turned back to the noise. They pressed on but with more caution than before. Perhaps someone had been there.

Two people began whispering several feet ahead.

"FBI. Show yourselves." Nick aimed his gun and the light toward the whispers. "Jesus H. Christ!"

A man and a woman appeared in the spotlight. Nick directed the light onto the floor and spotted the mattress and blankets along with used needles, a makeshift tourniquet, and dime-bag-sized Ziplocs containing what appeared to be drugs. "God damn it."

"Please don't arrest us. We'll leave right now."

"Patrick's not here." Nick turned on his heel. "Let's get the hell out of here." He started back toward the rear entrance.

"Maybe the others have had luck." Kate followed him through the door and both returned to the car.

"Those people have no idea how close they came to being shot." Nick started the engine.

"I'm not sure they cared." She picked up the radio. "Detective Sharpe, this is Reid. No luck yet; we're onto the next one. Anyone else have news?" She released the button and waited.

"Not yet. We're oh for four and onto the next ones. Sharpe out."

"Damn it." Kate hung her head.

"This isn't over yet. Just hang in there. Where are we going next?"

MARC PLACED THE MUG BENEATH THE DISPENSER AND PRESSED THE button marked "brew." A moment later, piping hot black coffee filled his cup. Two sugars and one creamer later, he began to drink the much-needed shot of caffeine. He left the breakroom and walked back into the lobby where a few die-hard reporters still lingered. Marc figured they were no different than he was. Waiting for the story to break. But the guys here, they'd heard news that Vince Sanchez was in custody. Someone must've leaked it because Detective Sharpe made it painfully clear that if word got out about it, heads would roll. Guess those guys weighed the risk versus the reward if it turned out to be true. He'd hoped to be given a chance to talk to Sanchez, but Sharpe put the kibosh on that request.

Marc came to the swift understanding that Sharpe wasn't there right now. Moore wasn't there and neither were any members of the BAU. This put him in a unique situation. Who would know that Sharpe made it clear no one was to talk to Sanchez? He didn't think that information would've reached the guys back in holding because they weren't the same ones who were there when Sanchez was brought in and Sharpe made this broad declaration.

As he surveyed the jilted faces of his counterparts, he began to consider that there could be a way for him to get back there. A few embellished words, feigning permission. It could work, and even if it didn't, what did he have to lose? They were all out looking for this poor woman. Maybe his old buddy might have some insight into that.

Marc took a few steps back, eyeing the people in the lobby who might be interested in where he was going. He continued with a casual step, eventually turning on his heel and pointing in the direction of the holding cells.

With a hand in his pocket, he walked back, appearing to have a purpose in the event someone asked about his destination. Half the battle of fooling people was to appear confident. Then it was far less likely he would be questioned. And that was what he did; all the way back until he reached the officer sitting at his desk. "I'm here to talk to Vince Sanchez. I helped bring him in earlier today."

The officer examined him with some reservation.

"Detective Sharpe suggested I speak with him, considering we used to work together. Just get a feel for if he's withholding any information."

"Are you his lawyer?"

"No. A former colleague. Feel free to call Sharpe and confirm, but I think he's working hard to find the woman who was taken hostage."

The officer still seemed to be reserving judgment, until finally he stood and reached for his keys. "Okay. But if I find out otherwise, you'll be out on your ass."

"I understand."

Marc looked upon the man who had once been a friend; an acquaintance at the very least. He walked inside and turned to the officer. "Thank you."

"You've got five minutes." The officer closed the door.

"What are you doing in here?" Sanchez sat on a bench attached to the masonry wall of the cell. He was alone.

"Just wanted to talk. Is that okay?" Marc sat down next to him. "How did you end up getting involved with the likes of that man, Vince? What the hell happened to you?"

"Please. Like you wouldn't have done the same thing if you thought it would make a good story."

"No, Vince. I wouldn't have. People are dead and you knew they were going to be killed."

"If you're in here to lecture me, then you can just leave. Oh, wait, unless they think you were involved in it with me? Is that what they think? Because you know I can tell them whatever the hell I feel like telling them and I'm pretty sure they'll believe me."

"Good luck with that. Those FBI agents who talked to you before? I happen to know them personally. One of them is a close friend. She knows the whole story."

"What you told her."

"Okay. You think what you want. But we both know the truth. There's a dozen people out looking for some woman that psycho took, hoping they'll get to her before he kills her and what, puts her on display as a part of some freak show."

"Hey, I didn't do that shit. That's on him."

"Right."

"Besides, they aren't going to find him."

"What makes you say that? You know where he is?" Marc sat up at attention.

"Not positive, but I can guess where he is."

"Care to share that information, or do you want more blood on your hands? A longer prison sentence? Maybe life?"

Sanchez looked away for a moment, then returned his attention to Marc. "Look, I told them everything I know about that freak."

"Then why didn't you tell them you know where he's going?"

"It's just a guess. And it didn't occur to me until you mentioned they were all out looking for him."

"Then tell me, where is he? Help them save that woman and they might take that into consideration."

"Like I said, I don't know for sure, but my guess is he went back to the old studio. I met him there once and he remarked how he thought it would make a good place for one of his films."

Marc turned deadpan. "What studio, Vince?"

"The old studio. You remember. The old KTLA building on Sunset Boulevard. I told him that would be a good place for us to meet because it was closer for me. I can almost guarantee that's where he'd go. No one's been in there for months."

Marc pushed off the bench and hurried to the cell door. "I'm ready to go now."

A moment later, the officer approached. "That was quick." Marc nearly pushed the officer over. "What the...?"

"Sorry. Thank you." He made his way outside to make the call.

Kate's line rang, but there was no answer. "Come on, come on. Pick up!" He tried again and her line rang. Finally, she answered.

"Marc, I don't have time."

He cut her off. "I know where he is."

"What? Where and how do you know?"

"Look, I know Sharpe will be pissed, but I finagled my way back to talk to Vince Sanchez. He said he was sure the guy would go back to the old KTLA studio where he used to work. I guess they moved to a new building several months ago."

"Oh my God. You think he's telling the truth?"

"I think so, yes. He seemed confident of it. Kate, you got to get down there and at least check it out."

"I have to go, Marc. Thank you. We'll figure this out." Kate ended the call and turned to Nick. "We have to go to the old KTLA building." She opened the maps app on her phone and typed it in. "Marc is sure that he's there."

"Aguilar? How the hell does he know?"

"He got it from Sanchez. We don't have time to debate this."

"We still have to check out the other theater. We're almost there, for Christ's sake."

"I know. Please, just trust me. I trust Marc and it makes sense. It would be something Patrick would do. Please, Nick, we have to at least try."

"God damn it." Nick turned the wheel. "Where is it?"

Kate spit out the address and immediately radioed Sharpe. "This is Agent Reid. We're headed to the old KTLA studio on Sunset Boulevard. We have new information to suggest Patrick could be there."

"Wait? The studio? Agent Reid, we're still searching the abandoned theaters where you were confident he would be. Now you're saying he's somewhere else?"

"Detective, please. We're already on our way. Sanchez was the one who gave us the information. If anyone would know, it would be him."

"Ten-four. We're on our way."

29

The abandoned KTLA studio was in sight. Kate squeezed the passenger door handle as Nick continued to approach. Her pulse raced and while it was cool in the car, she aimed the air conditioning vent at her face to dry the beads of sweat that formed on her brow. She feared this would end up being a wild goose chase and they would be too late to save Dina Knight. But what good would it do for Vince Sanchez to lie? It would only serve to harm his case and so Kate felt she had to believe him, even if it went against her better judgment.

"If he's here, he's going to see us pull into the lot." Nick turned the corner.

"Park over at the adjacent building, if you think it'll keep us from being seen." Kate still clung on to the handle with white-knuckled intensity. She peered over her shoulder at the rear window. "I don't see Sharpe yet."

"He'll be here. I don't think they were far away." He pulled onto the lot next door and cut the engine. "Aguilar better be right about his boy." He turned to Kate. "You ready to do this?"

She nodded and stepped out of the car. Her Kevlar vest felt like a cinched corset and her lungs struggled for air. It was nerves. Not from the idea of facing Benjamin Patrick, but from the idea that he wasn't here and this mistake would fall squarely on her shoulders. Making the wrong call would all but seal Dina Knight's fate.

Nick waved her over and the two began to approach the building. The ground floor was encased in glass. Some of it was boarded up, and some had been painted over, but exposure was still a concern. The main news had been broadcast from the ground floor studio near the back of the building. They continued in that direction.

Kate spotted no other cars, no sign at all that anyone else was there. Her heart sank, but she continued to follow Nick, steadying her emotions.

"Door." Nick pointed ahead to the building's rear entrance.

At that moment, the sound of a vehicle passing by caught Kate's attention. "That's Sharpe." She reached for the radio clipped to her shoulder. "Pull into the next lot. We're almost inside."

Nick turned the handle and tossed a glance her way, noting the door was unlocked, suggesting someone was inside. They crossed the threshold with weapons drawn and moved in with caution. Lights were visible in the distance. They were getting closer to the light and it appeared to be coming from the main studio area. The fact that there was still electricity to the building suggested it hadn't been abandoned for long or perhaps was running on a generator.

Kate whipped her head back at the sound of the door opening behind them. Detective Sharpe and Dwight were entering the building several feet back. She caught Dwight's attention and signaled ahead toward the lighted area.

A voice sounded behind the wall from which the light emanated. Kate looked at Nick. "It's him." Only her lips moved, but he'd heard the voice too.

Nick released the safety on his weapon and eyed Kate to do the same. He held back as they reached the end of the corridor. Another step and they'd be seen. With precise movement, Nick held his gun with both hands and raised it in front of him but still kept the barrel pointed toward the ground.

Sharpe and Dwight were almost upon them and Kate turned to place a finger on her lips and shake her head. They slowed a step but still moved forward.

In one swift motion, Nick raised his weapon, emerged from behind the wall, and spoke. "FBI, don't move." He stepped out into full view.

Kate moved next to him.

Benjamin Patrick held a camera pointed at Dina Knight. Her face was painted and she was propped up in a chair behind the anchor desk. Blood had already seeped through her clothing. He was startled by their arrival.

"Turn around and put your hands up! Now!" Nick aimed his weapon at Patrick. "Don't think for one second I won't pull this trigger."

"Oh my God." Kate noticed Dina Knight strapped to the chair and realized they were too late. "Do as he says!" She aimed her weapon at Patrick. Anger welled in her chest and she felt the pressure of the trigger beneath her finger.

Dwight and Detective Sharpe soon came into view, all weapons pointed head-on at Benjamin Patrick.

"Looks like you pulled out all the stops." Patrick set down the hand-held camera and turned toward them with his hands raised high. "What do you think? I think she looks great. Too bad I didn't quite get to finish my work." As he turned, blood spatters on his face and clothing became visible.

Kate looked at the camera and noted it was pointed toward them and saw the red glowing light. She shifted her eyes quickly to Patrick and, in an instant, watched as he drew a gun from his waistband. Time slowed and it seemed every movement that followed was happening as if she was watching a movie in slow motion.

Patrick's thumb pressed the side of the gun, releasing the safety, and his index finger wrapped around the trigger.

Kate's eyes grew wide as she turned to Nick because the gun was pointing at him. She blinked at the crack of a bullet flying from its barrel and the flash of light that followed. Her eyes shifted to Patrick and she watched him crumple to the ground and blood spill from his chest.

Everything sped up again and Kate turned to Nick. "Did he hit you?"

"No. I'm fine."

Detective Sharpe holstered his gun and jogged toward Patrick. He pressed two fingers against the man's neck. "He's dead."

Dwight had already rushed past them all to check on Dina Knight. He looked at his team and shook his head.

It was all Kate could do to keep from collapsing from her failure. "God damn it."

"I'm sorry, Kate. We did everything we could." Nick offered comfort and wrapped his arm around her shoulders. "You found him, though, and you stopped him."

~

AFTER WAITING FOR THE AMBULANCE, CSI TEAMS, AND EVERYONE else involved to converge on the scene, the team made all the appropriate statements. Reports had gotten out about the incident and the media was arriving in droves.

Within a few hours, the team was allowed to return to the precinct to a swarm of even more reporters, many of whom had pushed their way through the station and were unavoidably scattered around. Nick shielded Kate as they walked toward the captain's office.

She spotted Marc wandering the halls and stopped.

"Kate, come on. We need to brief the captain." He noted her glance to Marc.

Kate waited for Marc to approach. "I was too late."

He took hold of her hands. "You did the best you could. You always do. It was me who was too late. Too late to realize what I was dealing with in Vince Sanchez. But you stopped the killer."

"Sanchez used everyone he could to get what he wanted, including you. I need to go. I think the captain will probably make a statement if you want to hang around with your people in the lobby."

"My people?" He glanced past her. "I suppose they are. Come see me later, if you can. Or call me, okay?"

She nodded and turned away.

Inside, the captain's office was crammed with the entire team. Sharpe's people and her own.

"I want you all to know, each and every one of you played a vital role in locating Benjamin Patrick. And I especially thank the FBI for dedicating their resources to help us bring this to a close. We're preparing a statement now and I'll be holding a press conference within the hour. I know it's late and I think you all deserve to get some rest. Tomorrow's going to be much worse once word reaches the public."

"Has anyone talked to Andre Knight yet?" Kate asked.

"No. Not yet," the captain replied.

"I'll tell him." Sharpe turned to Kate. "It's my job and I'll take care of it." He turned his attention back to the room. "Captain's right. You all should go and get some rest. There'll be a lot of cleanup tomorrow. Agent Scarborough, will your team be staying?"

"Of course, we can help out tomorrow, but then I'm sure we'll be needed back in D.C."

"Then it's settled. Goodnight, everyone." Sharpe checked the time. "Or is it morning?" He clapped his hands, dismissing the room. "Agent Reid, can I have a word with you?"

"Sure." She turned to Nick. "I'll catch up with you guys in a few minutes."

"Why don't we go to my office?" Sharpe ushered Kate into the hall and back toward his office. "Sit down for a minute, would you?" Sharpe removed his leather jacket and draped it over the back of his chair. "I can see this wasn't how you wanted this to turn out. Well, me neither." He sat down. "But I want you to know something. I don't work well with others. Most people around here know that about me and have accepted it. So when you offered help, I immediately thought, hell no. I don't need help from the feds. But then, and please forgive me, I did a little research on you and discovered that you were probably the best person I could've had on my team for this investigation. I don't think I've ever known anyone who has gone through what you have and become a federal agent, let alone a BAU agent. That's an incredible accomplishment. And I know about Detective Avery too. You can't work here and not be made aware when an officer is killed in the line of duty. I'm sure he was a good man." He paused for a moment. "I don't mean to ramble on. I guess it is late and I'm as tired as the rest of you. This is just my way of saying thanks. Thanks for offering your help. And I truly believe it was because of you, your skills, and possibly even the people you know who were responsible for finding Benjamin Patrick. I am sorry Mrs. Knight died. I'm sorry the other women died too, but at least one was saved." He stood up and offered his hand. "Agent Reid, I will be letting your superiors know what a fine job you did here. You've opened my eyes to the possibility that maybe other points of view are good to have. I'm a stubborn cop, but maybe I can still change."

Kate took his hand. "Thank you, detective. It's been a pleasure to work with you and I learned a lot too. This isn't how I hoped it would end and I don't envy you having to tell Andre Knight that his wife died because of what he'd kept secret. I'm sure he'll suffer every day for what he's done to his family." She dropped her hand and turned to leave. "Goodnight, detective."

"Goodnight, Agent Reid."

THE TEAM ENTERED THE LOBBY OF THEIR HOTEL AND HEADED straight for the elevator.

"Sharpe asked us to be back by eight a.m." Dwight checked the time on his watch. "Should give us a solid six hours. That'll do for me." He smiled and turned to Nick and Kate, noting their blank expressions. "Okay. Looks like you're more tired than I thought."

They stepped onto the elevator and were silent for the next three floors. When the doors opened, Dwight was the first to exit.

"Guess I'll see you two in the lobby at about 7:30?"

"Yeah. Goodnight, Dwight," Kate said.

"Goodnight." He turned just as the doors were closing. "Night, Nick."

There was no point in hiding any of it anymore. Dwight knew and so what was the point in pretending she and Nick would be sleeping in separate rooms tonight? Still, Kate was uneasy at the assumption and current arrangement. They'd figured out nothing. Solved nothing. Both offered each other comfort without knowing how it would all turn out.

The doors opened once again and Kate stepped out first. They walked in silence toward her room and when she retrieved her keycard and slipped it into the slot, he placed his hand on her shoulder, standing inches behind her.

She opened the door and walked inside.

"You ready to tell me what's really wrong yet?" He continued past her inside and walked to the mini fridge to grab a miniature bottle of Jack.

Kate watched him pour a drink and refrained from noting that his first inclination was to reach for a drink. This wasn't the time to battle that demon, even if she believed, or rather, wanted to believe he kept it on a short leash most of the time. It had been a particularly brutal day and he'd killed a man. Perhaps a drink was in order. "I'll take one of those if you don't mind." She sat on the small loveseat and pushed off her shoes. "I'm sorry for what happened tonight. I know it's never easy when it ends that way."

Nick walked toward her with drinks in hand and offered hers up. "Just means the paperwork will be a bitch." He feigned a smile and dropped into the seat next to her. "Is that what you're upset about? I had to take Patrick down or was it because Dina Knight was already gone."

"I don't know, Nick. I guess it's all those things, but most of all, it was the moment that I froze."

"What do you mean? You didn't freeze up."

"I did. You were just too busy making sure Patrick didn't fire his gun. You were doing what you were supposed to do and that was making sure your team wasn't in any danger."

"That's part of the job. No different than if it'd been you."

"But it was different, Nick. For me, it was different." She gulped down half the drink. "I thought..." She shook her head and trailed off.

"You thought what?"

"I thought he was going to shoot you. I thought you were going to die."

"That's understandable."

"No, you're missing my point. I thought you were going to die and all I could think about was what if you had? What if he'd killed you?"

"Kate." He placed his hand on her knee. "I was wearing a vest. We all were. We're also all very highly trained in these situations and know how to protect ourselves and each other."

"You still don't get it. This is exactly the reason why—why I didn't want us to..."

"Get involved?"

"Yes. I just can't, you know I can't. Not again."

"What does that say of our friendship? That you'd have been okay if I'd been killed because we were just friends?"

"Of course not. You're my best friend and it would be devastating."

"Then I don't get the problem here, Kate. This is the job. You know it and I know it. Look, there've been plenty of times where I worried like hell you were going to get hurt. You're so damn pig-headed sometimes. You don't listen to anybody."

A faint smile formed on her lips.

"See? I'm right, aren't I? It's no different. We're close. That's a fact. All three of us are and it just comes with the territory."

"This was different, though. I hesitated. I watched you and I watched that bullet pierce your body and I watched you fall to the ground and all of this happened in my head. And it stopped me from doing what I needed to do to protect my team."

"So you want me to get that job at Quantico? Then you won't have to worry about me, is that right? It'll make things easier for you?"

"I don't know. Nothing's ever easy."

30

Snow had begun to fall when Kate arrived at the WFO. It was almost Thanksgiving and still a little early for the white stuff, but the sight of it made her smile, even if it melted the moment it hit the ground. And after having just returned from LA, it was nice to get back to a place that experienced seasonal changes.

Inside, it seemed business as usual, as if none of them had been gone for almost two weeks. They stayed for another three days after the investigation closed to assist with the mounds of cross-jurisdictional paperwork. But now, Kate was back and smiled when she spotted Agent Vasquez at her desk.

"You're back?" Vasquez noticed Kate's approach.

"We are indeed. And very glad to be."

"You mean you didn't miss being back in Southern California?"

"Not as much as I thought I would." Kate sat down and turned on her computer. "You see the guys yet this morning?"

"No. I haven't. But I've had my nose to the grindstone trying to keep up with your work and my own, so I haven't paid much attention to anything going on around me."

"Ha ha, very funny."

"Who's laughing?" Vasquez smiled.

"I'll check Scarborough's office, see if he's in there or Jameson's." Kate stood back up. "They're usually together."

"They might be with Campbell too. You'll have to check."

"Will do." Kate continued along the corridor, noting Nick's light was on, but he wasn't inside. She hadn't spoken to him since their return yesterday afternoon but couldn't recall if he mentioned not being in today. She kept going until reaching Dwight's office and that was where they were.

"Kate, come on in. Take a seat." Dwight motioned her inside.

"Morning. I was just looking for you," she said to Nick.

"Listen, I got a call a few minutes ago from Sharpe. He said he tried you but didn't get an answer," Nick began. "Andre Knight committed suicide in his cell last night."

"Oh my God." Kate raised her hand to her mouth. "How the hell did he manage that?"

"Apparently, he was determined and used the wires from his bedframe and, well, you get the idea."

"God, those poor kids."

"There was one other thing too," Dwight added. "Can you reach out to Marc Aguilar? I know he's running with the story, but just let him know that we can't comment on it. I'm assuming he'll call you if you haven't called him. We need to direct any and all inquiries back to Detective Sharpe. We're no longer involved unless called upon in Sanchez's trial."

"Understood. I'll let him know. Was there anything else?"

"Not yet. Although I think ASAC Campbell wants to meet with all of us later this afternoon. Are you free?"

"As a bird." Kate stood up to leave.

"Oh and hey, listen, Abby and I have decided to host Thanksgiving at my place. I've got the kiddos this year and I thought it'd be nice for you and Nick to come over. What do you think?"

Kate looked at Nick. "I'm good with that."

"Me too."

"Great. Then it's settled. Okay, Nick and I have a few things to go over, so we'll catch up with you later before we meet with Campbell."

"Sounds good." Kate left the office, wondering what it was those two needed to discuss alone. It must be the job at Quantico. She wondered if they were discussing mentioning it to Campbell yet, in the event Nick was awarded the position.

It would change everything, that was for certain, and Kate still hadn't gotten her head around it yet. On the one hand, Nick wouldn't be in the field as much, which she figured was a good thing. He needed a change. For the past year, maybe longer, she'd seen a transformation in him. He'd begun to lose confidence in what they were doing and why. He'd grown tired of hunting monsters and watching bad things happen to good people. Parents lose their children. People falling prey to the worst of mankind. She couldn't blame him. Her first-hand knowledge was enough to come to that conclusion.

But it was who she was now. Maybe she was supposed to pick up where he would leave off? Dwight was a remarkable agent in his own right and he'd been her mentor for a time. It wouldn't be a difficult transition. At least, not in that respect.

"You manage to track them down?" Vasquez said as she stopped Kate at the end of the hall.

"Huh? Oh yeah. I did. They're in Jameson's office if you need them."

"Thanks."

"WHEN ARE YOU GOING TO TELL HER?" DWIGHT ASKED.

"I don't know yet. Not for a while. I don't think I can."

"She needs to know, Nick, and the sooner the better." Dwight twirled a pen between his fingers. "Don't underestimate her. She'll handle it."

Nick began to shake his head. "You weren't there that night. After we got back to the hotel. After we got Patrick. You didn't see the look on her face, the tone of her voice."

"This too shall pass. Isn't that what they say? Come on now; we've all been through the wringer. It's time for some change. It's time to move on. She just needs closure on this. And so do you. In fact, I think I do too."

"I know this affects you too."

"Look, just think about it. Get it straight in your head and do what you need to do. You've underestimated yourself for the past year and I sure as hell don't want to see that anymore. Nick, you're one of the best agents I know. Certainly, the best I've had the pleasure to work with. If this is what you need to do, then do it. If this is what it will take to bring you back to the man you know you are, then do it. But this in-between stuff? You and I both know that's got to stop. It's not good for anybody."

Nick pushed up from the chair. "I hear you. I just need some time to process." He began to walk away. "So, Thanksgiving at your place, huh?"

"Yes, sir, and you'd better not miss it. I'm counting on you so I can have a buddy to watch the game with."

"Okay, man. I'll be there."

KATE STEPPED OUT OF HER BATHROOM, FLUFFING HER HAIR A FINAL time and smoothing down her skirt. "You ready to go yet? Dwight said to be there by two and it's almost 1:30." She emerged from the hall and into the kitchen where Nick stood, scrolling through his cell. "What are you doing? You're not even dressed yet?"

"I've got pants on," he said without looking up.

"Your shirt is lying on the bed. Please, go finish getting dressed. I don't want to be late. What will Abby think of us?"

He finally looked up. "You mean, apart from what Dwight has already told her?"

"Exactly." She pushed him. "Now please put your shirt on."

Nick thrust his shoulders back and sucked in his already firm stomach. "What? This not doing it for you, babe?"

"Any other time, yes, but not right now."

"Fine." He relaxed his muscles and still looked the same.

The past few days had been really good for the two of them. The case was over and they'd each been consulting on a few different tasks. Kate had continued to explore the idea of working toward profiling and had already registered for the extra training Quantico offered on the subject, which was extensive.

It all seemed perfectly normal, except it wasn't. Not once had they discussed the future, or the past, or anything in between. They'd avoided any topic that might evolve into what would happen when Nick left the team. It was coming, but it seemed neither was ready to tackle the subject. Maybe after Thanksgiving, she thought. The job would have him leaving at the first of the year, so it was easy to skirt the topic.

She did have to admit to herself that a part of her was relieved. She wouldn't have to worry about him getting hurt or worse. He was going to be in a heavy consulting role and his team would focus on that almost exclusively. Still, it would be strange for her not to be able to run to his office whenever she needed him or vice versa.

But she would have Dwight and that was okay too. It did bring to mind who might take his place, though. Dwight would be promoted to SSA, she'd keep her status, though no longer a probie. She'd decided to put Vasquez's name forward. While she was a part of the team, it was more of an administrative, support role. Although she had no idea if Vasquez would be interested, she suspected she would.

"Okay, I'm ready." Nick returned, buttoning the cuffs of his shirt. "All better now?"

"Much. Let's go."

DWIGHT OPENED HIS DOOR. "HEY! RIGHT ON TIME." HE STEPPED aside to allow Kate and Nick in. "Kate must've been the one responsible for that."

"I was." She kissed him on the cheek. "Happy Thanksgiving. Thanks for having us over, Dwight. Where's Abby?"

"In the kitchen. And you can open up that bottle of wine you're holding. I'm sure she'd love a glass. She's been in there all morning."

"Perfect." Kate kept walking toward the kitchen but stopped

short as she happened upon the kids. "Hey, guys. Haven't seen you in a while. How are you?"

"Fine." Dwight's daughter approached Kate for a hug.

"And what about you, dude? Can I get a hug, or are you too cool for that?"

His son reluctantly pulled himself from the sofa and wrapped an arm around her. "Hi, Kate."

She continued toward the kitchen. "Oh my. You've been busy."

"Kate?" Abby turned away from the stove and drew near. "So good to see you. How are you? Glad to be home?"

"Absolutely. And I brought some wine."

"The opener's over there and you know where the glasses are. I'll definitely take one if you're offering."

"You bet I am."

"Can I get you a beer or something?" Dwight took the coats and hung them on the rack near the front door.

"Sure. Yeah, I'll take a beer."

"Sit down. I'll be right back."

Nick perched on the edge of the sofa and began watching the game as the kids decided they'd be better off in their rooms.

"Don't stay up there all day now. We have company," Dwight shouted as they ran up the stairs. "Here you go." He handed over the beer. "Cowboys are up by ten. Might be a blowout."

"I'd expect nothing less for a Thanksgiving Day game. Thanks for hosting us, Dwight. It was nice of you, especially since Abby's probably had to do most of the preparations."

"Well, in fairness, I was out of town, but yes, she's done the bulk of the planning." He held his bottle up. "Cheers. Happy Thanksgiving."

"Happy Thanksgiving."

After watching the game for a few minutes, and watching the Cowboys score another touchdown, Dwight began, "Why don't we go see the girls? They might need some help."

"Help finishing the wine? I'm in." Nick smiled and followed Dwight to the kitchen. "It's sure starting to smell good in here." He walked to Abby. "Don't think I've said hello to you yet." The two embraced for a brief moment. "How are you?"

"Good, Nick. And you?"

"Great. Thanks." He walked toward Kate. "How's that wine? Any good?"

"Not bad. Not bad at all, actually. You chose well." She wrapped an arm around his waist.

They both looked on as they watched Dwight and Abby help each other make the meal. "They seem really happy, don't they?" Kate asked.

"They most certainly do." He continued to watch them. Hugging, kissing each other's cheeks, and he couldn't help but smile. That was what he wanted. And he wanted that more than anything with the woman standing next to him.

Nick never expected to be the kind of man who needed a woman or anyone, for that matter. But he needed Kate. It had taken years to come to that conclusion. Years and a whole lot of denial. But there it was. He was captivated by her beauty, by her intelligence, and most of all, by her sheer determination to succeed. He sipped on his beer again and cast his gaze toward the kitchen window. "Looks like it's snowing."

"So it is," Dwight said. "Might need to crank up the fireplace after dinner."

Nick pulled Kate closer and cast his gaze upon her.

"You okay?" she asked.

"I'm good." He stared into her eyes.

"What? What is it? You're looking at me funny."

"Kate. I've been meaning to tell you this since we got back last week, but I guess I couldn't find the right time."

Her expression shifted with marked concern.

"It's nothing bad. I mean, I don't think it is. You might think differently." He looked at Dwight and Abby again, then back to Kate. "I removed my name from consideration."

"What?" She pulled back.

"I withdrew my name. I don't want the Unit Senior Agent job at Quantico."

Kate appeared stunned or angry or maybe both. She released her grip and walked into the living room.

Nick quickly followed. "Hey. What's wrong? I thought this would be welcome news. We've been getting along so well lately and..."

"And what? You thought, hey, I'll give up my dream. I'll give up a great promotion to stay in a job I've been in for years just so I can hang out with my girlfriend." She walked toward the coat rack and opened the door.

Dwight appeared from the kitchen. "Everything all right?"

"Yeah. We'll be right back." He grabbed his coat and followed her.

She stood outside on the small patch of grass that fronted Dwight's row house. Flakes of snow fell on her hair, turning it white. "Why would you do that, Nick? I didn't ask you to give up your dream. I would never do that."

"Who says it was my dream? You keep saying that, but I don't remember ever saying that."

"What are you talking about? You've been wanting to get out of the field for a long time and you know it. Now's your chance and you're what? You're going to bail because of me?" Kate looked up to see Dwight and Abby staring at them through the window.

They quickly vanished when she caught them watching.

"I am so confused right now. I thought you'd be happy. Silly me. I thought you wanted me around."

"Oh my God. I do, you buffoon. But not at the expense of your career. You are an FBI agent. It's what you always wanted to be and I'll be damned if I take an opportunity like this away from you."

"You're not. Don't you see? I want to do this. Despite what you think, I do want to be in the field. Maybe not all the time, but yeah, I still get pleasure from putting the bad guys away."

She shook her head. "You remember what I said to you at the hotel? How I couldn't do my job because I was afraid of losing you?"

"Yes, I do. But I also remember telling you that you'd have felt the same way whether or not we were sleeping together. We both care very much about what happens to the other. Regardless of a physical relationship, it's always going to be that way. It has been since I got you out of that damn cellar." He stopped to take a breath.

"You realize that even if you had transferred, I'd still be with you. In fact, I'd have felt better about it. Knowing you were happy. Knowing you were safe. I mean, are you kidding me? It was the best thing that could've happened to us." She pressed her palms against her cheeks. "Oh my God. I can't believe you did this without talking to me first."

Nick moved next to her and gently took her by the shoulders. "I thought I was doing what was best for our relationship."

"That was best for our relationship."

"Well, it's too late now. What's done is done and they're giving the job to someone else. I'm sorry you're so disappointed in my decision."

"We're going to have to talk about this later. Dinner's going to be ready soon." She began walking up the steps.

"Kate. I love you. Don't walk away, please."

"We have to go inside. They're already looking at us."

He caught up to her. "I'm sorry."

"Did you even think about Dwight in this decision? Don't you think he wants to move up?"

"Of course, and we did talk about it."

"What did he say?"

"He said I should do what makes me happy."

"I agree with him." She took a deep breath. "Let's just get back inside."

"What if I could bring you with me?"

She stopped and faced him again. "The last thing I need from you is to hitch a ride on your coattails again. Thanks, but no thanks."

"Jesus. You are so damn stubborn. You want to learn profiling. That's what you want to do. That seems to be what makes you happy. You're already going to do some training at Quantico. This would just be a more permanent solution. Train under Unit Four's profiler."

"Right. They already have one. An expert who far exceeds my current skillset."

"I know. But they always need good profilers on the team. Learn from him. After what Sharpe has said about you to Campbell, there's no way they'd say no. As of the first of the year, you'll no longer be on probation. Doors will be open to you, Kate."

"What about Dwight?"

"He would get his promotion. He would be the new BAU Resident Agent at the WFO."

"You said you withdrew your name? Sounds like it's too late to me."

"I can tell them I've reconsidered. They haven't exactly made the decision yet. It wasn't supposed to be until the end of the year."

She studied him again. "I want to do things on my own, Nick. You of all people should know that about me. I can't go in there on your recommendation. I won't be that person again. I've already done that."

"Wow." He folded his arms. "How long is it going to take for you to realize you've been pulling your own weight since you started at WFO? Campbell knows it. We all know it. It wouldn't be me dragging you on my coattails. It would be you earning it and joining me at the same time." He could see she was considering the possibility. "We could buy a house. Together. Maybe someday, I don't know, maybe get married."

"Now you're just talking crazy." She held his gaze. "Dammit, Nick. Why are you telling me this now? We're standing on the porch of our friend's home in the snow on Thanksgiving. And you're making decisions without talking to me. It can't go down like that if you want us to be together. And we haven't talked about anything. Not the future, not how we ended up standing here right now. And now you're saying we should move in together. Move forward with our careers together. It just doesn't happen that way, Nick."

"I'm sorry. I'm sorry I didn't discuss this with you first and I'm sorry we're both standing in the freezing cold arguing about a future we never debated."

"A future neither one of us are sure is even possible. We fell into bed together without understanding why."

"We knew why. But neither of us wanted to admit it. Kate, you left Mike because you wanted to be with me. Even if you refused to admit it to yourself. I know it. I could see it in your eyes, but you held back. And we both let it lie. Look, I don't know how we got here. But why do you feel the need to analyze it to death? Can't we just accept it? We finally got out of each other's way and allowed ourselves to be happy. Would you rather spend the rest of your life pushing away people who love you? Because that's what you've been doing. And I've let you do it. But not anymore, Kate."

They both fell silent for a moment.

"I just don't know if I'm ready. I don't know if I can leave WFO, my house, my friends."

"Me?"

The door opened and Dwight slowly peeked his head through. "Um, hey, guys, dinner's ready if you want to come back in now."

"Kate?" Nick waited for an answer.

She turned to Dwight, raising one corner of her mouth into a partial smile. A moment later, she faced Nick. "I'll get out of my own way and see where this takes us, but as far as the rest of it, I do it on my own; without your help. And I swear to God, you'd better take that damn job. That's a deal breaker, you understand?"

He nodded.

"Then let's go inside and eat some damn turkey."

THE END

ABOUT THE AUTHOR

Robin Mahle has published more than 30 crime fiction novels, many, of which, topped the Amazon charts in the US, Canada, and the UK. And most recently, she has delved into the world of psychological thrillers.

Also a screenwriter, she has adapted some of her works into teleplays, which have gone on to place in film festivals nationwide.

From detectives to federal agents, and from killers to corruption, her page-turning tales grab hold and refuse to let go. Throw in tense action and thrilling twists, and it becomes clear why her readers come back for more.

Robin lives in Coastal Virginia with her husband and two children.

If you enjoyed Ms. Mahle's work, please share your experience by leaving a review on <u>Amazon.</u>

ALSO BY ROBIN MAHLE

The Kate Reid FBI Thriller Series (17 books)

The Chef (stand-alone psych thriller)

The Man in My Attic (stand-alone psych thriller)

The Compound (standalone psych thriller)

The Remy Fontaine Fugitive Hunter Thrillers (4 books)

The Det. Rebecca Ellis Thrillers (5 books)

The Allison Hart PI Thrillers (5 Books)

The Lacy Merrick Thrillers (4 books)

**Visit Robin's website, robinmahle.com and sign up for her newsletter so you can stay up to date on her new releases, events, contests and even exclusive new material!